"From the first line to the finale, I was immersed in all facets of this multi-plot drama." —*Dru's Book Musings*

"I was kept guessing until the final suspenseful reveal. I loved the first adorable book and I was more than delighted with this second installment in the series!" —*Cinnamon Sugar and a Little Bit of Murder Reviews*

"Those pages were really flying and so much was happening, there was no way I was going to put this book down until I reached the end. By the way, I was wrong and surprised by the ending. I loved it!" —*Dollycas Reviews*

"I would be thrilled to recommend this book to all mystery fans. I say buy it now and read it in the fall! A five-star hit and I can't wait for the next!" —*Bibliophile Reviews*

"Order a pizza, blow off dinner, and get lost in this book."
—*A Cozy Experience*

"I am looking forward to visiting Silver Hollow again, not only because Ms. Macy is such a talented writer, but because I love teddy bears as much as I love cozy mysteries."
—*Melina's Book Blog*

Kensington Books by Meg Macy

Bearly Departed

Bear Witness to Murder

Have Yourself a Beary Little Murder

Wedding Bear Blues

Bear a Wee Grudge

BEAR A WEE GRUDGE

MEG MACY

KENSINGTON
PUBLISHING CORP.

www.kensingtonbooks.com

KENSINGTON BOOKS are published by

Kensington Publishing Corp.
119 West 40th Street
New York, NY 10018

ISBN-13: 978-1-4967-2918-7 (ebook)

ISBN-13: 978-1-4967-2917-0

First Kensington Trade Paperback Printing: December 2021

10 9 8 7 6 5 4 3 2 1

Printed in the United States of America

For my Honey Bear and Sweet Pea . . .
we'll get to Scotland one day

ACKNOWLEDGMENTS

Thanks to my dad, who always took me and my siblings to the Memorial Day parade, where we watched the bagpipers—that music stirred my soul for all things Scottish, British, Irish, and Welsh. He also took us to Greenfield Village, where my love of history began. Miss you, Dad.

Thanks also to my wonderful editor, Wendy McCurdy, and her fabulous assistant, Elizabeth Trout; to Kensington's production and art departments (crack teams!); to my four daughters (three of them "adopted"); to Sharon for last-minute (and much-needed) help; to my faithful readers, family, and friends—you are all so important to me. Writers can be lonely, cranky, and elusive around a deadline. Be kind to us, because we need all the support we can get.

If the person you are talking to doesn't appear to be listening,
be patient.
It may simply be that he has a small piece of fluff in his ear.

—Winnie-the-Pooh *(A.A. Milne)*

Chapter 1

"Mama, Mama! My teddy bear—"

I quickly stepped out of the crowd of walkers and snatched up the furry toy before one of the focused joggers in the middle of Roosevelt Street could kick it away. Brushing a smear of dirt from the bear's nose, I dodged runners in shorts and sweaty shirts. My sister Maddie kept power walking toward the park, arms pumping hard, oblivious to my rescue effort. I struggled to avoid bumping others before I caught up to the woman, who'd halted her child's stroller.

She smiled in relief. "Thank you so much!"

"No problem," I said. "Sorry, but it's a little dirty."

"I want my bear," the little girl wailed, wriggling in the stroller's seat. She looked adorable, with light brown curls and huge chocolate brown eyes.

"That's the third time you dropped it this morning, Gracie," the mother scolded her child. "I think you're doing it on purpose."

"Gimme my bear!"

"Not until we get home. Which will be sooner if it rains

like last night." The mother stuffed the toy into the backpack hanging from the stroller's handle. "If you behave, I'll let you have your teddy bear in the car."

"I want it now!"

"No. And stop whining." She turned to me once more with a deep sigh. "Thanks again. I'm sorry if we messed up your timing this morning."

"Oh, not at all. I was just walking." I wiggled my foot. "I'm slowing down more and more with each step."

The woman nodded and pushed the stroller off, her child still wailing in misery. Had my sister noticed that I'd stopped? I shielded my eyes from the bright spring sunshine, trying to spy Maddie up ahead. I gave up and limped to perch on one of several large boulders that bordered a lawn. I should have worn socks and sneakers instead of sandals. My feet felt like ice, and a big blister had formed under the strap on my right heel.

Maybe I should have kept walking instead of taking a break. I rose to my feet and tugged my Silver Bear T-shirt into place. A chill breeze sent shivers up and down my spine. I untied my sweatshirt's sleeves from around my waist and pulled it over my head. It also had the Silver Bear logo printed on the back. As manager of a teddy bear shop and factory, I had to serve as a walking billboard for the family business.

"Are you okay, Sasha?"

Maddie suddenly appeared before me, looking cute with her pixie hairstyle temporarily dyed pink to match her jogging suit and sneakers. She wore a string of tiny flocked white teddy bears around her neck as well. My sister wasn't surprised about my blister.

"I told you to change into sneakers." Maddie handed me a strip of gauze from the fanny pack at her waist. "This should cushion it until we get home."

She waited while I wrapped the gauze around my sandal's

scratchy leather strap, then pulled me to stand. Maddie led the way to the street once more. The sun shone between the bank of clouds overhead, but that didn't mean winter was forgotten. Even this late in April, a few weeks short of May, Michigan could get overnight frost, a coating of ice, or even a blizzard.

Silver Hollow's small park was only a few blocks away. Good thing. I was dying to sit on a bench and take off these sandals. I texted my boyfriend, Jay Kirby, to bring socks and sneakers, if he had a free minute. Smart of him to spend the day working on a commission, and I didn't mind him begging off on the trot. Jay had signed up for the Kilted 5K in a few weeks instead, while I preferred a relaxed walk today.

I pushed a stray blond hair out of my eye, chugged a long drink from my water bottle, and wiped a few stray drops from my sweatshirt. Dirt streaked my leg below my capris. I needed a shower.

"Hey, Mads. Got a ribbon, by any chance?"

"I found this scrunchie on the ground. Not too dirty."

"Beggars can't be choosers." I gathered my long hair into a ponytail. One more thing I'd forgotten to do this morning. "Okay, let's go."

"You can make it, right?" Maddie asked, eyebrows raised.

"I'll manage." I gritted my teeth and limped forward once more. "I feel like such a baby. The Teddy Bear Trot is only what, two miles?"

"Three, I think," she said. "The joggers' route is five. I did half of it while I waited for you to show up this morning."

"You're a glutton for punishment."

Ignoring my blister's sting, I focused on the trees overhead. They'd already filled out with tiny leaves after a rain-soaked March. Clusters of yellow daffodils and the earliest tulips had bloomed and left their green stems behind. Late-blooming tulips of every color would soon brighten the village flower tubs and line the fronts of houses and sidewalks. Azalea bushes sprouted pink or purple flowers, and forsythias danced with bright yellow blooms.

I loved spring in Michigan, except for the heady scent of hyacinths and Easter lilies. Every time I walked past them, inside a store or outside, I sneezed hard. Luckily, I didn't suffer as much as Jay, whose spring allergies to tree pollen drove him crazy. Right now I relished the flowers, the distant barking of dogs around the village, and the scent of freshly mown grass.

The newly formed Silver Hollow Entrepreneurs and Business Association, commonly shortened to the acronym SHEBA, was hosting a Scottish-themed Highland Fling soon. The committee didn't have much choice with Mother's Day and graduations filling up the May schedule, so they settled on the first weekend of May. Once the decision was made, they rushed to shape up their plans.

Local bakeries prepared to sell scones, oatcakes, and other Scottish treats. Vendors had been approved to offer goods from kilts to Renaissance-type costumes, along with swords and armor. Dancing and music, herding dog trials, the Kilted 5K run, plus athletic games filled the tentative schedule. My mother, recently elected as mayor, had joined forces with Amy Evans, the village coordinator, to assist SHEBA. A huge crowd was expected.

"We both missed the latest committee meeting for the Highland Fling," I said to Maddie, wincing as a stray pebble hit my sore toe. "Not that much happened, from what I read of the minutes Mom printed off. Why did we volunteer to help?"

"Because we let her twist our arms. Total pushovers, both of us."

I laughed. "That's true."

Maddie steered me around a group of seniors, all wearing parka-like jackets with gloves and scarves, who rolled their walkers along the street. I didn't think it was *that* cold, but maybe it was part of the territory in getting old. Many had strapped large teddy bears onto the aluminum frame tops. That looked sweet. The seniors chatted together, enjoying the fresh air and the sight of young mothers with toddlers or babies in strollers.

"They need a better name. 'Silver Hollow Highland Fling' is boring," Maddie said.

"I don't know what else they'd call it," I said. "The games and food will be bigger draws than the dancing, in my opinion. We've gotten tons of pre-orders already for our bears in kilts. That should make Uncle Ross happy."

"I'll put a photo of the sample bear in the promotional flyers."

"Did you know Scotland holds their highland festivals on the Isle of Skye, and all around the country?" I asked her. "The Ceres Games in Fife is the oldest."

"Let me guess. You Googled that."

"Nope. Gavin MacRae told me, and that Robert the Bruce gave the village of Ceres a charter in the fourteenth century. Now *that's* old."

Maddie shrugged. "I'll try to remember those facts for trivia night next week at Eric's brewery. Maybe he could get some Irn-Bru for people to taste, besides his mead."

Her boyfriend Eric Dyer owned the Silver Claw, a brewery and wine producer, with help from his dad. I wasn't sure my sister was committed to their relationship, however. She seemed enthusiastic now, but Maddie's previous liaisons usually waned long before reaching a one-year anniversary. I wasn't sure if she was fickle or if it was a coping mechanism to avoid heartbreak. For now, they both acted like they were into each other.

"I'm thinking Eric ought to get some haggis for them to try," Maddie said.

"He can't import it, though," I said. "The USDA doesn't allow any products made with sheep lung. I bet we can find a different recipe for it on the web."

My sister slowed her pace again to match mine. "Okay, then. You ought to talk Uncle Ross into making teddy bears using plaid fabric instead of fur."

"Hmm. Good idea, so I'll bring it up at the next staff meeting."

Maddie circled me a few times, dancing around to expend extra energy, while I limped past the park's entrance. "I thought you prepared for this Teddy Bear Trot. Like using my Pilates machine, right? And walking at least thirty minutes, minimum, each day? That was your New Year's resolution, starting in January."

"Aren't they meant to be broken?"

"Sasha!"

"Hey, you know it's been crazy at the shop."

I didn't have to explain further. While the Silver Bear factory staff worked overtime producing wedding bears and accessories for spring and summer, plus kilted bears for the Highland Fling, the shop itself was closed. We'd hired a paint crew to refresh the exterior and interior, a long overdue project. That meant I had to deliver bears to sell at shops around the region. I logged over three hundred miles in the last month alone.

Plus I'd helped with shipping, stuffing, and a host of other jobs, except for sewing, to get so many items finished on time. I also delivered teddy bears to local shops—Mom's gallery, the bookstore, the Queen Bess Tea Room, and almost every other shop in our small village. I'd also forgotten all about preparing and filing my tax return. Aunt Eve helped me out at the last minute. We'd spent several days going through paperwork before I filed online, using her temporary "office" in a small corner in the factory.

That created another huge problem over the last month. Aunt Eve and Uncle Ross had recently remarried, and the closer proximity day and night was taking a heavy toll on their sanity. Production staff usually tolerated Uncle Ross's barked orders and bristly manner, but Aunt Eve craved peace in an isolated working atmosphere. Any attempt to change his grumpiness led to flare-ups between them. Acting as a liaison, more than a dozen times since the painting project began, had not been easy.

The last thing I'd thought about was finding time to exercise.

"Oh, man." Maddie sighed. "I paid for your yearly gym membership as a Christmas present, Sasha. You've used it what? Twice?"

"How do you know that?" I asked, more curious than annoyed.

"You're on my plan, remember. I know when you check in," she said airily, "but I've got another idea. Remember how Kristen Bloom opened Blissful Yoga? She bought that little rental house from Barbara Davison that you wanted for Jay's studio."

"Yeah, I remember. Mom's too busy being mayor and she doesn't seem to miss Barbara and any lunch meetups."

"They talk once a week on the phone. Anyway, Kristen offers a goat yoga class."

"GOAT? As in 'greatest of all time'?"

"No, not GOAT. Real goats, baby ones, that jump around during class," Maddie added. "She teaches out at Richardson's Farms. You should sign up, since you're clearly unmotivated to go to the gym. I love it, it's a blast."

"I'll think about it." Two gym visits in three and a half months was pitiful, I had to admit. My jeans felt tight from eating so many Christmas cookies. My sister took after Mom's family, slender and petite, while I'd gotten the thunder thighs from the Silverman side. "I'm not thrilled about goats jumping around while I'm doing yoga. Sugar Bear and Rosie cause enough trouble wanting attention whenever I do Pilates."

"Dogs are a distraction, but the goats don't care. Ignoring them is a good challenge to keep your focus on each pose."

I almost laughed at my sister's sincerity. I had challenge enough finding time—well, making time—to exercise. I wasn't a morning person and often skipped walking the dogs at lunchtime or after work. Maybe goat yoga would help.

Maddie jogged up the sloping wooden bridge that spanned the narrow Huron River. After meandering through several tiny lakes farther north, the Huron entered Silver Lake behind the Kilted Scot boutique—formerly the Davisons' residence—then skirted the village's eastern edge and flowed through the park. Beyond that, the river widened on its way toward Ann Arbor. The banks tended to overflow in spring, unfortunately. Many local roads would either be marked as one-way or closed due to flooding.

Our village park was a misnomer, given it was only a few acres. Evergreens and other trees bordered the open sward, with picnic tables at one end, a volleyball net near the parking lot, and the dilapidated metal jungle gym playscape.

Not nearly enough space for the Highland Fling.

"The committee expects a couple thousand people," I said. "This park can barely handle our annual Teddy Bear Picnic crowd over Labor Day weekend."

"True enough. Let's ask Mom if they found another place to hold it."

Maddie walked over to join our parents, who stood at the Teddy Bear Trot registration table. Isabel French handled the job since early this morning; we both worked late last night putting all the name tags in lanyards, alphabetizing them, and tucking them into envelopes along with fee payment receipts. Then we'd stapled on a flyer that listed Silver Hollow's summer events. A portion of the money raised from the Trot would benefit a volunteer group who made fleece blankets for sick kids at the Ann Arbor children's hospital.

The Silver Bear Shop planned to donate a small bear to go with each blanket, as well. So far I had to package seventy-one bears and then drop them off next week. Isabel handed me a revised list that brought the number up to seventy-four teddies.

"Great, thanks," I said. "Hey, Mom. Did you enjoy the Trot?"

She nodded. "Of course. It's all for a good cause."

"We should have stuck to the route. Your mother slipped on a wet patch when we cut across the village green." Dad showed off grass stains on his khaki pants and sneakers. "Judith pulled me down with her when I tried to catch her."

"Oh, Alex! You didn't have to tell them how we cheated." Mom brushed the back of her jeans with a frown. "I admit, that was a mistake—"

"What is Teddy Hartman doing here?" Dad glowered past my shoulder.

I whirled to see the former owner of Bears of the Heart, once a rival teddy bear company out east, ambling over the park's bridge. My stomach clenched at the familiar sick feeling. Teddy Hartman no longer resembled the genial actor Billy Crystal; his temperament was the exact opposite, in fact, and his hairline had receded so far that he was nearly bald. His face sported more wrinkles, too. He wore faded jeans, red canvas sneakers, and a fancy red wristwatch.

I hadn't seen him since last fall, when he'd passed out flyers for his company, Bears of the Heart, at the Labor Day parade. Teddy Hartman never passed up a chance to compete with the Silver Bear Shop, even after selling his company. That had to be why he wanted to buy Richard and Barbara Davison's house and turn it into a specialty bed-and-breakfast inn, with themed rooms showcasing his teddy bears. Thank God that plan failed.

I figured Hartman would leave us alone. Clearly, I was wrong.

"Here comes trouble," Maddie muttered under her breath. "Who's that with him?"

The woman beside Hartman wore a blue velour jogging suit and headband holding back her shoulder-length dark hair. Her clothes matched the teddy bear she carried under one arm, along with a blue leash attached to a small brown and white dog.

"Teddy and Lucy Hartman," she said to Isabel, who riffled through the manila envelopes.

Several walkers lined up behind the couple. "What an adorable Yorkie," one crooned to the little animal, who bared its teeth.

"He's a Morkie." Annoyed, Lucy Hartman scooped up the pooch into her arms and turned to her husband. "This is taking forever. I need to get back to the store."

"I'm sorry," Isabel said, clearly flustered. "Wait, here it is, out of order."

Teddy grabbed the envelope. "We already walked the route, but I need the receipt for tax purposes. Do I have to sign anything?"

"Nope. You're good to go."

"What a waste," Lucy muttered. She reminded me of the crabby cartoon character from *Peanuts*, Lucy Van Pelt, who always pulled the football away from Charlie Brown and called him a blockhead. "Hey, Teddy. Isn't that the corrupt mayor you were telling me about?"

Hartman snickered. "Yeah, babe. And her lame husband."

"Hey," I said, bristling at his insult.

"Still full of yourself, Hartman?" His voice firm, Dad had

turned around and now eyed his former business rival. "I hear you opened a pet shop in Silver Hollow."

"My wife did. She's finding out just how cozy your wife has it here, taking advantage of the mayor's perks and throwing her weight around. She's got plenty of that."

Dad shook his head at me when I clenched my fists, as if warning me not to speak. "You haven't changed, putting others down and spreading venomous lies."

"I'm telling it like it is. Especially after talking to residents here," Hartman said, "plus a few village council members."

My mother shoved past my father. "Who are you referring to, Mr. Hartman? Because if there's any problems, I'm right here. You can discuss the issue directly with me, and tell these unnamed village council members to air their grievances in person, as well."

Hartman eyed my mother and then me, his thin brows furrowed. "Why do I have to tell you what they said? Go talk to them yourself—"

"I'm talking to you right now," Mom replied tersely, "since you mentioned corruption. If you make a claim like that, you better back it up with facts."

Lucy stepped forward and shushed the dog when it growled. "The SHEBA business owners told me you've been ramming stuff down people's throats."

My mother cocked her head, her auburn hair glinting in the sun, and placed a hand on Dad's arm before he could speak or react. "Thank you for telling me. I'll schedule a SHEBA meeting so we can resolve the issue. I heard your husband took over leadership of the group without a vote. Isn't that right?" she asked, her tone saccharine-sweet.

Hartman shrugged. "So what? Nobody in SHEBA said they had a problem with that. We'll be keeping an eye on you and Alex Silverman, plus your network of cronies." He suddenly snapped his fingers, flashing that Michael Kors red watch in my face. "Now I remember you. From a while back, running around that trade show in New Jersey—you were what, fifteen or sixteen? A little spy, taking notes for your dad."

Both my parents stiffened at his words. I stepped back and waved a dismissive hand in the air to keep them from losing their tempers. "Pure research," I said. "Dad planned to open the Silver Bear Shop, and I was gathering ideas to help him."

"Stealing ideas, you mean." He grinned at my father's growing anger.

"I didn't steal any ideas from you, Mr. Hartman," I said. "You might want to watch what you say given what happened back then."

"Nothing happened," he cut in. "I wouldn't touch such a fat, ugly girl—"

Maddie quickly darted forward and landed a hard punch right on Teddy Hartman's nose. Howling, he clutched his face. Bright red blood streamed between his fingers. Lucy screamed and dropped her dog on the ground.

At the same moment, I reached out to stop my sister from a second punch. The tiny Morkie snapped at my outstretched hand several times, however, biting my fingers and thumb. In shock, I shook it off and stumbled backward.

Lucy hauled on the leash and jerked her pet away. "First you assault my husband, and now you're trying to hurt my dog? I'll sue you for this!"

I reeled, staring at the red drops that dripped to the ground. More blood trickled down from the ragged wounds on my hand. Mom tore off her light jacket, wrapped it around my fingers, and then rushed me over to the registration table. I was oblivious to whether Teddy or Lucy Hartman had retreated from the scene. My shock ebbed away, and pain at last seared my foggy brain. I'd never been bitten by any animal, dog or cat, in my life. I shivered, unable to understand how this had happened so fast.

"Breathe, Sasha," Dad said, crowding me. "Judith, call 9-1-1."

"Already did, Mr. Silverman." Isabel French waved her cell phone.

I took a few deep breaths. Big trouble was certainly brewing now.

Chapter 2

Still in shock, I unwrapped my hand to look at the wounds. "It's not that bad. I only need a bandage, really. It's fine."

"You are not fine," Maddie said, her cheeks pink, and rubbed her skinned knuckles. "I'm glad I popped that jerk for his insults to you and Mom! What an a—"

"Stop, Madeline, right now," Mom said. "You'll be lucky not to land in jail."

"It's her own fault," Teddy Hartman yelled from afar. "She tried to hit our dog!"

"She did not, you liar!" Maddie's bellow brought more onlookers to the scene.

"Stay away from my family," Dad said, his voice tinged with fury, so unlike him. "I'll file charges of harassment if you persist."

"Sasha, sit down. Alex, what will happen to Maddie?" Mom asked, clearly frantic.

"It's her first criminal offense, Judith. I'll talk to the judge and prosecutor about a DPA," Dad said. Possibly noticing my blank stare, he added, "A deferred prosecution agreement.

Otherwise Hartman will insist on felony assault and battery, or even a misdemeanor charge."

My father had practiced law before he opened the Silver Bear Shop & Factory, so he knew all the ins and outs of legal procedures and jargon. Good thing, too. I was far more worried about Maddie going to jail than my own injuries.

My mother caught me when I swayed on my feet. "Sasha, you're shaking like a leaf. Sit down, please! Alex, make her sit in that chair behind the table."

I obeyed, since I saw Hartman better as he held a fistful of paper towels against his face. His wife fussed over him. Lucy's little dog strained on the leash looped around her wrist and yapped. Isabel French hovered over me with anxious eyes, while Maddie paced back and forth before the table in agitation.

"I couldn't help myself, Sash. I've been dying to get back at him for what he did to you at that New Jersey trade show."

"You'll regret this," Hartman shouted again. "The cops will arrest you—"

"I don't care," Maddie yelled back.

"You assaulted me! No, I won't calm down." Hartman waved off a bystander who'd attempted to intervene. "Look at my shirt. It's soaked with blood."

"There's two sides to every story, dude," the stranger said.

"What do you know about it? Get lost!"

I ignored Hartman and slumped on the chair, emotionally numb but feeling every bit of the stinging pain in my fingers. Mom surveyed my hand.

"It doesn't look too bad," she murmured. "I hope you won't need stitches."

Isabel, panting from fetching wet, soapy paper towels from the park's public restroom, watched in concern while Mom washed the blood away. Maddie opened a fresh bottle of water and rinsed my fingers. Dad fumbled to open a first aid kit, spilling items over the box of envelopes on the table, and pawed through the contents. His hands shook when he held out a tube of antibiotic and some gauze.

"Sorry about the mess."

"No problem, Mr. S," Isabel said. "We're all a little upset."

"Where are the police?" Dad muttered. "We'll have to file a report about the dog bite and provide statements about Hartman's injury."

"Do you really think Maddie will face criminal charges?" I asked him.

"Hartman provoked her, but we'll see what Chief Russell says."

I winced at the throbbing pain in my hand. I'd been stung by a wasp and a few yellow jackets, but my own dogs had never snapped at me or my family and only barked at strangers. They loved visitors. I'd gotten used to their welcoming enthusiasm. Maybe I should have known better. That little Morkie had given a few warnings, baring its teeth and growling. But I certainly hadn't hit that dog.

Lucy Hartman's pet seemed high-strung. She'd also been upset, which may have brought on that reaction from the Morkie. The dog lunged at *me*, after all, and Lucy failed to keep him under control. A telling point. I was glad that Isabel witnessed the event along with the outspoken stranger. Other observers milled around and talked in low whispers.

"There." Mom finished wrapping an entire roll of gauze around my hand and fingers. "Alex, hand me some adhesive tape—"

"Here's three pieces. I ripped them since there's no scissors in the kit."

Maddie paced again. "Why hasn't an EMT unit shown up? Or the cops, either."

"I'm okay," I said. "I don't need more than this bandage."

"I'll get you a doctor appointment, Sasha. You need a

tetanus shot," Mom said. "That Morkie better be current on its vaccinations, too. We better get proof from the Hartmans' vet, an actual printout, not just their word for it."

"No one can leave until the police allow it," Dad warned, his voice low.

"Here's a patrol car now, pulling into the lot." Maddie sounded relieved. "Good, it's Digger instead of Officer Hillerman."

"I hope he doesn't spread the news around to everyone in Silver Hollow," Mom muttered under her breath. "He's one of the worst gossips."

Officer Douglas Sykes, whose nickname of "Digger" had stuck with him since high school, strolled our way in his easy gait. That might change once he learned what happened.

"What's going on?" Digger eyed me, Maddie, and my parents before he glanced over at Teddy Hartman. "You guys get into some kind of fight?"

Lucy Hartman stabbed a finger. "They started it! That girl tried to punch my dog, and her sister broke my husband's nose."

"Teddy Hartman started everything," Maddie yelled back.

Dad held up both hands for peace. "Officer Sykes, thank you for coming. Sasha was bitten by their dog—"

"That's nothing compared to getting punched in the nose!" Hartman raised the damp, bloody paper towels in protest. "I want to press charges, officer."

"Sasha hit you?"

"No, that shorter girl did."

"Maddie?" Digger snorted with laughter and then pulled out a notebook from his pocket. "Okay, hold on. Give me your names and addresses."

"He's Teddy Hartman," I offered, "former owner of Bears of the Heart—"

"I can answer for myself." Hartman sounded annoyed.

"My wife and I participated in this stupid Teddy Bear Trot to help out the community. So what do we get in return? A broken nose, from the corrupt mayor's daughter."

"I'm tired of you insulting my wife," Dad said, "and your dog bit Sasha. We want proof of current vaccination records."

"Whoa, hang on now," Digger said, trying to reclaim the conversation, and pointed at my bandaged hand. "Okay, Sasha, you can file a report with the Michigan Humane Society. Or come into the station and file it there. Your choice."

"For a little nip?" Hartman sounded disgusted. "Oh, come on."

I showed him the blood-stained gauze wrapped around my fingers. "All this is not from a little nip, Mr. Hartman."

"Teddy told me long ago how the Silvermans always made trouble for him and Bears of the Heart." Lucy sniffed in disgust. "No wonder this happened today."

"You need to arrest that other Silverman girl," Hartman said. "Right now."

Digger turned away from Hartman and squinted at my sister. "Maddie, you better go into the station and talk to Chief Russell. I'll get the witness statements."

"Handcuff her, right now, or I'll report you," Hartman called out.

"She's not a flight risk, she'll cooperate—"

"You're on their side, aren't you?" Lucy shook a fist at Digger. "Come on, Teddy. We won't get anywhere with this crooked cop. Call our lawyer."

She stalked off, followed by her husband. Digger only shook his head. "Okay, Maddie, you'd better explain what happened."

While she reeled off the events, Digger took notes and asked several questions. Then he joined Dad, who'd been quietly chatting with the onlookers. Digger gathered more names and contact information before he headed over to talk to the Hartmans near the park entrance.

Teddy and Lucy seemed well matched—combative, manipulative, with a double dose of bad temperament. Memories from the past flooded my mind. Hartman had swaggered around the New Jersey trade show, the first one I'd attended, and boasted of his company's huge success and sales. He also accused several people, not just me, of spying or stealing ideas from him. Dad learned later that people filed complaints about his behavior at that show and others.

Hartman never changed his habits until the Disney lawsuit last year. Angry about our win in a magazine's Keepsake Contest, he'd concocted his own version of our Beary Potter wizard bear. It looked too similar to the wizard apprentice Mickey Mouse in *Fantasia*, however. Once Disney lawyers sent a cease and desist letter, Hartman quickly sold his company. Maybe he figured that was the only way to prevent further litigation.

But now I focused on the present. Given a leadership role in SHEBA, Teddy Hartman was stirring up trouble in Silver Hollow. And his bold claims of corruption didn't bode well for my mother or her goals to accomplish as mayor.

I sighed. Bad enough we had so much to deal with at the Silver Bear Shop & Factory.

Isabel pulled a chair over next to mine. "Hey, Sasha. Your uncle said sales have been sluggish, so I've been thinking about how we could set up a tent somewhere to sell bears. Like in the village green, maybe?"

"We already have our bears for sale in several shops," I said. "Plus, we shouldn't rely on what Uncle Ross says."

Maddie hooked a thumb toward a group of women, who slowly walked over the sloping bridge into the park. "Ask Aunt Eve about sluggish sales. She'd know if that's true."

"She's a godsend on our staff," I said. "Her friends are all so funny, and it's exciting to see them take part in community events."

I also enjoyed seeing the group's colorful outfits decorated with teddy bears. They wore red and purple, being Red Hat Society ladies, either velour jogging suits or sweats. Aunt Eve had added a frothy red tulle skirt over her purple pants, plus red beads. Her wide-brimmed straw hat's crown carried a ring of our tiny bears in a rainbow of colors. She also held an iPod, which belted out a Paul McCartney song, and joined in on the last verse.

"I may be turning sixty-four this year, but it's only a number," Aunt Eve said after the music ended. "I feel forty-two, so I'm sticking to that."

"Go ahead, live in denial. I'm proud of all these wrinkles!" Vera Adams, Aunt Eve's best friend, cackled aloud, and everyone joined in. She had on a red sequined sweater that matched the cloche on her head, plus a huge purple feather boa with two red bears dangling on each end. "I loathe birthdays, though."

"I'll take 'em. Better than being six feet under." Susan Jones adjusted her red-and-white-striped hat with a purple bear perched on top. She also had a purple and red scarf with several tiny dangling bears. "But some of us are less than sixty, remember."

"Yes, we know you're only a baby at fifty-eight," Vera retorted. "We allowed you and Shea into our Red Hat Society to keep it alive after we're dead and gone."

"And we're honored to be included." Shea Miller was married to one of Silver Hollow's volunteer firefighters. "But you'll be sticking around for a while, Vera."

"She'll outlive us all, for sure," Aunt Eve said and then rushed over to the registration table. "Sasha! What happened to your hand, did you fall?"

My face burned when the rest of the ladies crowded around me. I flashed a warning look at my sister and Isabel before they could answer. "No, nothing like that. Hope you enjoyed the Teddy Bear Trot. We love the bears you're carrying, they're adorable."

"We wanted to be unique," Aunt Eve said. "I brought this tutu skirt for Shea to wear, but she refused at the last minute."

"Because my sweatshirt is too bulky—"

"Oh, come on. You didn't want to look silly, admit it."

Shea waggled her hands. "Okay, okay. Isn't it enough I'm wearing a necklace of teddy bears?" She jingled the array of tiny plastic bears hanging on a chain. "Fashionista, I'm not."

"So what happened?" Aunt Eve raised an eyebrow. "It must have been something, or you wouldn't have that big of a bandage."

"Dog bite," Isabel said quickly and then clapped a hand over her mouth. "Oops, sorry. You all should have been here to see that!"

"My goodness," Vera said. "Tell us the story, then."

Isabel embellished the tale too much, in my opinion, but her enthusiasm rose near the end. "You should've seen how Maddie punched Hartman—*ka-pow*! That was amazing."

My sister shook her head. "Enough about me. I wanted to ask you a question, Aunt Eve. Is it true that teddy bear sales have slacked off?"

"Who told you that?" She cocked her head, hands on her tulle-covered hips.

Isabel waved a hand. "Your husband—"

"Oh, please don't listen to Mr. Doom and Gloom," Eve said. "He's so negative about everything that I've been calling him Chicken Little. The sky is always falling."

"That's good to know," I said, "because I'm worried if this paint project will ever be done. The crew isn't rushing to finish. Uncle Ross had a fit when the company's estimate included three shutter replacements, railing repairs, and a support post, which sent the cost skyrocketing. Customers keep calling to ask when we'll reopen, too."

Aunt Eve shook her head. "Online sales are strong, and we're shipping out more than the usual number of teddies every week. We've also got a huge number of pre-orders for the kilted bears. I placed a few ads in teddy bear magazines, so that's really paying off."

"Bears in kilts?" Vera looked excited. "I'd like three for my grandkids."

"We're selling them at the Highland Fling next month," I said, "but you can pre-order now to make sure we don't run out."

"Wonderful. I hear there's a new Scottish-themed boutique in town, right?"

"The MacRaes moved here from Edinburgh and converted Barbara Davison's house into the Kilted Scot. I'm dying to see the inside, but I've been so busy."

"I'd like to go," Maddie said. "The MacRaes are close friends of the Queen Bess Tea Room owners. Art and Trina Wentworth helped them contract for the renovations."

"The entire first floor is their shop," Isabel said, her eyes snapping with excitement. "And Bonnie MacRae put in a huge commercial kitchen so she can bake shortbread, scones, and baps, plus sandwiches for the tearoom."

"Baps? What are those?" Shea Miller asked.

"Buttery rolls," Maddie said, "from what Trina told me."

Susan Jones tugged my elbow. "I want to know more about this dog bite, Sasha. What kind of dog was it?"

"Morkie, a mix of Maltese and Yorkie," Maddie said before I could reply. "It totally went berserk and bit Sasha's fingers. She bled like crazy."

"I bet it was that same yappy dog we saw back by the Village Green," Vera said. "It was snarling when we walked past, remember? And it snapped at me, too."

"The one who bit Teddy Hartman?" Aunt Eve laughed. "We walked behind them for half a mile or so, and saw him kick the 'nasty little cur,' as he called it, when it got in his way. Can't say I blame the dog for chomping his ankle. His wife said he deserved it."

Interesting. So I wasn't the only one bitten today.

Chapter 3

Maddie pumped her fist. "Ha! Now we know that dog has a history of biting," she said, "even if Teddy Hartman provoked it first. Sasha was only trying to help me, but then the Morkie attacked her. Lucy failed to control her dog."

Dad meandered over, and I noted his pleased expression. "I overheard your conversation, Eve. Would you sign a deposition about witnessing the earlier dog bite? You might have to testify in court if the case isn't settled before then, however."

"Of course, to both," Aunt Eve said. "I believe I heard Lucy Hartman mention that her little Sparky was only being sassy. Teddy didn't seem to agree, though."

"Whoa. I can testify to how crazy that dog acted when it bit Sasha," Isabel said, her voice hushed. "I wouldn't call that sassy, not one bit."

Dad wrote down Isabel's name and phone number. "Great, thanks."

"Do you think Maddie will be arrested?" I asked him.

"No way," she said. "I'll go to the station and talk to

Chief Russell, like Digger said, so chill out. Maybe we need ice cream."

"Sounds good to me."

I noticed the crowd had thinned over by the brand-new Silver Scoop truck. A few parents with young children stood in line, their children running around in excitement while they waited. Lucas Vanderbeek's dark blond head bobbed behind the counter. He handed out treats and then counted change, countless times. The young entrepreneur had bought both the name rights and inventory from Isabel French and Kristen Bloom's village shop, and added frozen popsicles and other items besides hand-dipped cones.

Isabel had a familiar starry glaze in her eyes while she watched him. "He's so cute," she said. "I've tried to talk to him, but he acts so distant. I don't know what to think."

"Too busy with his business, maybe?" I sympathized with her frustration. "Maybe he'd appreciate a few sales tips."

"I tried that already." Isabel sighed. "He said he's got his own ideas. He thanked me, but maybe Lucas has a girlfriend."

"Mint chocolate chip for Sasha, and Rocky Road for me," my sister said. "Did you want something, Isabel?" When she shook her head, Maddie raced over to join the line.

Isabel handed out packets to the last few Teddy Bear Trot participants. Asia Gibson, an employee at Maddie's graphics business, Silver Moon, walked my way. She looked spunky in an orange hoodie and jean capris, with dark sunglasses on her head and a mass of tiny braids pulled into a long ponytail. Her coffee-hued skin glowed in the sunshine.

"Hey, Sasha! Heard you got bitten by a dog. Are you okay?"

I wasn't happy that gossip had already spread, but smiled. "Yeah, I'm good."

"Hope it wasn't too bad. I still have a scar on my calf when that happened to me." She pulled up her patterned capri fabric on one leg to show off a jagged line that hadn't faded yet. "I had to get a dozen stitches, right here. That was no fun."

"When was this?"

"Last fall, at the Labor Day parade. Some tiny little thing. A Morkie—"

"Lucy Hartman's dog—brown and white, floppy ears, and a curly tail?"

"How did you know?" Asia listened to my story with wide eyes. "Me and my boyfriend Miles walked by the court-house when Teddy Hartman passed out flyers. His wife was with him. She had the dog on a leash, one of those extending ones. Little devil chomped on my leg, all of a sudden. Without any warning."

"Wow! What did you do?"

"Told her she'd better pay for the doctor's bills," Asia said, adjusting her sunglasses, "or they'd have to put down the dog. Miles works for a lawyer, so the Hartmans decided to settle out of court."

"I'm glad you made them pay." I held up my bandaged hand and winced. "This trumps the blister on my foot from walking in sandals instead of sneakers."

She nodded. "You ought to try some organic foot massage cream. I love that stuff. Do you eat berries and fruits high in vitamin C? Those are great for feet health. And I swear by using raw honey for any bites or wounds. Heals up the skin fast."

"Maybe I'll try that. I've got a jar of Debbie Davison's honey."

"It even works on poison ivy rashes," Asia said. "I was tearing out vines at my parents' house last summer. Nothing the doctor gave me worked, and nothing over the counter. So use honey. But make sure you cut down on caffeine—"

"I can't do that," I interrupted. "It's impossible!"

Asia laughed. "Cut down, not totally eliminate, although you'd get used to it if you started drinking green tea all the time. Eat more salmon, too. Or take a supplement to boost your omega-3 intake. I cut all carbs and sugar out of my diet."

I shook my head with sorrow. "Another impossible thing, because I'm addicted to cookies. They know my name. I still have a box of Girl Scout Thin Mints left in my freezer."

"I hear ya, girlfriend. I was so hooked on sugar, but I lost sixty pounds two years ago." Asia nodded at my disbelief. "Yup. Had a bad hernia and couldn't eat for months. Cottage cheese, soup, that was it, until surgery fixed it. Now I'm careful about eating healthy. Processed foods don't appeal to me anymore. Fruits and veggies, chicken, turkey, fish. Smoothies with kale and broccoli. Mmm."

Kale? Ugh. I was not feeling the love.

Asia flexed from side to side, lifted one arm to stretch beyond her shoulder, and then the other. I envied her suppleness and vowed to do more stretching. Maybe in the morning, before I slid out of bed. And maybe goat yoga, like my sister suggested. A few friends had been raving about Kristen Bloom's classes. One thing was for certain. I now had more fodder for dealing with the Hartmans, given Asia's story about being bitten by their Morkie.

I changed the subject, though. "How do you like working for Maddie?"

"I love it! Zoe and I teamed up to work on the next ad campaign for Silver Claw, Eric Dyer's business—but you know all about him. And we're doing billboard designs for Flynn Hanson and his law firm. That's gonna pay big bucks."

I barely hid my surprise. Why would my ex-husband hire Maddie instead of a graphic arts business in Ann Arbor? I also hadn't heard whether Flynn had set a wedding date with his fiancée, a local weather forecaster. After the murderous fiasco the Antonini-Davison wedding spawned a few months ago, I planned to avoid any others.

"Sounds like Maddie has her hands full, then," I said, eyeing my sister, who chatted with my parents, Aunt Eve, and her friends.

Asia nodded. "I'm set to work on the flyers for the Highland Fling."

"I can't wait for that," Isabel said, although a man walked over to address her.

"Excuse me, I'm looking for the Hartmans. They're registered for this event."

"Oh, I'm sorry. They left already."

The gentleman looked out of place in a tailored business suit and red tie, given the Teddy Bear Trot participants in casual dress. He frowned. "That's odd. Teddy told me they'd meet me here at the park."

Dad hurried over and extended a hand, clearly recognizing him. "Kevin Whittaker! Good to see you again. I'm Alex Silverman."

"Yes, I remember. You retired from running the Silver Bear factory, right?" Whittaker grinned. "You must know I bought Bears of the Heart, then. Teddy Hartman is my brother-in-law, in fact. I helped my sister out and saved the business."

"I see. How's it going?" Dad asked.

"That crazy Love Shack bear is selling like hotcakes. Otherwise, I wouldn't be all that happy. I'm planning to change the name, though."

"Still located in New Hampshire?"

"We moved operations to Maine, actually. How's the Silver Bear business? On the way into town, I noticed a crew doing repairs to the shop's exterior."

"Just a quick paint job to freshen up, inside as well. My

daughter Sasha is managing everything now." He waved a hand in my direction. "I'm only a consultant."

"Nice to meet you, Sasha."

Whittaker nodded in my direction, so I smiled back. He reminded me of square-jawed Ted Danson portraying Michael in *The Good Place*, whenever I caught the TV show, given his black eyeglass frames and nice suit, but without the bow tie. Kevin Whittaker even had the same white hair combed back from his high forehead and similar voice tone. After pushing a button on his cell phone, he waved it at me.

"You scored a huge hit with that Beary Potter wizard bear," Whittaker said, his tone bordering on jealousy, and tapped the image. "Teddy made a big mistake trying to copy that Disney design, and his social media posts backfired. I warned him not to do that, but he ignored my advice. And my sister Lucy."

I only nodded, since I suspected he wouldn't care to hear my real opinion about Teddy Hartman or Bears of the Heart. Whittaker and my father walked off, discussing business.

"Sorry, they didn't have mint chocolate chip." Maddie set down half a dozen ice cream sandwiches on the table. "There's Neapolitan or plain chocolate. Lucas Vanderbeek said he's waiting for a local dairy farmer to get back to him, and plans to make real custard. Help yourself, Isabel and Asia."

Isabel chose Neapolitan, but Asia backed off. "No thanks, I'll pass. What did I say about sugar and carbs? The worst thing for you."

"Your call." When I fumbled with the paper, Maddie took pity and unwrapped the ice cream for me. "But how can we eat all these by ourselves?"

Asia glanced around furtively and then snatched a sandwich. "If Miles sees me, he'll rag on me for hours. I'm always gettin' on his case about junk food."

"So did you hear that Teddy Hartman and his wife

opened a pet shop?" I asked her. "In the store that used to be the Silver Scoop."

"No, and I'm staying far away from them." Asia leaned closer, her voice low. "But I did hear that he's telling people that your mom's corrupt and plays favorites. And how she shuts down anyone who opposes her when she rams things through the council."

"That's so unfair," I said, snatching another ice cream sandwich.

Maddie unwrapped it for me. "Why is Hartman always making trouble?"

Isabel agreed. "I heard he was mad about the shop's rental fee, but Barbara Davison wouldn't budge. Good thing she's in Florida now and doesn't have to deal with him in person. He ought to be thrilled the pet boutique is located right next door to the Pretty in Pink bakery. Tons of women go there. You know they'll stop in and browse for their pets."

"But this town doesn't need another boutique," Asia said. "There's the antique shop, the new Scottish-themed shop, the Silver Bear Shop. Even your mom's Vintage Nouveau gallery has plenty of gift merchandise besides artwork."

"The Bird Cage sells a lot more than seed and suet cakes, too," I said, finishing my ice cream. "Like stationery and earrings—you name it."

"Don't forget the Queen Bess Tea Room offers teacups, pots, tea tins. Fresh Grounds has specialty coffee items," Maddie said. "And Ham Heaven has pig-related items."

"See what I mean?" Asia licked her sticky fingers. "Too bad he didn't open a hardware store. Miles and I are always running to Chelsea or Ann Arbor for stuff. We're renovating our bungalow over on Edith Street."

"The one with the black shutters, right? That's a cute house," I said. "I love the front yard with all the perennials."

"We worked so hard to plant them. Miles has a green

thumb, but not me." She tossed her ice cream wrapper in the nearest trash can. "I saw that crew ruining all your flowers. You should have heard Miles, ranting and raving, because that really burned him. He said your shop could have won a land-scape design contest. That'll be a job and a half redoing it."

"I guess we're stuck with Teddy and Lucy Hartman as business owners in the village," Maddie said, returning to our original topic. "Garrett Thompson told me his uncle is steamed that Hartman managed to be appointed as the leader of SHEBA."

"The what now?" Asia asked.

"Silver Hollow Entrepreneurs and Business Association, shortened to SHEBA. At first, Dad refused to join the organi-zation," I added, "because he really loathes Teddy Hartman. Uncle Ross agreed with him, too. But Mom said it would look bad if our family business was a holdout, so we had to join and pay dues. Not that any of us have attended a meet-ing yet."

"We better not, after today," Maddie said.

Asia nodded. "I don't blame you one bit."

My ears perked up, however, when Dad and Kevin Whit-taker returned from their stroll around the park. They dis-cussed several teddy bear and toy shows at a distance, and then moved on to the Hartmans' bid to open a bed-and-breakfast.

"The financing fell through, from what Lucy told me," Whittaker said. "She preferred a pet shop business anyway. Lucy said they've already cleared a profit."

"I wish them well," Dad said, but I sensed his tone fell short on sincerity.

Maddie pursed her lips, eyes on the sky, holding in silent laughter. I had to grind my teeth and freeze my face to keep from reacting. At last, Kevin Whittaker shook hands with Dad and strolled toward the parking lot. Dad rejoined Mom, Aunt Eve, and her friends.

"Talk about awkward," Asia said, eyes wide.

"You bet Dad was cringing the whole time, listening to that drivel," Maddie said.

"I was, too, dealing with the Hartmans and their lawyer." Asia winced. "Lucy's worse than Teddy, if you can believe it. I better get home and see how Miles is doing in the garage. You know how guys love to tinker with anything broken. See you Monday!"

She rushed toward the park entrance. "Jay gets wrapped up with his carving," I said to Maddie, "but is Eric like that in his brewery?"

"Hours go by, and he forgets to eat. Forgets what time it is, forgets we'd planned to meet for dinner." My sister sighed. "Just the other day, Eric said he'd pick me up after work. Granted, I lost a few hours finishing a graphics project, but at least I was done by seven. He never showed, so I went home. Eric called me the next day, apologizing up and down, because of this mead he's working to perfect. He's obsessed."

"I bet he could sell that at the Highland Fling." I waved my bandaged hand at Maddie and Isabel. "Hey, does anyone have an aspirin or two?"

"Yeah, I do—and Mom said she's taking you to the doctor so he can check those bites. You need a tetanus shot, remember."

"But they're only open until noon on a Saturday," I said, "and it's past that."

"You have a three o'clock appointment. What was that about Asia having to deal with the Hartmans and their lawyer?" Maddie asked.

I explained about how the Morkie bit her at the Labor Day parade before Digger stalked up to the registration table. He hooked a thumb at Maddie. "Ready?"

"Yeah. Did you know *The New York Times* and *The New Yorker* won a Pulitzer over that awful Harvey Weinstein scandal? That's why I got so mad about Hartman, Sasha. I'm all for the MeToo movement and not letting guys get away with bad behavior."

"But don't you think you overdid it?" I asked.

"Hartman insulted you and Mom today," she said, "and he deserved to get punched out for acting like such a creep. Stop worrying about it. I'll be fine."

Maddie sounded cheerful, but I had a feeling this situation might spin out of control. Her assault came before the dog bite, after all. Knowing Teddy Hartman, he'd press charges. That meant I'd have to come clean about what happened at the New Jersey trade show.

"Now that the Trot's over, I'm going home," Isabel said.

Instead she sauntered over toward Silver Scoop's truck and smiled at Lucas Vanderbeek. I swallowed an aspirin tablet that Maddie found in her fanny pack, despite the dirt specks on it, with the last few sips in my water bottle. I dreaded stitches.

"Let's go, Sasha." Mom jangled her car keys. "Don't give me that hangdog look."

I really hated needles.

Chapter 4

Fuzzy headed, I reached for my buzzing cell phone and caught it before it slid off the bedside table. The alarm clock showed eight-something. I fumbled to swipe the phone with my bandaged hand to answer before my voicemail cut in.

"Ow. Hello?"

"Sash. I heard about your dog bite." Flynn Hanson, my ex-husband, sounded cheerful so early. I stifled a groan, aware that I should have recognized the special ringtone I'd programmed for his calls. "Sorry it happened. I know you'll want to file a lawsuit—"

"What time is it?" I interrupted, squinting at the clock.

"Uh, quarter past eight."

"Coffee. After coffee."

"Want me to call you later? Like, after church?"

"Tomorrow," I mumbled.

"But you need to get the ball rolling on the lawsuit," Flynn said. "It's important to file quickly in a dog bite case. Michigan is strict with their one-bite policy, and it sounds like the owner is clearly responsible. Have you gone to the doctor yet?"

"Yeah. Got a tetanus shot." I rubbed my sore arm.

"Have the office fax the report over, along with the dog's vaccination record."

"But—"

Click. He'd already hung up. I sighed in dismay, since I hadn't decided what to do about the incident at the Teddy Bear Trot. Especially given the complication about Maddie's assault. My ex-husband never considered anything except winning a case, though. I rolled over. My hand throbbed, along with my arm, and I had a hard time getting back to sleep. I also couldn't block the memory of that little Morkie's jaws clamped on my fingers. The shock lingered.

And when Rosie and Sugar Bear greeted me yesterday after I arrived home, their tails wagging, I felt myself hesitating to respond. That worried me. Now my sweet little dogs slept at the bed's foot, instead of near my pillows like usual, as if sensing my need for space.

Throbbing pain brought me to my feet. I ambled to the bathroom, picked up the ibuprofen bottle, and popped a few pills with a glass of water. I didn't want an upset stomach, so I chowed down on crackers from the waxy plastic sleeve I'd left on the counter last night. Then I massaged the injection site on my upper arm with its raised lump. I saw once more the wild look in the small dog's eyes. The flash of his canine teeth. And the blood.

No way did I want to unwrap my hand and check the stitches.

The doctor insisted on half a dozen, given the jagged edges on my thumb and fingers. Church would have to wait. No way did I want to rehash what happened with anyone who'd heard the gossip. Not even to set the record straight, in case the story had gone off the rails. That seemed likely, given Digger and plenty of other villagers who fed the network. Let them talk.

I was in no mood to deal with all that today, so I slid back into bed, pulled the covers over me, and closed my eyes. I needed time to forget. To heal, and come to grips with the Hartmans moving to Silver Hollow. Why had they chosen our village? It didn't make sense. After losing out on the bed-and-breakfast option, why hadn't they found some other small town for a pet shop? Unless Teddy Hartman planned revenge against my family.

Rosie crept forward and snuggled against my back, while Sugar Bear inched her way to a warm spot near my chest. Within minutes she snored. I smiled. My sweet dogs gave me comfort without conditions. I reached over and petted Rosie and then cuddled with Sugar.

How had Flynn heard the news about the dog bite? He'd moved his offices to Ann Arbor, after all. I had a feeling he'd either talked to Mom or heard from someone else with ties to Silver Hollow. Maybe his fiancée? I wasn't sure where she lived, however, or her parents.

"Knock, knock!" Maddie stood at the door, eyes bright, fully dressed. "Breakfast is ready. It's almost nine, and I figured you wouldn't want to go to church with that bandage on your hand. How do you feel this morning?"

"Sore. I took a few pills."

"Better change the dressing with fresh ointment." She pulled on my good arm until the dogs reluctantly moved, untangled the covers, and dragged me out of bed.

I yawned, wishing I'd gotten more sleep. "Maybe—"

"Jay's downstairs having breakfast. He came to check on you, and said he's going to Riverside Park to practice tossing a few cabers. The Highland Fling committee chose it for the event, so you should tag along and check it out. Ready to change this bandage?"

Maddie also helped me get dressed afterward, despite my protests. I followed her downstairs to the kitchen, where my honey bear of a boyfriend, Jay Kirby, sat with a huge mug of coffee and a plate of pancakes. He looked adorable. His light brown hair hadn't been combed, and he wore his usual plaid shirt and cargo pants, but his hazel eyes twinkled.

"Morning, sunshine!" Jay jumped up and hugged me. "How are you doing?"

A talented woodcarver who accepted commissions and often worked at various other jobs to pay the bills, Jay was now part of the family. We'd been seeing each other for over eight months, exclusive. I basked in his love and tight hug.

"I'm good."

"I never got a text reply from you earlier, so I came over."

"I haven't checked my phone for anything. I'm so wiped out."

He grinned. "That's okay. I brought you those flowers."

"Thanks!" I kissed him and drank in the gorgeous display of colorful tulips in a huge glass jar. "They still have their bulbs, so I can plant them."

Once I sat down, Mom set a plate with fluffy buttermilk rounds and pushed over the butter and syrup. "Need me to cut your pancakes?" she asked, hovering by my elbow.

"I'm not an invalid," I said, half-joking, and mangled the pile with my knife and fork. "Too bad that dog bit my right hand, not the left."

"Here's your coffee." Mom slid the mug closer. "Listen, honey. You had a big shock yesterday. Rest and relax today."

I couldn't relax, however, with all the hammering noises outside. A few workers passed outside the window, carrying lumber. "Why are they working on Sunday, and what are they doing? I thought they finished the exterior repairs."

"Yesterday your father talked to the construction manager," Mom said. "He saw that the corner turret and rotunda had several rotting boards, so now they're replacing those. They'll have to repaint that area, too. The crew should have noticed them in the first place."

I grumbled to myself while pouring cream and sugar in my coffee. "They trampled our beautiful dogwood shrub to bits. We'll have to replace that, plus several flower beds. And there's paint flakes everywhere. They better clean up before they leave."

"Never mind all that. I want you to see how much room there is at Riverside Park," Mom said, "for all the music and dancing, plus the athletic games."

"Isn't it north of here?" I swallowed a bite of blueberry pancakes. "I thought Amy Evans wanted to host the event at the Chelsea fairgrounds."

"Their manager couldn't guarantee that the RVs stored over winter would be retrieved that early, so Amy had to go with Riverside Park. The committee plans to build a permanent pavilion instead of paying a rental fee to use the grounds."

Jay sipped his coffee. "The park is kind of long and skinny in shape. How are vendors going to get electricity?"

"They'll have to rely on generators." Mom fetched a travel mug. "Chief Russell is still negotiating a fee for directing traffic and crowd control, and Amy has plenty of other details to hammer out yet. Finish eating, Sasha—"

"She can take her time." Jay winked at me. "Want me to feed you?"

I stuck out my tongue, even though I knew he was teasing. After finishing my pancakes, I set my plate in the sink and accepted the travel mug with more coffee. But at the door, Mom helped me shrug into a light jacket, laced up my boots for me, and kissed my cheek. I sighed, feeling like a kindergartner on the way to school.

"Are you going to pin a note on my chest, too?"

"You're the walking wounded. Milk it while you can," Mom said.

I accepted the inevitable when Jay had to buckle my seat belt in his truck. He even rubbed my upper arm to ease the tetanus soreness. My phone pinged. I read a text message reminder from Flynn's law office to fax over the Morkie's current vaccination record. I wasn't looking forward to tracking the Hartmans down but called the K-9 and Kitty Korner pet store. The phone kept ringing. Rats. Clearly, they hadn't set up voice mail yet for messages.

Faint bells pealed from Silver Hollow's clock tower when we drove past the village outskirts. I filled in Jay about yesterday's Teddy Bear Trot, and how the Hartmans' dog had also bitten Asia Gibson last year at the Labor Day parade.

"I'm sorry I wasn't there to punch Hartman's lights out as well."

"Violence is never the answer," I said, and meant it. "You'd be facing charges, too."

Jay shrugged. "True, but he needs some sense knocked into him."

When we arrived at the park, he drove past a dozen or so people chatting near the entrance. The Highland Fling committee's chair, Amy Evans, stood in their midst. Jay parked close to the first baseball diamond—if you could call it that, being a bare patch of dirt without bleachers or any white chalk marking the bases. I remembered playing softball here during high school, either as first baseman or pitcher.

Three different groups milled on the fields, both men and women. One group on the soccer field's far end practiced axe throwing at several wooden targets. A cheer rose whenever someone hit a bull's-eye. In the baseball diamond's outfield, three men dragged wooden logs over the grass. A third cluster of athletes, far enough away on the second baseball diamond, swung long-handled pieces of wood over their heads and then let go. They sailed out to land between markers in that outfield's grass.

I shielded my eyes from the bright sunshine, wishing I'd brought sunglasses. "Wow, there's a lot more people here than I expected."

"My younger brother is over there, the short guy. Nathan was up north when my parents invited you over after Christmas. He works at the Quick Mix factory, but Mom hopes he'll get serious about choosing a better career," Jay said. "And that's Charlie Volker over there, tossing the hammer. Never too early to start practicing."

He parked the truck and led me to meet both men. Nathan Kirby, probably five foot five or six at most, but husky like a football tackle, saluted me with two fingers. He looked like Jay's twin, with light brown hair and blue eyes, the same mischievous smile, and a friendly manner.

"Hey, you must be Sasha. Jay told me about you, and so did my sister."

"Nice to meet you," I said. "How's Lauren?"

"Good," he said, "although I never see her much."

"So, Charlie," Jay said, "you gonna beat me at caber toss?"

"You bet, but first I'm practicing the hammer throw." Charlie sported long dark hair and a beard, a flimsy T-shirt over well-defined muscles, a tartan kilt, and heavy boots. "Watch and learn, bro! Watch and learn."

He spun around and then flung the long wooden handle out toward the markers. "I'm surprised you don't get dizzy and fall over," I said. "But why is it called a hammer? It looks more like a croquet mallet."

Nathan laughed. "Yep. Only a lot heavier."

I suddenly noticed Teddy Hartman break away from the group at the soccer field. He leaned down to retrieve an axe— actually, a short-handled hatchet. I hadn't noticed him before among the others, but recognized him now by the white adhesive strips over his nose. His wife Lucy jogged behind him, wearing a dark fleece jacket over her jeans, but their little dog was nowhere in sight. Thankfully, they walked back to rejoin their friends.

I watched them, keeping my distance, curious about the sport. Hartman stared at one wooden target with its red rings. He drew the hatchet, one-handed, high over his head, and then let it fly. The weapon bounced off the board and fell into a patch of weeds.

Lucy laughed, although her attempt fell short of the target, too. Another man ambled over to retrieve their hatchets, lean yet muscular, with a scruffy beard. He reminded me of the actor Chris Pratt of the *Jurassic* films, but taller and far more solemn.

Still curious, I tugged at Jay's elbow. "Who's that guy?" I asked. "The tall one who's holding those axes in his hands."

"No idea," Jay said. Charlie and Nathan didn't know either and turned back to practice.

Jay and I watched Teddy Hartman's next hatchet strike the board well below the target. Lucy's cackling laugh drifted our way. She swung the small axe back and forth, as if loosening up, and then raised it over her head using both hands. But her throw sailed wide.

"I wouldn't laugh so hard, babe," her husband called out.

"Your dad was practicing axe throwing," Jay said, "and he looked really good. Charlie said he's the best amateur around, and has a good chance to win."

I stared at him. "*My* dad?"

"Yeah," Charlie said, rejoining us. "Alex told me he won a few contests in the past."

"At axe throwing." I still couldn't process that. "You're not kidding?"

He laughed at my puzzled frown. "Guess you didn't know, huh?"

"Nope. Did you?" I asked Jay, who shook his head.

"Surprised me, and that's why I'm sticking to the hammer throw and caber toss at the Fling," he added. "Nathan, too. You should try tossing a caber, Sasha. I heard they'll have a women's-only toss in a separate contest."

"If I lifted boxes all day in the shipping department, I might. All I do is sit behind the sales counter." I poked my upper arm muscle. "I'm lucky I can heft up Mr. Silver, the giant bear in the loft, when I need to move him. Go ahead, laugh it up," I said when they snickered. "That reminds me. I need the vaccination record for Lucy Hartman's Morkie. I might not get another chance, so I'll catch them now."

Hoping Teddy and Lucy wouldn't bite me for interrupting, I walked over to the soccer field. "Best one yet, Ted," the other man called out when Hartman's next throw landed in the target's outermost ring. "Come on, Lucy. Try it one-handed."

"I'm not used to this sandy ground in the park. I can't get a good stance." She grunted hard and then released her hatchet. It sank into the board's top right corner. "Damn."

Taking a deep breath, I marched toward the Hartmans and waved my gauze-wrapped hand to catch Lucy's attention. She frowned and glanced at her husband.

"Flynn Hanson, my lawyer, wants your dog's vaccination record," I said.

"That Flynn Wins guy?" Hartman hooted with laughter. "Always bragging about how many cases he's won. Arrogance doesn't always translate to success."

"This is our lawyer, Andrew Kane." Lucy waved at the

Chris Pratt look-alike. "He may not do TV commercials, but he'll beat your lawyer in court."

"Now, Lucy." Kane brushed bits of grass and dirt off his khaki trousers. "Ms. Silverman hasn't filed a lawsuit yet, that I've heard, but you need to comply."

Lucy rummaged in a backpack. "Too bad his rabies shots are up to date. Catch!"

She tossed a small object my way, so I caught it without thinking—and regretted it, given the slimy fur. Apparently, their dog had recently chewed on a Benny Bear. I could tell it was the infamous toy, given its front seam and sitting position. That style of teddy bear, no longer produced by Bears of the Heart, had been used by a group of pedophiles to videotape children at home. The company discontinued sales long before the men awaited trial for the crime.

I dropped the bear on the ground with a scowl.

"Can't take a joke?" she said, grinning wide. "Never mind, here." Lucy dug in her jeans pocket and retrieved a folded piece of paper. "Sparky's current on all his vaccines."

Gritting my teeth, I wiped my damp hand on the grass before I scanned the sheet. It looked official, with the vet's signature and seal. I crammed the folded paper into my pocket and turned on my heel, leaving without a reply. Flynn could deal with the Hartmans. They followed me all the way over to where Jay waited, however. I turned around, my good hand on a hip.

"What do you want?" I asked.

Teddy Hartman pointed to his taped nose. "If the cops won't charge your sister with assault, I'll slap her with a civil lawsuit. She can't go punching people out of the blue."

"It wasn't 'out of the blue'," Jay shot back, "because you insulted Sasha and her parents. Plus, your dog bit my girlfriend."

"You weren't there, what do you know about it?" Lucy

swung the hatchet by its handle, but Andrew Kane wrenched the weapon away from her.

"Don't make this situation worse," he said to her in a low voice.

"Don't be a jerk." She tried to retrieve it, but he held tight. "Let go, for God's sake. I'm not gonna do anything stupid."

"It's stupid to insult people," I said.

Ignoring her profanity-laced comeback, I followed Jay past the hammer throw group to watch Charlie Volker in the second baseball field. The caber toss athletes handled huge logs that resembled telephone poles. One man struggled to lift a caber, grunting with the effort. After he tossed it, the log flipped only a few feet. Jay waved to several other men, their shirts already damp under their armpits, who'd also practiced a few tosses.

"Ready to try it, Jay?" Charlie asked. "Start stretching."

He grinned. "I don't think that's gonna help."

"Hey, Sasha. Did you know Jay was a star pitcher of the high school baseball team?" Charlie gathered his long, curly hair into a man bun. "Killer fastball. Won't help him in the caber toss, but maybe the hammer throw."

"I remember him playing baseball," I said, to Jay's surprise.

"You do?"

"Sure. Watched a few games, especially the state championship—"

"Where I blew it in the final inning," he said, sounding morose. "Tore a ligament in my shoulder, and that ended any chance at a college scholarship. We lost the game, too."

I hugged him. "Nobody blamed you for the loss."

"Yeah, I'm grateful for that." Jay rolled his shoulders. "I still feel bad about it, though. There goes Charlie into his warm-up routine."

We watched him loosen his black T-shirt and stretch his hamstring muscles. His navy and green kilt swept the ground when he lunged several times and then flexed his arms. Charlie stretched his leather-gloved fingers, took a few deep breaths, and marched over to the caber. He balanced it against one shoulder and closed his eyes. After several more breaths, clearly preparing himself, he slowly walked forward.

Charlie sped into a run, his spiked golf shoes marking the grass. Then he gave a mighty shout and heaved the log away from his body. The long pole tipped forward, flipped over, and landed. All three men rushed to measure the distance. Nathan whistled.

"Even farther than your last toss, dude. Wow. I'm gonna try that."

Jay's younger brother repeated everything Charlie had done, but barely managed to balance the caber against his short torso. Nathan walked forward, but before he could speed up, the heavy log tipped sideways. He tried to heave it, except that made things worse. Nathan shouted a warning, since the log didn't flip but plummeted downward.

Straight toward Teddy Hartman.

Chapter 5

At Lucy Hartman's shrill scream, her husband jumped out of harm's way. "Hey! Watch what you're doing," Teddy Hartman shouted.

"He gave a warning," Charlie called out. "You should have heard it."

"That kid tried to kill me!"

Amy Evans rushed over, since she'd witnessed what happened. Her dark hair wasn't pulled back into the usual ballerina bun, and she wore jeans and a sweater instead of a navy pantsuit. But her commanding voice lent a formidable presence.

"I'm certain that was unintentional, Mr. Hartman."

"Bunk! He aimed right for me," he shot back. Andrew Kane plodded over to join him, holding several hatchets. "You saw what happened, right?"

"I heard a shout and saw the log fall. But I couldn't tell if it came close to you." Kane shrugged. "Sorry."

"My brother lost control," Jay said in Nathan's defense. "It's all gravity. What goes up, must come down."

Hartman snorted. "And I bet you put him up to that trick."

"No way, man." Nathan shook his head, clearly nervous. "Nuh-uh."

I faced the Hartmans. "What are you doing over here, when you're supposed to practice axe throwing in the soccer field?"

"We have a right to walk wherever we want," Lucy said.

"Only as long as you pay attention," Amy said. "Accidents can happen. Don't forget one of your group almost hit that little dog earlier today."

"That's why we put Sparky in the car."

I glanced at the parking lot, hoping they'd left a window cracked open. While the spring weather wasn't too hot, a closed-up car could be uncomfortable with today's sunshine. Even though Sparky had bit me, I didn't want to see any animal suffer in the heat.

"Okay, already." Teddy tapped his red watch and turned to his wife. "We'll need more practice if we're gonna beat Alex Silverman. He's a champion, remember."

"In throwing axes?" Andrew Kane sounded skeptical.

"Yeah. He won the last big tournament in Ohio, and I came in sixteenth. That blowhard won't get the best of me this year."

Amy Evans rejoined her assistants at the park's entrance. Once the Hartmans were out of earshot, Jay turned to his brother. "You didn't aim for Hartman, right?"

"I should have," Nathan grumbled. "What a jerk."

"Maybe so," I said, "but we've had enough trouble."

"Athletes tossing a caber are more likely to strain a muscle in their core," Charlie said, "or end up with a hernia more than hurting a bystander."

"What's this about hurting a bystander?" Gavin MacRae

strolled over with his wife, Bonnie. They both glanced in appreciation at Charlie's kilt. "A MacArthur tartan?"

"My mom's heritage goes way back to the Highlands," he said. "Dad's German all the way, with a surname like Volker."

"How's business at the Kilted Scot boutique?" I asked Gavin.

He seemed pleased to reply. "Great so far—am I right, Bonnie?"

"Could be a wee bit better, but we're hopin' more people hear about us after the Fling," she said in her lyrical accent. "We're doing all right for now."

Bonnie MacRae was a short, plump woman with salt-and-pepper hair and bright blue eyes, wearing a long dress over stirrup tights, plus a denim jacket. Silver earrings dangled near her neck and matched a necklace with an unusual pendant.

"That's gorgeous," I said. "Isn't that a thistle in the center?"

"Aye. *Outlander* fans love these. It's a wax seal, and we sell them at the shop."

"So cool."

"I've been orderin' far too many souvenirs, mostly Loch Ness monster ladles," she said with a hearty laugh. "Even photos and paintings of the Isle of Skye and Edinburgh. I hope that won't step on your mother's territory. Will she host a vendor booth?"

I heard a touch of worry in her tone and shook my head. "The local artists who sell their work at the gallery will have their own booths, so it won't be a problem. Mom will be busy representing the village as mayor."

"I saw several lovely paintings at the gallery. And Gavin's been teachin' me all about Michigan, and how to pronounce the bridge as *Mack-i-naw* and not *Mack-in-knack*."

"Then you're way ahead of others who've recently moved here."

Bonnie leaned toward me, the corners of her eyes crinkling, and hooked a thumb at Teddy Hartman. He was tossing an axe at the target in the distant soccer field. "Have you heard the daft stories he's been spreadin' about us in the village? That our products are pure rubbish, and overpriced to boot."

I nodded. "He's been saying that about our teddy bears for years."

"Tell me more about this Hartman. I hear you're the one to ask."

"Well, it's a long story."

Bonnie threaded an arm through mine, careful not to bump my bandaged hand, and winked. "You can tell me while the boys play their games."

Gavin, Jay, Nathan, and Charlie, all joking and laughing, had moved on to the hammer throw in the next baseball field. We strolled past the cars in the narrow parking lot, avoiding any other people walking around the park. I explained everything, within reason, of Teddy Hartman's jealousy over our contest win last year, and his years–long rivalry with the Silver Bear Shop regarding product quality.

"He's copied my sister's promotional ideas on social media, our accessories for bears, and even tried to steal our sewing pattern last fall."

Bonnie shook her head. "A right scunner. And he's livin' here in the village now?"

"Yep. It can't be coincidence. Maybe he won't compete directly with our products any longer, but my parents are pretty sore about it."

I suspected the Hartmans offered small teddy bears with

squeakers inside for pets in the boutique. More power to them. No doubt the toys would be easily destroyed if they were cheaply produced overseas. And that wouldn't sit well with customers.

"Um, what's a scunner?" I asked.

"Disgusting bloke," she said airily. "A dobber, a bampot, a roaster."

"And a huge troublemaker."

Bonnie led the way back to watch the men. "I'm glad Trina talked us into comin' over and opening our wee shop. That certainly put Hartman in a tailspin, from what the Davisons told us. Ever since, he's been sayin' we don't belong here, that immigrants aren't welcome."

I shrugged. "I guess the best thing is to ignore him."

"We do, since everyone else in Silver Hollow welcomed us." She gestured toward her husband as Jay handed Gavin the wooden hammer. "Your young man is so talented. We love our shop sign, and want him to carve us a Scottish terrier next. We miss our little Molly. He did your mailbox with the mama bear and cubs, right? In front of your shop."

"Yes," I said with pride. "He's gotten several commissions around the village. Like the eagle at the lawyer's offices on River Road."

"Oh, I saw that when we first arrived," Bonnie said, "but your mailbox gave me the idea of putting Molly on top of a new one for our shop. She was the best little terrier. Loved eating scraps from the table, especially haggis."

"That reminds me. Do you happen to have a recipe that doesn't require sheep's lung? It's banned here. That's why we can't import it."

"You can use any type of sausage instead—"

At a hoarse shout, we both jumped to our feet in alarm.

Gavin limped our way, holding his side. Bonnie ran over to him. "What's happened, love?"

"Och, it's nothin'," he said. "Pulled a muscle when I threw the hammer. But Jay let go of his too soon, and it landed in the soccer field."

Fearing the worst, I broke into a dead run. Jay, Nathan, and Charlie circled Teddy Hartman, who sat on the ground. He ran a hand over the balding spot on top of his head, as if confused and dizzy. I saw Lucy tugging his arm until he finally rose to his feet.

She turned to Jay. "You aimed for him on purpose!"

"I swear I didn't. I'm really sorry—"

"It looked like an accident to me," Andrew Kane said. Lucy glared at him.

"Whose side are you on? First his brother tried to smash Teddy with that log, and now Sasha's boyfriend tried beaning him with that hammer! She's getting back at us for Sparky biting her. Maybe we need a new lawyer."

Teddy Hartman waved a hatchet. "Good thing I reached for this on the ground, babe. Maybe you're right. They're trying to run me out of Silver Hollow."

"Nobody's running you out of town, Mr. Hartman," I said.

"Yeah, right."

Gavin MacRae bristled at that. "I was trying to show Jay proper technique—"

"To split my skull open?" Hartman demanded.

"I told you we shouldn't have come here in the first place, Teddy," Lucy said. "Alex Silverman's wife interfered in the sale of that house you wanted for the bed-and-breakfast. She and Barbara Davison are best friends, after all."

"I heard the financing fell through," Bonnie said.

Lucy turned on her. "Who told you that?"

"Your brother, Kevin Whittaker, mentioned that fact to my dad yesterday," I said before she could reply. "At the Teddy Bear Trot."

"Why would he—"

"Time to go home," Andrew Kane said firmly and steered Lucy out of range. "We don't want things to get out of hand again."

Teddy Hartman had the last word, however, his voice raised while he followed them. "It's gonna take a lot more than a stupid hammer to take me out!"

Jay sighed. "It really was an accident, Sasha. Maybe I better stick to the caber toss and the Kilted 5K in the Highland Games."

"You can't let him scare you out of competing," I said, although I knew Hartman would take full advantage of spreading the word around Silver Hollow. "Wait and see."

Gavin MacRae gestured toward the cars parked near the baseball diamond's fenced backstop. "Isn't that Alex Silverman now?"

I twisted to see both my parents walking from the parking lot along with Gil Thompson. Gil opened Fresh Grounds long before coffee shops had increased in popularity. A smart move, along with taking on his nephew Garrett as manager and co-owner. Soon after Gil hired Mary Kate, Garrett's girl-friend, to bake delicious pastries, Garrett married her. Mary Kate was one of my best friends, and had given birth to a new baby with a toddler underfoot.

Gil Thompson looked jolly due to his half-bald head, loose jowls, and broad smile. He favored button-down shirts and slacks with polished shoes, no matter the occasion. Too bad he hadn't brought coffee. Instead, he carried a canvas bag with several wooden handles sticking out, no doubt the sharp hatchets. I guessed that Dad had gotten into axe throwing under Gil's influence, since they both shared hobbies of fishing and golf.

"Hi, Dad. How did you get started throwing axes?" I asked.

Gil chuckled. "Alex needed to let off steam back when he practiced law, so we tried our hand at it and the rest is history. Even won several tournaments, too. Maybe one of us will win the contest at the Highland Fling."

"I'm not letting you display another trophy if you do, Alex," my mother said. "I finally got rid of those awful things. You should have seen the dust they'd collected."

"I wouldn't mind tossin' a few," Gavin said.

"Sophie's on duty at the shop, remember," Bonnie said to Gavin and tugged his sweater. "Come on, now. We can't leave all the work to her."

Once they hurried off, Jay hooked a thumb toward the soccer field. "You just missed the Hartmans, Mr. Silverman. We had a little run-in with them, and they left with their lawyer."

"Oh? What's his name?" my father asked.

"Andrew Kane," I said promptly.

"I know him. We've met in court several times."

"So what happened with Hartman?" Mom asked Jay, clearly concerned. "We can't afford worse gossip around Silver Hollow after yesterday's trouble."

I let Jay and Nathan explain about the caber's odd fall, and how Jay's hammer had narrowly missed Teddy Hartman's head. Mom looked horrified, but Dad shrugged.

"He blows things out of proportion, Judith, you know that. Hartman likes to twist things to his own advantage. That's his standard MO."

"But Alex—"

"Let's not talk about him anymore," I interrupted and changed the subject. "We think the soccer and baseball fields are big enough to hold the athletic games, Mom. Exactly where are they going to build the pavilion for the music and dancing?"

"Close to the park's entrance, near the public restrooms. It's not too far for people to walk to the fields and see the games," she said. "The committee is thinking of having a pony ride for young kids, too, but there isn't much for teen-agers."

"How about a Hurl the Haggis contest?" Jay suggested. "I know it sounds crazy, but it might be fun for that age group."

"All ages, actually." I snickered. "Totally nuts."

"I'll mention it to Amy Evans," Mom said. "I've got a meeting with her in fifteen minutes, Alex, so you'll have to find another way home."

She hurried off. Charlie headed back to the caber field along with Nathan. Jay and I chose to follow Dad and Mr. Thompson over to one of the soccer field's wooden targets. But instead of watching them, I pondered today's ominous events. How had things gotten so out of control? My hand ached, remembering yesterday's confrontation with the Hartmans.

Startled by a loud *thunk*, I turned to see that Dad's axe had landed in the board's bull's-eye. Gil Thompson folded his jacket with care and set it on the grass. Then he hefted a hatchet, corrected his stance, aimed, and threw at a second target. Another bull's-eye.

"Whoa," Jay said, his voice low. "Hartman doesn't have a chance to win."

"I'm starving," I said. "Want us to fetch some lunch?"

"I'm game." Mr. Thompson pulled several twenties from his embossed leather wallet. "My treat, but don't forget to bring back the grub."

Jay and I headed out while they continued to practice. Luckily, Ham Heaven wasn't too crowded. We drove back to Riverside Park, delivered two thick ham-and-cheese sandwiches and Gil's change, then parked the truck on the winding road along the riverfront. We ate our lunch while sitting on a fallen log and soaking up the sunshine. Jay and I hiked in the shady woods, enjoying the birds and other critters, and then returned to his truck.

My cell phone jangled with Dad's ringtone. "Hi, what's up?"

"Meet me on the road, outside the park entrance. It's an emergency." He hung up.

Confused, I slid the phone back into my jacket pocket and turned to Jay. "Uh, I guess Dad needs me. We better hurry."

"Sure. I wonder what's going on."

"I don't know, but it didn't sound good."

Once I climbed to the passenger seat, Jay shut my door and raced around to climb behind the wheel. He made a U-turn on the road in a swirl of gravel, jamming his foot on the gas until we drove back to the park. Within minutes, we saw Gil Thompson flagging us down. An EMT ambulance with flashing lights blocked the way, with several other cars and a van. The county forensics team swarmed around the area.

I gasped when I saw Detective Phil Hunter, lean and lithe, in a bespoke dark suit, leading my father, his hands cuffed behind him, toward a patrol car. "Hey! What are you doing?"

Ignoring me, Hunter stuffed Dad into the back seat. I watched the detective exchange a few terse words with Gil Thompson, who quickly headed to his car. He also ignored our calls to stop, and swerved around Jay when he attempted to flag him down.

"What happened? Can't you tell me anything?" I asked an officer.

"Sorry, miss. You'd better stay back until we're done with the investigation."

He assisted two other policemen in stretching yellow crime scene tape between several trees. I glimpsed a body on the ground, surrounded by technicians, and strained to see from a distance. My heart thudded when I caught sight of a red Michael Kors watch on the victim's wrist. Plus red canvas sneakers—I swallowed hard. It had to be Teddy Hartman.

With a hatchet planted in his back.

Chapter 6

Since we couldn't get closer to the scene, or question any of the officials about what happened, Jay and I drove back to Silver Hollow. The police station, a low, brick building, had two front windows hidden by tall shrubs, and a low overhang shaded the entrance on Roosevelt Street. Detective Phil Hunter had once described the building as a bug trap. I had to admit his description wasn't far off the mark. Jay parked in the lot behind the building.

My mother rushed over to the truck before I slid out of the passenger seat and hugged me. Eyes red and puffy, she wiped her damp cheeks with a crumpled tissue. "So you heard what happened to Teddy Hartman?"

"Yes, but why did the police arrest Dad?" I asked.

We both turned at the screech of tires. Maddie jumped out of her car, parked haphazardly in two spaces. "Mom, what happened? No way would Dad kill anyone!"

"I know, honey. Gil Thompson called me on the way here, of course. I can't believe that awful detective arrested Alex—"

Mom hesitated when Uncle Ross's vintage Thunderbird pulled over to the street's curb. "Oh, good, he got the message. I called Flynn Hanson, too."

I groaned in silence over that news. Uncle Ross locked his car and joined us. "Gil didn't tell me much, Judith, so what happened?"

Mom gulped back more tears. "After they finished practicing axe throwing at Riverside Park, they walked to the road where Gil parked his car. That's when they saw the body, half-hidden under a thicket. Good thing, too, because otherwise no one would have seen it."

"But we saw Teddy Hartman leaving the park," I said, "with his wife and lawyer."

"Huh," Uncle Ross mused. "Why would Hartman be there?"

"I have no idea." Mom sighed. "Gil said he never heard any cars or saw anyone, not from the soccer field, with all those trees lining the road. They first noticed his red shoes under that bush. That's how they found him."

"Red car, red shoes, and a red watch," I said. "Power red."

Uncle Ross snorted. "So how was Hartman killed? Murdered, I mean—"

"With a hatchet in his back," Jay and I interrupted at the same time.

Maddie looked stricken. "Is someone trying to frame Dad?"

"I don't know," Mom said, tears streaking her cheeks. "I guess when that detective showed up, Phil Hunter, he arrested Alex on the spot. He claimed it had to be Dad's axe, and he wouldn't listen even though Gil showed him that none of theirs were missing."

"Don't worry, Judith. They won't find his fingerprints on the handle, and the police will have to let him go."

"Gil said I'd better call a lawyer, so that's why I contacted

Flynn. Why won't the police let me see Alex or talk to him? I didn't know what to do or think."

"Here's Gil now," Uncle Ross said.

The door squeaked shut behind Gil Thompson when he stalked out of the police station. His shirt had wrinkles, grass stains marked the knees of his trousers, and his shoes had been scuffed. Gil wasn't smiling, and he looked tired. Worried, as well.

"How's Alex?" Mom asked. "Why can't I see him?"

He scratched his jaw. "No idea. Chief Russell's up north for a long weekend, and I can't get him on the phone. Tried half a dozen times."

"Didn't he pick up coffee at Fresh Grounds yesterday morning?" Maddie asked. "I saw him there before the Teddy Bear Trot."

"Yeah, and then drove to his cabin in the Yoop." Gil shrugged. "Tom goes up there to catch whitefish, since it's open season all year."

"Spotty service up there, if any," Jay said. "I wouldn't be surprised if there's still snow. That means he may not be back until Tuesday or Wednesday."

"Lenore's not a fan of winter. That's why she stays here and keeps the Sunshine Café going," Gil added. "I bet Tom didn't expect further trouble with the Hartmans. How crazy that Alex has been arrested for murder now."

While Mom and Uncle Ross peppered him with more questions, I turned to Jay. "What time did we drop off those sandwiches from Ham Heaven?"

"Uh, I dunno. Why?"

"If the time of Hartman's death is anywhere around when we drove back, that would give them both an alibi. We tossed the sandwich bag, though, with the receipt," I said. "Maybe Mary Walsh kept a copy, though."

"Whatever helps clear your dad," Jay said. "Didn't Detective Hunter date Kristen Bloom for a while before Christmas?"

"Yeah," Gil piped up. "Skinny guy, who wears a suit all the time."

"Pale eyes like a snake, too," Uncle Ross said.

"Snakes have dark eyes."

"Some constrictors and boas have blue eyes," he retorted, "and a snake's dark eyes can turn blue when it starts shedding its skin—"

"Forget the science lesson," I interrupted my uncle, angry that Phil Hunter was once more muddying up a murder. "Hunter's the worst person to run an investigation. He always jumps to conclusions. Detective Mason takes his time and gathers all the facts first."

"Hunter arrested Alex without a shred of evidence," Uncle Ross said.

"But why did he show up on the murder scene in the first place?" Maddie asked. "Or did someone call the county to send a homicide detective?"

"I dialed 9-1-1, soon as we found the body," Gil Thompson said, "but Hunter arrived before Digger Sykes. Said he happened to be in the area. Asked a few questions, read Alex his rights, and arrested him. Then he told me I'd better tag along here."

"Hunter probably figured Alex is the best suspect," Uncle Ross said, "due to the rivalry between Bears of the Heart and the Silver Bear Shop. He probably heard how Maddie broke Hartman's nose, too. So where's Flynn Hanson? He should be here by now."

"I called his Ann Arbor office," Mom said, biting her lip. "One of the staffers said they'd get back to me, but that was over an hour ago."

"I'm calling Mark Branson." I waved my phone. "Forget

Flynn, Mom. He told me he doesn't want anything to do with more murders in Silver Hollow."

"Maybe that's for the best. He specializes in personal injury, after all." She sighed. "How could this have happened in the first place? Poor Alex. I was shocked when Flynn and I found Cal Bloom at the Christmas parade last year. I'd never seen a dead body except after being laid out in a funeral home."

"Remember, Sasha and Maddie found Will Taylor," Uncle Ross said. "And that girl in the parking lot behind Fresh Grounds last fall. And then the best man a few months ago, at a wedding rehearsal dinner, over at the Regency Hotel. Your girls have been through a lot more than either you or Alex."

I plugged one ear since Mark Branson answered at the Legal Eagle office. He promised to drive over right away. Unfortunately, I fumbled my phone while sliding it into my pocket and watched it bounce a few times on the cement. Jay snatched it up.

"Screen's broken," he said, waving it aloft. "Might be an easy fix, though."

"If it's just the glass protector—oh, no." I'd peeled off the thin layer with its jagged crack, but realized the screen had shattered also. Things had gone from bad to worse.

"Maybe the screen can be replaced, though."

"I'll worry about it later." I turned to Gil Thompson. "So how come Detective Hunter didn't arrest you for murder, too? You were with Dad when you found the body. And you both practiced with those axes."

He shrugged. "Your guess is as good as mine."

I started tapping a text message but stopped when a familiar SUV, bearing the Dexter County logo on the side, pulled into the police station's parking lot. Detective Greg Mason climbed out, wearing a suit, white shirt, and a plain blue tie. He always reminded me of a teddy bear, with his rounded build and light brown hair. I trusted him far more than Phil Hunter. Mason had always acted fair and impartial during investigations.

Given the suit, Mason probably had a court appearance or some official errand. He flexed his shoulders, clearly not comfortable, and loosened his tie. "Heard something about a murder on the village outskirts. Is that true?"

"Yes," Mom said, rushing to answer, "and that other detective arrested my husband for murdering Teddy Hartman! Which is totally ridiculous."

"Huh." Mason glanced at me with a frown. "I was sent over when the department got the call earlier. So how did Phil Hunter find out?"

Once I explained, I waved a hand at the station's door. "He said he was near the scene. And since Chief Russell's on vacation, Hunter's taken over and more than likely thinks he can do whatever he wants. He won't tell us anything. My dad's a lawyer, remember—"

"Hold on, Sasha. Let me find out the details."

Mason vanished inside the station. I folded my arms, musing over the day's events. If only I kept better track of time this afternoon. We'd dropped off lunch at Riverside Park, between two o'clock and half past three, and gone on our hike. Nowhere near the road where Dad and Gil Thompson practiced, though. Someone had killed Hartman there, or dumped the body in order to frame my father.

I turned to Gil Thompson, whose face glowed from the bright lamp light above the station's entrance. "I still don't get why Hunter zeroed in on Dad as the killer."

"Probable cause, so he said, for motive, means, and opportunity."

"But Hunter doesn't know what time Teddy Hartman was killed, or anything."

"I know that, but he questioned us both. We weren't together the whole time," Gil said, eyes on the sidewalk. "Alex visited the restroom near the park entrance. He was gone a while, and admitted it. Hunter thinks he had plenty of time to murder Hartman."

"But that means you were alone, too," Maddie pointed out. "You had the same chance, in the same time frame."

"I suppose, but I hardly knew the guy."

Uncle Ross pushed his flat cap back on his head. "Oh, yeah? What about you being more than a little peeved when Hartman took over as head of SHEBA? Come on, Gil, you can't deny it. Lots of people heard you complaining to Lenore Russell the other day."

Gil's face and neck flushed beet red, and he wiped his palms against his trousers. "Nobody expected that! Teddy Hartman showed up early, took over the gavel, and acted like he was in charge. You'd think someone would have protested, but nope. By the time I got to the meeting, he'd gone through half the agenda."

"Okay, but why didn't Hunter wait to question people around the village before arresting Dad?" Maddie asked. "Like maybe find witnesses who saw you or Dad at the park. Who knows if anyone will come forward with important information now."

"Let's hope the killer didn't wear gloves," I said. "Once they determine someone else's fingerprints are on the axe handle, that will prove Dad is innocent."

"Hunter claims he caught Alex red-handed. That's crazy."

Jay agreed. "And there was no blood on his hands or clothes?"

"No. I didn't see much blood at all at the scene," Gil said.

"Then maybe Hartman was killed somewhere else, only Hunter decided it was easier to make an arrest," I said. "First Maddie, and now Dad's in trouble." My shoulders slumped. "Who knows when Detective Mason will find out what's going on."

"Too bad Teddy Hartman complained so much about Alex around Silver Hollow," Gil said. "He unloaded at the SHEBA meeting, before and after we voted to adjourn. Even hinted that the Silver Bear Shop would soon close down."

"What did he mean by that?" Uncle Ross smacked a fist into his other hand. "I wonder if Hartman was behind that paint crew taking their sweet time! They keep finding stuff to repair, when it's supposed to be a simple job."

"Except Dad found some rotting boards after they'd already finished one area," I said, "and they removed a wasp nest. Some of the shutters needed replacing, too."

"Minor stuff. They claimed the sheathing was bad under the rotunda's roof, so I climbed up their ladder. Total bunk. The planks looked and felt solid. So did the soffits, and those gutters should last a few more years. Good thing I checked it out before we paid extra."

I turned to Maddie, who leaned against the brick wall, arms folded over her chest. "What happened yesterday after Digger brought you here? Chief Russell was already gone."

"We managed to call him. No big deal." Maddie avoided my gaze, and her face was shadowed since she stood with her back to the lamp light. "He asked me a bunch of questions, and Digger wrote up the report. That's all."

"Was he shocked that you punched Teddy Hartman?"

"Yeah, but he agreed with Dad about the first offense. I'm not a two-bit criminal." Maddie's laugh sounded hollow. "I'll submit to the judge's terms, like probation or community service. That way I won't have a permanent record."

"Thank goodness for that," I said, relieved.

"But since Hartman can't press an assault and battery charge any longer, the whole matter might be dropped."

My eyes widened. Uh-oh. What if Hunter believed that Dad killed Hartman to avoid any legal problems for Maddie? And if the detective learned what happened to me years ago at the New Jersey trade show, Hunter would cite a second motive.

"Sash, what are you gonna do about that dog bite?" Maddie asked. "Lucy Hartman is still liable for it, even if her husband's dead."

"Flynn wants me to file a lawsuit, but I don't know."

Mom shook her head. "Your father told me that's a level-four dog bite, according to Michigan law, and that animals aren't put down unless it gets to a level six—an outright attack, on or off leash."

"But the Morkie bit Teddy Hartman, too," Maddie said. "And Asia Gibson told us the dog bit her at the Labor Day parade. At least file a report at the Humane Society."

I didn't reply. I hadn't made up my mind, since I didn't know how Lucy Hartman took the news of her husband's death. Then again, the police might consider her a suspect. She'd been with Teddy at the park, along with their lawyer, Andrew Kane. They could have worked together to kill her husband and set Dad up to get the blame.

So many questions, and too few answers.

I paced the sidewalk, thinking over everything I'd learned. Mom looked wan. Her shirt had a coffee stain, and she twisted the sleeves of her pale blue cardigan with nervous energy. Even the messy bun behind her head had come partially undone. She tucked a wisp of her auburn hair behind one ear, but that proved futile. Mom suddenly grabbed the station's door handle.

"I'm going in there to protest Alex's arrest," she announced. "I know it might do more harm than good, since I'm the mayor, but I don't care!"

"Now, Judith. Calm down, take a deep breath." Uncle Ross pulled her back into our circle. "It's better if you don't interfere. Detective Mason will take over—"

"Wish I could." Mason suddenly emerged from the entrance, and the doors squeaked shut for the second time. "Hunter's been assigned to the case. I can't interfere."

"But couldn't you assist him in the investigation?" I asked.

"Phil somehow convinced Sergeant Michaels that I'm biased in Alex Silverman's favor," he said, his tone patient. "I tried to refute that, but no go."

"That's ridiculous," Mom said, clearly furious.

Uncle Ross and Gil Thompson looked even angrier by the news than my mother. "That's crazy," my uncle said. "If I have to, I'll drive up north and hunt down Chief Russell. Maybe he can get that incompetent detective off my brother's case."

"I'd advise waiting." Mason ran a hand through his hair and adjusted his wire-rimmed glasses. "Once the coroner determines the time of death, and gathers hair and clothing fibers, the facts might exonerate Mr. Silverman."

"That makes sense," Gil Thompson said. "We all know Hunter seemed too eager to pin the blame on Alex. He's gotta find proof."

"I'll keep an eye on any developments," Mason said.

That raised my spirits. I didn't trust Phil Hunter, given his smarmy manner and laziness in tracking down any leads. Greg Mason had always balked at my help in the past, but at least he listened to my theories and considered all the options. He also gave me credit for intelligence. Phil Hunter's superior attitude and coldness grated my nerves.

"I bet he wants this case so he can get back at you," I said. "Hunter looked bad when you investigated the murder before Gus and Cissy's wedding."

Mason shrugged. "Keep me updated if you learn anything important, Sasha. Send a text or leave a voice mail on my cell."

He strolled off toward his car. How odd that he hadn't reminded me to "stick to selling teddy bears." Not that I needed much encouragement to snoop around and find the truth.

No way would I let Dad be railroaded into a murder charge.

Chapter 7

"Sasha Silverman?"

I whirled around at the terse voice behind me. Speak of the devil. Detective Hunter stood in the station's open doorway, pale eyes narrowed. After glaring at Mason's retreating figure, he glanced at my mother as if he suspected she might rush him and bust her way inside to see Dad.

"Yes?"

"I have a few questions for you. Come this way. Please."

Clearly he'd added that last word due to my mother's icy stare. Uncle Ross headed to his car, muttering under his breath, but Mom nudged me forward. My heart pounded in my chest while I walked past Hunter into the station and squinted in the bright interior lights.

"What about my boyfriend? Jay was with me at the park—"

"Just you." He locked the door behind us.

Detective Hunter led the way into the lobby and punched the door's code into the wall keypad. I waved to the chief's son, Dan Russell, who worked at the front desk behind Plexiglas, and followed Hunter down the hallway hung with notices and lists of rules. A large FBI MOST WANTED poster had faded and grainy photographs. My boots squeaked on the shiny linoleum. The air smelled stale with lingering scents of burnt coffee and sweat. I glimpsed several tables through the small window of one closed door—possibly a lounge.

Another room had a row of monitors and a dispatch clerk wearing headphones. Hunter stopped farther down the hall at a windowless door and unlocked it. He gestured me inside the cramped room, its four walls bare, depressing, and claustrophobic. No doubt that first impression was deliberate. I prepared myself. Was I a suspect? I couldn't tell what Hunter was thinking, given his severe poker face.

I eyed the tiny table and recording device, along with a padded chair behind it and a metal folding chair near the wall. "Will anyone else be here?"

He frowned. "I'll fetch Officer Sykes."

Good thing I'd asked. No way did I relish being alone with Phil Hunter. The door clicked shut behind me. The knob rattled when I twisted it—locked again. Somewhere in this building, Dad sat in a holding cell. Maybe Hunter had brought him here first for questioning. Then again, maybe he hadn't bothered. A large mirrored rectangle hung on the nearest wall. I guessed it had to be a two-way, but wasn't sure if anyone watched behind it.

I blinked at my reflection. Right hand bandaged, my blond hair windblown, in need of a good trim at the Luxe salon, and worry plain in my eyes. I turned away. This mess had all started only yesterday at the Teddy Bear Trot.

Digger Sykes entered the room. "Hey, Sasha."

"No small talk," Hunter snapped and shut the door behind him. "Please sit down, Ms. Silverman, and we'll begin."

Digger stood by the door, forearms crossed over his wrin-

kled uniform, and sweat stains in his armpits. Phil Hunter
blocked me when I headed to the padded chair, waited for me
to sit on the metal one instead, and then claimed the more
comfortable seat. He slapped a closed file folder on the dull,
scratched, Formica-topped table. Eyeing me, Hunter punched
a button on the recorder. I noted the tape spinning inside.
Talk about old-fashioned.

I bet he assigned someone else to prepare transcripts of his
interviews.

"State your name, please, and address," he said.

I did, then cleared my throat. "First of all, why—"

"Remember, Ms. Silverman, you're here to answer my
questions. What time were you at Riverside Park?"

"I didn't look at my watch." Which was true, but I added,
"Jay drove us out there around eleven, I guess. We stayed several hours, watching the athletic games."

"Where you confronted Mr. Hartman and his wife."
Hunter's tone was harsh.

"I needed their dog's vaccination record. It bit me on Saturday," I said and waved my bandaged hand. "They gave it to
me, no problem."

"Oh really." He sounded almost gleeful now. "I've already gathered statements from several people that Jay Kirby
targeted Teddy Hartman with a weapon—"

"That's not true!"

"Don't interrupt, Ms. Silverman. You cannot deny that
you were involved in a second altercation with the Hartmans
at Riverside Park today." Hunter tapped a finger on the
manila file folder. "Two witnesses swore to what happened."

I straightened my shoulders. "Let me guess—your witnesses are Lucy Hartman and Andrew Kane? Did you talk to
Jay's brother or his friend, Charlie Volker?"

Hunter shrugged. "They're biased witnesses."

"You can't be serious. Lucy Hartman is biased," I added hotly. "What about Gavin and Bonnie MacRae, who own the Kilted Scot boutique? They witnessed what happened."

"Couldn't understand a word they said."

My jaw dropped. "Are you kidding me?"

"Remember, Ms. Silverman, I am asking the questions." His aggravation held a warning along with his cold blue eyes. "What time did your father arrive?"

"Right after Teddy and Lucy Hartman left. You must have talked to Gil Thompson at some point. He was there, and my mother."

Hunter ignored that. "What time? Answer the question."

I bit my upper lip. "Maybe one o'clock or one thirty? Jay and I left to get sandwiches at Ham Heaven, but I didn't check my phone for the time then, either."

"Did you see Teddy Hartman again? Or his red Camry?"

When I shook my head, he changed the subject. "Ms. Silverman, is it true you were once sexually molested by Mr. Hartman?"

"What?" Both Digger and I chimed in at the same time, and my heart thudded harder. "No! Who told you that?" My cheeks burned, and my stomach clenched tight.

Hunter leaned back in his chair, his steely gaze fixed on Digger. "Keep your mouth shut, Officer Sykes." Then he looked at me. "I believe the incident happened back in New Jersey, at a trade show. You were fifteen or sixteen at the time."

Angry that he'd even brought it up, I folded my arms over my chest. "I'm not answering anything unless you tell me why it's relevant, first of all."

"You're smart enough to figure out why it's relevant.

Mrs. Hartman told me about the incident, so I'd like to hear your side of the story."

"But Teddy Hartman denied it!"

"Is that true?" When I didn't answer, Hunter added, "Your sister punched him in the nose, after all. And Hartman threatened to press charges against her."

"He also insulted my mother, and called me a spy," I retorted, "and their dog bit me. But I haven't filed a lawsuit against Lucy Hartman. Why would she tell you about something he claimed never happened?"

"Your father wanted revenge, could that be why? It would help if you explained."

"Help who, that's what I'd like to know."

"Help me, Ms. Silverman," Hunter said, but I caught his sly glance.

I resented his flippant attitude and stared him down. Hunter glanced at Digger Sykes, who watched us with a bored expression. I knew him better than that, however. Inside he was probably itching to spread this new dirt in Silver Hollow's gossip network. If he did, I'd have to file a complaint with Chief Russell. Police interviews were supposed to be confidential, after all. But I couldn't assume that.

When I stood, the metal chair clanged against the wall. "I'm going to contact the county sheriff's office about your bias, detective. Clearly you're favoring the Hartmans."

"Sit down, Ms. Silverman."

"Am I a suspect?"

"It's possible that you aided and abetted in Hartman's murder," Hunter said, "so I can hold you forty-eight hours for questioning. Might give you time to think over the consequences of not cooperating with the police."

"Me, not cooperative?" I glanced at Digger, who motioned for me to sit down. I shook my head. "I've told you everything I know. Jay Kirby can verify it."

"Your boyfriend would naturally cover for you."

"The forensic team hadn't even started collecting evidence before you made your arrest," I snapped back. "What kind of homicide detective does that? An incompetent one."

"I can hold you for forty-eight hours, like your father." Hunter sounded as if he held all the trump cards. "Now sit back down, Ms. Silverman."

I sank onto the chair. "I want to call a lawyer."

"First take a look at these photos. You didn't get a close-up view earlier."

I sensed his confidence wavering, as if he knew he'd overplayed his hand. Hunter opened the manila folder and slapped several glossy black-and-white photographs on the table. He leaned back, as if he expected me to be shocked. Instead, I studied them, although the stark images made the corpse and scene seem unreal. My curiosity rising, I leaned over to survey the odd angle of the hatchet sticking out of Teddy Hartman's back.

No bloodstains showed beneath the body, and his clothing wasn't drenched, either. In a second photo, the forensics team had turned Hartman over. He stared blankly at the sky, eyes wide, as if he hadn't expected to leave this earth.

Or suffer a betrayal.

I pointed at a third glossy square. "What's this thin line around his neck? It looks like he may have been strangled with something thin. Like a cord of some kind."

"That's just a shadow—I'm asking the questions, remember," he added, more annoyed than ever. "How many axe-throwing tournaments did Alex Silverman win in the past?"

"No clue. I just learned about his hobby today."

"I find that hard to believe." Hunter waited, but the minutes ticked by. "Come on, Ms. Silverman. Your father was proficient enough to—"

A loud rap on the door interrupted him. Digger Sykes yanked it open at the same moment that Hunter ordered him to ignore it. When Mark Branson walked into the small room, I breathed a sigh of relief. Older than his sister Mary Kate, the lawyer had a pale, freckled complexion and sandy hair above bright blue eyes. He matched Digger Sykes in height, who barely cleared the department requirement, but Mark wore a trim gray suit, red tie, and highly polished wing-tip shoes. Hunter stuffed the photos back into the manila folder.

"I'm representing Sasha Silverman and her father," Mark said. "I spoke to Alex earlier, in case you're not aware. We can leave now, Sasha. Unless you have any questions."

"Just one. Am I a suspect in Teddy Hartman's death?"

Hunter scowled. "Not at this time."

"Why didn't you question Gil Thompson, or anyone else at the park? The MacRaes may be from Scotland, but they speak perfectly good English," I said. "So you only talked to Lucy Hartman and her lawyer. If that isn't total bias, detective, I don't know what is."

"I'll rely on Officer Sykes's notes," Hunter said, but Mark waved a hand.

"I've read those. Sorry, Digger, but a few short paragraphs hardly does justice to explain the incidents today at Riverside Park. As for Hartman's murder, you should have investigated further before arresting my client."

Hunter bristled at his criticism. "It's plain as day who killed Teddy Hartman."

"On what evidence?" Mark's tone was challenging. "You won't win over the judge at a preliminary exam hearing with probable cause, if the district's prosecuting attorney even allows the case to proceed that far. And my client will file a complaint for false arrest once evidence exonerates him. Now. If you're ready to leave, Sasha."

I marched past Digger Sykes, who flashed a quick wink. Mark followed in my wake. Once more, my boots squeaked loudly through the hallway and past the empty lobby, until we left the station. I breathed fresh air deep into my lungs outside.

Jay rushed over to meet us, his worry disappearing. "Are you okay, Sasha? Maddie took your mom home—to your place, not her condo. She was almost hysterical when Hunter took you in for questioning."

"Oh, no. Mark, can you get her in to visit Dad?"

"I'll see if I can arrange it," the lawyer said and then checked his phone.

"I figured you'd be released," Jay said. "That's why I hung around."

"I'm glad." I kissed and hugged him back. "You should have heard Mark give Detective Hunter the third degree about arresting Dad too soon!"

The lawyer shrugged. "Innocent until proven guilty, remember. But it may take a while for forensics to process the crime scene evidence. Unfortunately, people around Silver Hollow may jump to the same conclusion as Detective Hunter."

"What can we do to help?" Jay asked him.

"First, we need to establish Alex's alibi. Ask anyone who saw him at Riverside Park—what time, where exactly, that kind of thing," Mark added. "I need to know everything, Sasha. But I also need to hear about this business rivalry between your father and Teddy Hartman. Maddie assaulted him because of something he did at a trade show, right? I need to know the specifics of what that was all about. Somewhere private, though."

"Come back to the house."

With a heavy heart, I prepared myself for worse grilling. I remembered Dad telling me about being blindsided by information that came out about clients during their trial. He loathed learning deep-held secrets that could undermine a case. Dad preferred them to be honest upfront. Now I'd have to explain not only what happened, but why I balked at telling the whole story.

Even to my father.

Chapter 8

In the kitchen, Maddie and Mom sat over cups of coffee at the island. Rosie and Sugar Bear barked at Mark, but I blocked them from jumping against his legs. After scooping up my tiny poodle, I guided Rosie away and sat at the table instead. Rosie settled near my feet, and Sugar calmed down on my lap. Mark and Jay took seats opposite me.

"How bad was it, Sasha, with Detective Hunter?" Mom asked.

She looked pale, so I kept it brief. "I managed to get through it. Mark saw Dad, and I'm sure we'd like to know how he's holding up. Is he okay?" I asked.

He nodded. "In good spirits. Your dad gave me a detailed timeline for the afternoon, and all the people he and Gil Thompson saw there. I don't know why Detective Hunter didn't ask him that and check their stories before arresting Alex."

Jay scowled. "Hunter's an idiot."

Mark ignored that. "So tell me how the business rivalry

started between the Silver Bear Shop and Teddy Hartman's Bears of the Heart. How long has it been going on?" He directed those questions at me, but Maddie spoke up before I could reply.

"Right after Dad opened the factory. You must know the history about Grandpa T.R. Silverman, and his homemade teddy bears."

"Everyone in Silver Hollow knows that story. Alex explained how he wanted to retire from practicing law, and start fresh with a new enterprise." Mark smiled at me, as if sensing my hesitation. "He told me you tagged along to trade shows, Sasha, and helped him gather ideas for the business. Tell me how you first met Teddy Hartman in New Jersey."

"He claimed Sasha was spying," Mom said, "but she was only taking notes and photos with a camera, to get ideas of what was popular with kids."

"Okay, but let her tell me the details."

I appreciated Mark's patience and took a deep breath. "It wasn't a big deal, really. The vendors explained everything about quality and prices to me, and I wrote it all down for Dad. He wanted to know the different fur fabrics that companies used, stuff like that. He'd already decided to produce teddy bears with natural-color fur, like real bears. Brown for grizzly, black for black bears, white for polar bears."

"Alex was stubborn about that, even though I told him a lot of kids want pink or blue bears," Mom said. "And he didn't want to sell accessories back then. Right, Sasha?"

"Yeah, Uncle Ross felt the same. Aunt Eve and I talked them into it, though. Costumes for bears are big sellers in the shop," I added with pride. "And Mom said we should make our smallest bears in a variety of colors, for kids who couldn't afford bigger ones."

"So what happened at the trade show?" Mark reminded me.

"Hartman caught me taking a photo of his display. It wasn't

like I only wanted pictures of his," I said. "I'd been doing the same thing at all the vendor booths. Dad gave me a new Sanyo flip phone with a camera—it cost four hundred bucks, one of the first phones with a lens. He wanted to compare all the vendor displays and see how he could do his in a unique way. But Hartman knocked the phone out of my hands—"

"That's malicious destruction of property!" Maddie looked incensed.

"Vandalism in New Jersey," Mark said calmly, taking notes.

My sister slapped the island's counter. "I'm glad I broke his stupid nose. Hartman lied, because he *did* assault you back then."

"It wasn't a sexual assault, though," I said, my cheeks hot.

"But why didn't Alex tell me about it?" Mom asked, clearly upset.

"I begged him not to, or call the police and report it," I admitted. "Maybe I should have. None of this would have happened if I had let him."

"I doubt that, Sasha," Jay said. "Seems like Hartman had a habit of acting petty and vindictive, to a lot more people than you and your family."

"You told me he called you a 'slutty little spy' and looked you over like a piece of meat," Maddie reminded me. "But he hit you, too."

"He—well, he smacked me. On the backside."

"That's physical assault," Mom said, horrified.

"He didn't use his hand," I mumbled. "It's so embarrassing."

"Spit it out, Sasha." Mark's tone wasn't angry or irritated. Leaning forward, he squeezed my shoulder and then let go when I met his gaze. "No matter how long ago this happened, or how embarrassing. Just explain and then let it go."

After another deep breath, I straightened my posture. Jay moved his chair next to mine and slid an arm around my waist, which helped me to relax. Mark poised his pen over his small Moleskine notebook, although he remained silent and focused on the page.

"It sounds silly now. All the vendors saw what happened, but Dad wasn't there. Hartman was such a bully. I was so shocked when he knocked the flip phone out of my hand, but it didn't break. Thank God. When I bent over to retrieve it, he hit me. With a toy paddle."

"I wish I could break his nose again," Maddie said, indignant.

"Hartman had ripped off the elastic string and rubber ball."

"I take it a vendor had those on display?" Mark's eyebrows rose.

"Yeah." My cheeks burned, and I focused on the tile floor. "Almost everyone around us burst out laughing. I wanted to crawl under a table. One woman didn't laugh, though. She had a booth of hand-sewn teddy bears, dressed in beautiful clothes. She stood up to Hartman and told him to back off and stop targeting me."

"Good for her," Jay said.

"Hartman laughed in her face and asked if she wanted a spanking, too. That's when another vendor stepped in, a man. He said Hartman crossed the line with that."

"So abusing a fifteen-year-old is okay, but an older woman is not?" Mom's disgust was clear. "I am thankful she intervened, though. And I'm sorry I didn't accompany you and Dad to that year's trade show."

I nodded. "Dad said Hartman was a coward, and that he only did it because I was alone and vulnerable."

"So what happened next?" Mark asked.

"Nothing. I pretended it didn't happen."

"So you blocked out the worst of the trauma."

Jay sighed. "That's common. My sister Lauren had an incident where some guy tried to drag her away from a group of friends at the mall. She managed to escape, but didn't recall what happened until a few months ago."

"What made her remember?" Mom asked, clearly concerned.

"Her ex-boyfriend did the same thing at a party, so it all came flooding back."

"Don't blame yourself, Sasha," Maddie said. "Hartman victimized you."

"Oddly enough, Lucy Hartman told Detective Hunter that Alex accused her husband of cheating customers and employees, spread rumors online, and posted bad reviews on their website." Mark rubbed his jaw. "Is any of that true?"

I almost choked with laughter. "Dad wouldn't know how to post an online review. He doesn't even check his email regularly. Right, Mom?"

"Oh, it's terrible. He must have over a thousand unread messages," she said with a groan. "I've tried to flag the important ones for him. And Alex never cared what Teddy Hartman did—Bears of the Heart is in New England, after all. Our sales were never affected by them. The business rivalry was blown way out of proportion, in my opinion."

"Then I'd say whoever killed Hartman took advantage of Alex's axe-throwing skill to frame him as the prime suspect," Mark said. "I can't guarantee the judge will set a reasonable bail amount for your husband, despite his good reputation in the community."

Mom sighed. "We'd planned to visit my brother in Arizona soon, but I guess that trip's on the back burner."

"At least until the murder is solved. Be patient, that's my advice. One more thing." Mark rose to his feet. "Alex mentioned how the Hartmans' lawyer, Andrew Kane, served as the defense attorney for a big tax fraud case that he prosecuted years ago—"

"The long, slow death march case?" I interrupted with excitement. "Dad said he had to dig deep to get enough evidence, since the primary witness was the defendant's loyal friend. The guy was hostile during testimony, and fought against answering every question. He told me it was like pulling teeth from a rabid raccoon."

"Sounds like one tough case. Alex said Kane constantly objected, too, although he failed to get much of the evidence dismissed."

"Do you think Andrew Kane wanted revenge on Dad, and maybe framed him for Teddy Hartman's murder?" Maddie asked. "Or is that a stretch?"

Mark shrugged. "Let's see what evidence comes in before we talk theories. I plan to keep badgering Detective Hunter before any arraignment hearing. Hang in there, Judith."

"Can you text me that list?" I asked. "Of the people who saw Dad at the park."

"Sure, and then update me with any information."

Once he departed, Maddie and I gave Mom a group hug to boost her spirits. Sugar Bear danced around our legs, yipping with excitement, so I scooped her into my arms and dodged a few sloppy dog kisses. Rosie, her tail wagging, gave a soft *woof*.

"Aww. It's like she knows Dad will be all right," Maddie said.

"I know he's innocent." Mom pushed a strand of auburn hair out of her eyes. "I've gotten lots of calls from people supporting him."

I let my dogs out, watching Mom's headlights bounce when she pulled out of the parking lot and onto Theodore

Lane. Orange barrels roped off the curve toward Main Street. The council had finally voted to remove the barriers at our street's dead end and repave the street. I was so relieved after letting go of the guilt and shame from that New Jersey trade show. Now I had to trust Mark to handle dealing with Detective Hunter.

Rosie and Sugar Bear raced each other back inside. Jay planted a kiss on my hair, a little cautious with another hug, but I kissed him hard.

"I'll see you tomorrow, okay? I think I need some time alone."

"Sure, no problem. Night."

Jay walked out to his truck. Maddie had already retreated to her bedroom, but her black cat hissed at my dogs. Onyx soon slunk toward the stairs. I rubbed my eyes and yawned. I'd lost so much sleep the last few nights, but tomorrow was the start of another busy week.

First of all, since we took pride in our shop's exterior appearance as well as its interior, I'd have to hire a landscaper. Once the paint crew finished, I had to return the shop to its usual orderly display of teddy bears and accessory racks downstairs. Along with tracking down the people who saw Dad at Riverside Park, in order to prove his innocence.

My cell phone buzzed with an incoming text from Mark Branson. I scrolled through the short list of names, glad to have a starting point. Then I blocked Rosie and Sugar Bear from rushing upstairs, aware that Onyx crouched at the top.

"Go on, Nyxie. Go to bed."

Disappointed, she slipped inside Maddie's room. I pulled that door shut, knowing the cat wanted revenge for Sugar Bear's not-so-playful bites. Those two always fought for dominance. It was too late for cat–dog wars. I needed sleep. A

Guilty Pleasures Gossip Club meeting would help me relax. I loved spending time with my friends, and they'd help relieve my anxiety about Dad and Maddie, too.

My dogs curled up near my pillow, so I closed my eyes—for a few minutes, or so it seemed. I realized sunshine was pouring into the room. Refreshed and far less worried, as if unicorns pooping rainbows romped in my world, I stretched in contentment.

Maybe facing Teddy Hartman's abuse years ago, and relating it aloud, had lifted a heavy cloud of darkness off my soul. Even my dogs seemed ready to face Monday. Sugar Bear jumped off the bed and then yelped in pain. Rosie sniffed her in concern.

"Aww, poor baby." I checked the poodle's thin legs and paws, but she seemed fine and squirmed free. "Ready to go outside, girls? Breakfast time!"

I padded downstairs, still in my bare feet, and inhaled the delicious fragrances of coffee and bacon. Seeing Jay at the stove totally surprised me. He flipped bacon like an expert, then cracked half a dozen eggs into a bowl. Jay hadn't shaved, and his hair stuck up in a few places. He grinned at me and tossed in chopped onions and peppers, then stirred the eggs with a whisk. How sexy was a man in the kitchen, cooking over a hot stove?

"Hey. Hope you're hungry as a hibernating bear."

"I am! And I didn't expect to see you this soon." I walked over and planted a kiss on him. "You're always welcome to make breakfast, of course."

He removed the crisp bacon to a paper towel-covered plate and then poured the eggs into the skillet. "Been so busy on all my commissions, my fridge is empty. I texted you two about meeting at the Sunshine Café, but Maddie said to come over instead."

"Could be my phone's wonky. I don't see any other texts besides Mark's from last night. Guess I missed Maddie's call earlier. It didn't play her *Peanuts* ringtone."

My sister emerged from the pantry, a ten-pound package of sugar in hand. "So that's why you ignored me. Better get that phone checked out, or upgrade to a new one. I've got a batch of muffins in the oven, so get dressed. Wait a minute, it's only eight—what are you doing up so early? Mondays are your toughest days."

"Hey, don't complain that I'm awake. Come on, girls. Outside."

I headed to the back door. Rosie and Sugar Bear rushed ahead of me out to the porch and down the steps into the dewy grass. A cloud suddenly obscured the sun. Not enough to shadow the miserable disarray of the trodden irises, tulips, and other smashed flowers beside the house. A dilapidated van pulled into the parking lot, spilling a crew of workers with lidded coffee cups in their gloved hands. They tramped toward the picket fence's gate.

"Wait, please! Until my dogs come back inside—"

"They should know us by now," a worker called out. Both dogs barked like mad, but the crew ignored them.

"Sugar Bear, leave it! Rosie, come. Right now."

I sighed in frustration when they ignored me. I ignored the crew when they smirked at my sweatshirt and pajama pants. Why should I feel uncomfortable? They'd never showed up this early before, and I didn't care what they thought.

Rosie continued to jump against the fence, so I marched over to her. "Down, girl. Focus!" She dropped to her haunches and gazed up at me, sad-eyed and confused. "Poor baby. You're a good watchdog, but I know they're here."

I herded both dogs back into the kitchen. While Jay divvied up the eggs onto three plates, I fetched the muffins from the oven. Maddie set mugs of coffee on the table. After a few bites, however, my stomach felt a little odd. I leaned back from the table, fighting the queasiness, eyes closed, until that faded.

"You all right?" Maddie asked.

"Yeah." I shrugged off her concern. "Why is the crew early?"

"Because Uncle Ross called the company's head honcho and gave him hell. He's not gonna pay anything if they don't finish by Wednesday. No matter what," she added with a chuckle. "Suddenly they've morphed into eager beavers."

Chapter 9

"I bet they'll finish in record time," Jay said, smearing toast around the puddle of bright yolk. The sight of it made me feel sick again. "You okay, Sasha?"

Confused, I pushed my plate aside and toyed with a poppy seed muffin, breaking it into little pieces. "I'm fine. They better not rush things and mess up worse. I hope Mom can visit Dad today. Have you heard from her yet?"

"She called me around seven," Maddie said, "but she didn't get much sleep. Not good, because Mom has a bunch of meetings lined up this morning."

"So. What are we doing today?" Jay asked me.

"Talk to the people who saw Dad, and find out what time and for how long."

My good mood had turned sour, partly from not finishing breakfast along with being caught outside in a sweatshirt printed with BEARLY AWAKE on my chest. My hair looked awful, given my reflection in the window, sticking up every which way. I needed to change my bandage and rewrap my hand, too. I sighed. Perhaps I should have stayed in bed.

Jay devoured a muffin, wrapped two more in a napkin, then crammed the bulk into his sweatshirt pocket. "Okay, let's get started."

"I thought you had that wolverine carving to finish."

"Yeah, I do. So you don't need my help?"

"Not that I don't want help, but I'll be running errands for most of the day." I checked the list in Mark's text again. "Oh, boy. He wrote 'some guy walking his dogs,' and I do remember seeing them at the park. How am I going to find out who that was? I kept my distance. No way did I want another dog bite. Do you remember seeing him?"

Jay nodded. "Reuben Johnson. He has a few pit bull rescues, and his sister Janet works at the Sunshine Café. You could ask her for his phone number."

"Okay. I know I saw Ryan Martinez riding on his skateboard."

"Yeah, and Larry Sykes was with him. As always."

I'd missed seeing Larry, Digger's older brother, who had a mild form of cognitive disability—or possibly autism. Village residents supported both brothers and admired Digger's loyalty to Larry. Whenever Digger was patrolling, he paid Ryan, a local teenager, to keep Larry company after school and on weekends. Sweet and polite, Larry focused on baseball statistics and other sports and rarely interacted in conversation.

"Is he still sweeping floors at the Quick Mix?" I asked.

"Not anymore. Ben Blake hired him to stock shelves, tidy the pharmacy, and even help customers find things," Maddie said. "Larry's happier doing that job."

"Ben has infinite patience, too," Jay said.

"Remember how Will Taylor refused to hire Larry at the factory?" My sister sighed. "Then again, Uncle Ross isn't patient with staff at the factory, so maybe that worked out. And don't forget Flora Zimmerman, too. They're both so bossy."

"Hey, did you ask Mom about Aunt Eve's birthday party?" I asked, changing the subject. "I forgot to mention it last night."

"She talked to Uncle Ross, but he was no help," Maddie said. "He figured the usual dinner at a nice restaurant. Bouquet of flowers. Box of candy."

"Guys don't plan parties," Jay said with a grin. "We'll show up, though."

"As long as there's beer," I teased him. "Sixty-four's not a milestone birthday like sixty-five or seventy, Mads. Not that I'm against hosting a party, but we have to make sure Aunt Eve won't mind us making a fuss."

Maddie nodded. "I don't think that's a problem. She loves a good party. I'm so grateful she packed up and moved back here after Will Taylor's murder. I appreciated Aunt Eve's help converting the accounting system into the computer, too. That was a lifesaver. We owe her big time, so she deserves a nicer celebration."

"I bet you didn't expect her to get hitched again to your uncle," Jay said, refilling his coffee mug. "Weren't they at each other's throats when your aunt first got back?"

"For weeks," I said, "and then, poof! They acted like lovebirds."

"Sometimes we still see the sparks flying between them. Aunt Eve is such a social butterfly, and he's the total opposite," Maddie said and then cracked a joke. "Just like how Eric's popular at his brewery, and I'm the dud."

"Oh, right." I threw a crumpled muffin wrapper at my sister, which landed in her yolk-smeared plate. "You both are very sociable. I'm more of a dud in the family."

"I better get to the studio," Jay said, "but dinner's on me tonight. How does Amato's Pizza sound?"

"Not gonna argue with that." Maddie finished her coffee.

"Me either! As long as you order the Hawaiian for me," I said.

After rubbing Rosie's ears and scratching Sugar Bear's curly back, Jay kissed me and strolled out the door. My sister raced upstairs to brush her teeth. I rinsed the plates and filled the dishwasher, jammed the coffee mugs into the only spots left inside, and set up the machine to run later. Luckily, my stomach had settled. I picked at the muffin pieces I'd left on a napkin and then dumped the rest. The stress must be getting to me.

I couldn't relax until Dad was off the hook.

After racing back downstairs, Maddie grabbed her purse and jacket. "So Mom said she'll help plan the party. How about inviting Aunt Eve's friends in the Red Hat Society, and the two or three couples they play games with on weekends?"

"Okay. Are we making it a surprise party?"

"No way can we pull that off."

"You're probably right." I sighed. Aunt Eve had an invisible antenna and always seemed to know whatever went on in the family or village. "She loves the Beatles. We could use their birthday song, and even print up some posters of the Fab Four."

"Yeah, and hang old vinyl records from the ceiling. I'll check Abby's antique store," Maddie said. "I'll spray paint them with 'sixty-four' in glitter. Should we order a specialty cake at Pretty in Pink, or ask Wendy Clark to bake one?"

"She's so busy at Fresh Grounds, since Mary Kate's off work."

"True." My sister unwound my bandage. "Good, it's healing up. We ought to celebrate your birthday at the same time, you know. Oh, stop your whining."

"I'm not whining—*ow*." I winced when Maddie prodded

a few bruises around the stitches. "You think that's healing? It looks terrible."

"It's just dried blood. You're taking the antibiotic, right?"

I nodded, although I'd forgotten last night's dose—and my birth control. Again. Once Maddie left for work, I swallowed the antibiotic pill and headed upstairs to fetch the round plastic disk from my nightstand. Oops. I'd forgotten I needed a refill. I showered and dressed, dried my wet hair until it was merely damp, and shook it free over my shoulders.

Not that I was late for work, given how we'd closed the shop, but I'd promised Aunt Eve to choose a fabric for our tartan bear. After applying makeup, I added silver teddy bear earrings. I stuck my feet in flats, and then braided my blond hair in a plait down my back. I'd have to make an appointment at the salon, given the split ends. Downstairs in the shop, I dodged ladders, paint-spattered drop cloths, and huge buckets, along with other paraphernalia. The crew had clearly sped things up, and now the foreman beckoned me into the back office.

"Ms. Silverman, right? I'm ready for you to sign off on the job." He held out a clipboard. "And pay the balance, of course."

"Sorry, but my uncle hasn't inspected your work. He'll sign the papers," I said. "You'll find him supervising at our factory, behind the house."

"Not an easy guy to approach, is he?" The man wiped sweat from his face and neck with a soiled rag. "Nearly ripped my head off last time we talked."

I only smiled and headed to the kitchen. Pleasing customers was part of any job, after all. I knew that after years of managing the Silver Bear Shop. The foreman would have to figure out a way to satisfy Uncle Ross and correct any problems.

Once I settled Rosie and Sugar Bear in their crates, I headed to the factory. I had plenty to accomplish this morning. I didn't regret canceling our usual Monday morning staff meeting, given the weekend's events, and added "screen repair" to the calendar app on my phone. Then I scrolled for the nearest store's location. I relied heavily on my cell—for notifications, texts, calls, photos. Technology—how did the older generations survive without it at my age?

Inside the factory, I waved to Chevonne Lang, Karen Anderson, and Evelyn Dolan at their sewing machines and threaded my way to the back corner. Aunt Eve had moved all her office equipment here a month ago. The noisy environment had frazzled her nerves, and she seemed happy to repack her things and move back.

"Good morning, Sasha." Aunt Eve pushed a strand of blond hair from her eyes. "It's far from good here. Don't even look at Ross if you can avoid him. He's in a rare mood."

"What's going on?"

"That woman again."

She'd hissed those three words under her breath. I whirled to watch Flora Zimmerman, her frosted bob tucked behind her ears, standing behind Joan Kendall's sewing machine. She often wore the same turquoise earrings day after day, along with a silver-shot cardigan over her white blouse and black knit pants, plus a chunky multi-beaded necklace and multiple gaudy rings on veined hands. Her shrill voice carried across the factory floor.

"Joan, you sewed those pleats crooked again—"

"I've told you before, Flora," Joan interrupted, "many times. If you have a problem with my work, report it to Mr. Silverman."

Her terse voice rang alarm bells in my head. Joan and Flora often butted heads over minor things, but this time their spat sounded far more serious. I glanced around the large room, but apparently, Uncle Ross was in hiding. That meant I'd have to intercede.

"Can I help?" I asked.

When Flora flashed her usual frown, I remained calm. She often considered my input into any factory dealings as interference, but Joan seemed relieved. Her blue eyes flashed.

"Flora's driving me crazy, always criticizing my work."

"She didn't pin these pleats correctly, and now they're wrong." Flora held up a teddy bear. "Look at this kilt. You have to admit it's a mess."

"The pleats look straight to me," I said. "Where's the sample?"

"The kilt isn't supposed to hang that low in back."

"Yes, it is!" Joan sounded cross. "We discussed the pattern at the last meeting."

The older woman shook her head. "You're wrong. Remember you messed up the bridal veils on the wedding bear, too. Almost half a dozen of them."

"And I fixed them. Don't forget your bouquets fell off."

"Isabel hid the sample bear somewhere," Flora sailed on, ignoring Joan.

"I did not," Isabel French called out. She left her machine to join us. Cheeks flushing pink, Isabel planted both hands on her hips. "The last I saw, you had the sample."

Flora denied that. "I haven't seen it in over a week."

"I'm tired of you poking your nose everywhere when you ought to be sewing your own bears," Joan said. "Mr. Silverman is our supervisor, not you."

"And he's busy right now," she snapped back.

"That doesn't mean you get to be in charge—"

"No more drama." I spoke so severely, all three swiveled to face me in shocked surprise. "Isabel, please search for the sample on the fabric shelves. Joan, I want you to check the shipping department. And Flora, you can go through the supply cabinets. That kilted bear didn't walk off by itself. It must be somewhere around here."

"Perhaps Mr. Silverman has it—"

"I doubt it," I interrupted, "but please, no more arguments."

Still peeved, I checked the cutting area and then headed to the enclosed room holding the stuffing machine. Uncle Ross stood before it, filling kilted bears with polyester, and looked up in surprise when I tapped his shoulder. The whirr of the machine died out when he turned it off and faced me, arms crossed over his chest, scowling. He wouldn't meet my eyes.

"Thought I locked that door. What's up, Sasha?"

"Another argument between Flora and Joan," I said, my patience thinning. "I'm supposed to help Aunt Eve choose the tartan fabric—"

"That's gonna cause more problems," he interrupted. "They already squabble over those stupid kilts. Now you want them to sew tartan bears!"

I gazed at the ceiling and counted to ten. "Do you know where the sample bear might be? And it's not a good thing to hide from Flora. She wants to take over as supervisor, and that's only causing more problems."

Uncle Ross tipped his cap back on his head. "I swear that woman's driving me into retirement. She won't listen, no matter what I say, and nitpicks everyone. Even Deon and the other kids in shipping. They hardly ever make mistakes."

"Maybe Flora should retire instead."

"Maybe so. She and Joan are always at each other's throats."

"Flora threatened to retire last year, remember, but I doubt if she really wanted to after all," I said. "How about using a suggestion box? If anyone has a complaint, they have to write it down. Believe me, most people won't bother."

Uncle Ross rubbed his grizzled beard. "And if Flora fills the box up, I wouldn't have to read them. Sounds good. I'm getting too old for all this fighting."

"You're what, fifty-seven? Fifty-eight? Positively ancient," I teased him. "Have you been to the doctor lately? Maybe you need a complete physical."

"Don't start in on me. Eve's pressured me plenty. First you came up with that wizard bear, then one wearing a kilt. Don't forget all the wedding bears, too, with a vest and tie on the groom, a veil and bouquet on the bride. All sewn on by hand."

"You don't do the sewing. Just find the sample bear, and that way they can't argue."

"I got it here." He thrust his hand behind the plastic bags of stuffing on the shelf above my head and drew out the beige teddy. "Thought they'd quit yammering if the sample wasn't around, but I was wrong. Thanks for acting as referee, Sasha."

"Sure, this time, but I can't keep—"

Uncle Ross had switched the stuffing machine back on, however, and the whirring noise drowned me out. I shut the door behind me, the sample bear in hand, and marched over to the back corner, where Aunt Eve was sealing a box with packing tape.

"How bad is it between Flora and Joan?" I asked.

"Bad enough. Ross hates having to stop their constant bickering, which only makes it worse. My presence here makes him uneasy, too. I keep telling him to stop being cantankerous, but that's what the staff is used to hearing."

"Hmm. Maybe so. Let's choose the fabric for the tartan bears."

"The samples came in on Saturday." Aunt Eve pushed up her sweater's sleeves, her flared floral skirt and crinoline swishing, and unrolled the first bolt across a table she'd been using

as a temporary desk. The pretty green and red plaid was shot
with gold. "I think it's too Christmas-y. And busy."

"I agree, so set it aside."

She arranged several more plaids in a semicircle. "I took
out a few flimsy cottons, so these others might be the best for
stability. Price-wise, too."

"I like this pattern with dark blue and green squares and
white thread, but maybe a lighter background would make a
more cheerful teddy bear. How about this one?" I pointed to
the plaid with blue and green threads bordering white squares.
"That might work."

"The Madras, my favorite!" Aunt Eve showed me the tag
and then drew another bolt out of a wheeled cart. "This is a
MacGregor plaid, without any blue in it."

"Which one is quicker to order? We'd better get started
sewing or we won't have any ready for the Highland Fling.
I'd like to have at least fifty to sell, if not more, using the nine-
inch-size teddy bear pattern."

"Okay. I'll call the vendors and see how quick we can get
it delivered."

"I'll tell Uncle Ross to assign Joan and Flora to sewing
those bears. They won't be able to quarrel over the kilts or the
wedding bears, either. And their sewing machines aren't next
to each other, so that will help keep the peace."

"Ross moved them apart last week, like little kids in a
classroom. Honestly, they tattle so much on each other, it
drives him batty. I cannot wait to get back to my office." She
handed me a sheet of paper. "Can you drop off this press release to Dave Fox at the *Silver Hollow Herald*? To announce
the shop's reopening."

"Sure thing, since I'm going that way on a few errands." I
hesitated and then tapped the table to get my aunt's attention.
"Do you think Uncle Ross wants to retire?"

She laughed. "No. We've talked about it, but he's not ready."

That was a relief. I headed back to inform Flora and Joan about sewing the tartan bears. They wouldn't be happy, and I hoped it wouldn't turn into a competition to see who could produce the most. Then again, that might be a good thing. Both were reliable workers.

They'd be out of my uncle's hair. I hoped so, anyway.

Chapter 10

Before heading to the newspaper, I walked across the street. My sister had opened her graphic arts business, Silver Moon, in a former restaurant. The brick building boasted floor-to-ceiling glass windows around the front, which allowed plenty of natural light.

Jay's studio took up the back half of the structure. Skirting the mud and tracks left by his truck, I peeked through the open sliding doors. The scent of burning wood tickled my nose. Jay bent over the wolverine carving that stood on a long plank table. I hated to interrupt him, but I'd forgotten to mention that Bonnie MacRae wanted a commission. Everything that happened before Teddy Hartman's murder had been completely driven out of my mind.

"That looks fabulous!"

Jay slid his goggles to the top of his head and set aside his electric tool. "Thanks. Didn't you have errands to do today?"

"Yup, but I need to tell you about Bonnie MacRae—"

"Her Scottie dog?" He hefted his cell phone and showed

me the screen. "She sent me several photos of the pooch and the specs, and a text explaining how she talked to you. Next time, Sasha, run it by me first. Not that I can't do a small job like that, but my schedule gets booked up fast. And this wolverine has been nothing but trouble."

"Sorry. I meant to tell you yesterday."

"It's okay. I've sent people to the Silver Bear Shop, promising they can find tie-dye or rainbow bears," he admitted. "Only you don't carry them. Sorry."

I laughed. "What kind of trouble are you having with the wolverine?"

"First I chose a bad piece of wood. Couldn't even get the general shape before it splintered under the chain saw." Jay waved his burning tool in frustration. "Then the second piece I chose had a major flaw in the grain. I'd gotten halfway, but that kind of problem can't be fixed. This one better work out. I'm getting tired of this project."

Glancing around the studio, I admired Jay's talent to fashion realistic animals from wood or ice. Massive tree stumps served as work surfaces on one side of the room. On the opposite side, a long wooden counter was littered with half a dozen trays of carving tools. Bigger tools, chain saws for the most part, sat on the floor along with tins of oil. A row of track lighting above boosted illumination. The studio back here had smaller windows instead of floor-to-ceiling, but overall, it had far more room and light than a garage or Jay's parents' old barn.

The wolverine was carved in a crouched position, teeth bared, claws extended. It looked so ferocious and realistic, it took my breath away.

"This is one of the best sculptures you've done, in my opinion."

"Thanks. I wish they weren't insisting on delivery next

week, because I'd rather help you track down whoever saw your dad at the park. His arrest really bugs me. I'm not in the mood to be creative, either."

"I get that." I circled the table, noting the detailed lines of the animal's hide. "So burning the wood makes the fur's shading, huh? Dark here on the muzzle and the legs, but lighter on the body behind the ears?"

He grinned. "Yep. Tricks of the trade."

"What's under this?" I moved toward a sheet-draped table, but Jay waved me away.

"The next commission, and the buyer wants to keep it secret from prying eyes. Check out the teddy bear carvings on the shelf, over by the door. I wanted to ask if you'd sell them for me at your Highland Fling booth."

"No problem. I'd better get out of your hair. I packed my car with all those bears for the Ann Arbor children's hospital, and I've got to get my cell phone's screen replaced. Guess I'll see you later at dinner. Pizza, right?"

"Already ordered. I'll pick it up at six."

I blew Jay a kiss after he replaced his goggles. A sweet and thoughtful guy, given how swamped my sister and I were lately with work. I headed back to my little Chevy in our parking lot. Good thing I had a jacket in the car, given the cold wind that chilled me to the bone.

Dave Fox rented a small cement block building on Roosevelt Street, near the American Legion. An empty lot stood between the newspaper office and a veterinary practice. Dave also operated a photography studio with a separate entrance on the side, plastered with photos of newlyweds like Gus and Cissy Antonini, family groups wearing holiday clothing, plus senior photos of high school kids who posed on the Village Green.

My tires jounced over the gravel parking lot. "Dave

should pave this," I muttered aloud. Two other cars sat near the building. A frantic yapping stopped me cold. "Oh, no."

Sparky, Lucy Hartman's little Morkie, clawed at one car's window glass and flashed its teeth. No doubt it remembered the taste of my blood. I rushed to the newspaper office and closed the door behind me, feeling silly but safer.

Inside the building, I surveyed the setup of multiple desktop monitors, their towers sitting below a long table, a few laptops, and small laser printers. Despite producing an online edition, Dave Fox ran off a hundred or so copies of the *Silver Hollow Herald* for the local assisted living and nursing home's residents, using the larger press machines of German origin situated on the room's far side. Most of the seniors had never become savvy with computers.

Lucy Hartman and her brother, who'd bought Bears of the Heart, stood chatting with Dave Fox. Lucy wore a black long-sleeved sweater and pants. She'd swept her dark hair to one side with a silver clip. Sunglasses topped her head, and a sleek black leather purse hung on one shoulder. She held a sheaf of papers along with her cell phone. Despite his white hair slicked back with gel, Kevin Whittaker looked casual in a polo shirt, slacks, and polished loafers.

Everyone in the village knew Dave Fox by his gray ponytail, blue denim shirt and chinos, plus trademark sneakers that looked ready for the trash. Dave loved those ripped shoes and often pointed out fresh damage with pride. He laced them tight so he wouldn't trip, however.

"There's room for your husband's obit in the next edition, Mrs. Hartman." Dave pushed up his black-framed glasses. "Cost is included in the Bloom's Funeral Home package."

"Good," Lucy said. "But send the obituary to the Ann Arbor newspaper, and the New England newspapers—"

"No can do," he interrupted. "You gotta contact them directly. They charge their own fees for an obit. Ask Dave Richardson at the funeral home, see if he'll do it."

"I'll have to pay through the nose for that, I bet," Lucy said bitterly.

Kevin Whittaker slid an arm around her shoulders. "Whatever the cost, I'll pay until you can access your bank accounts. Why didn't Teddy put your name on them?"

"Because of what happened in my previous marriage." She sniffed. "Peter divorced me after I splurged on a new car and a better wardrobe. Teddy said he couldn't afford to be wiped out the same way. He's got—had so many business transactions going on, he didn't want to jeopardize the accounts. But I should have insisted."

"So you'll end up in probate court?" Dave Fox asked.

"Yes, because I haven't found his will yet." Lucy looked close to tears. "I don't know what I'd do without you, Kevin. This whole situation is a nightmare."

I remained near the door, although Dave had noticed my presence. Before I could back out and come back later, Lucy turned around and spotted me. Her eyes widened.

"I heard your dad was arrested," she said, although her tone wasn't gloating. "I don't understand why, because Alex Silverman didn't kill Teddy."

Surprised and feeling hopeful, I walked over to join them. "I'm glad you think that. I'm sure he's innocent."

"Well, Andrew thinks it. Not me. I mean, he was practicing at the park," she said with a casual shrug, "but Andrew said it seems too obvious to fix the blame on him."

"Teddy didn't have enemies," Whittaker said. "Not here, anyway."

"No, we just moved to Silver Hollow." Lucy tucked a receipt into her bag. "The only person we did know was Alex Silverman. Teddy always saw him at trade shows."

"And they often disagreed," her brother said.

She nodded, as if sad to admit that. "I can't think of anyone else who might want to kill him," Lucy said. "That detective questioned Andrew, but we dropped him off at his car in the village that afternoon. He had calls to make and an appointment at his office in Ann Arbor."

Kevin Whittaker nodded. "Teddy was meeting me at Quinn's Pub around five o'clock, remember, but he never showed up. I'm not sure he wanted my advice about letting you make decisions about the pet store, but at least he agreed to listen."

"I couldn't get through to him about anything. Changes at the shop, putting my name on the bank accounts, and he never even told me that his loan for the bed-and-breakfast fell through. He had more financial problems than he ever let on. No wonder he always worried."

"And when Sasha's boyfriend threw a hammer at his head—"

"That was an accident." I interrupted Whittaker.

"Sure," Lucy said, her sarcasm plain. "Right after his brother tossed the caber and almost hit Teddy. Two accidents, so close together? Teddy was so upset, we had to leave. And he went ballistic when we found Sparky had chewed up the back seat. We left him alone too long, and he gets so nervous. Come on, let's go before he chews through his crate."

I decided not to bother arguing with her, and was relieved when the door slammed shut behind them. Dave Fox eyed the press release about our shop and shoved a blank form attached to a clipboard. He motioned to a cup of pens on a nearby desk.

"Pre-payment is the new rule."

I dug out a credit card from my wallet. "Okay, run this through."

"Want a photo included?" he asked.

"Yes, if you can run over and take a new one since the shop's been repainted. How much will you charge for that?"

Dave shrugged. "I'll cut you a break, given what's happened to your dad. As if Alex Silverman would kill anyone." He ran the card through the reader attached to his cell phone and handed it back. "I don't care what Lucy Hartman believes, either. She doesn't know squat."

I appreciated his support. "Did Pete ever get into that rehab program?"

"Nope, he wouldn't go. His brother let him work at the vet office, trying to straighten him out, but Pete blew that. Stole some controlled substances, the stupid kid. Cops found out he'd been dealing bath salts to his friends, too. He's sitting in Wayne County's jail."

"I'm sorry to hear that."

I felt bad for Pete, who'd once worked with Deon Walsh in the Silver Bear Factory's shipping department. Poor Dave—and Pete's older brother Mark, who could have lost his license and business over his brother's theft.

"I'll be posting the new issue of the *Herald* on Wednesday," Dave said, "so you can check out the announcement about your shop's reopening, with the photo."

"Great, thanks."

Shivering in my thin coat, I rushed to my car. Storm clouds had gathered in the west, and it smelled like rain. I skipped walking the dogs during lunch break. I drove to the freeway and managed to get to the hospital, lugging eight plastic bags of teddy bears, before the sky opened up. On the way back, however, I soaked one shoe in a deep puddle.

"Dang. Glad I didn't wear my sandals."

I popped open my glove box. Maddie had taught me long

ago to keep a spare pair of socks handy, along with extra sneakers in the back seat. Dry and warm again, I headed for the nearest cell phone store. The knowledgeable saleswoman quickly talked me into upgrading my phone rather than repairing the screen. The newer camera was worth the price. And I rarely spent that much money on myself.

I was so fried after this past weekend, I deserved a new model.

The tech expert set everything up and synced all my contacts as well, another bonus. After thanking her, I signed a flyer for the Highland Fling event with a discount code for a kilted teddy bear.

"If you can't attend, give it to a family member or friend."

"Wow, thanks! My little sister would love one," she said happily.

After that, I headed back to Silver Hollow. I'd planned to check inventory at a few stores in Ypsilanti and Chelsea but decided to wait for another day. Traffic heading out of Ann Arbor had snarled due to an overturned semi. A small car, similar to mine in size, had major front-end damage. An EMT unit's lights flashed as it sped past to the hospital, no doubt with the driver and passengers. I hoped no one had been seriously hurt.

While waiting for traffic to resume, I caught sight of a roadside billboard. Good grief. My ex-husband's image looked huge, along with a snarling dog perched above the memorable phone number for Hanson's law firm. And below that, in even bigger letters, FLYNN WINS.

No wonder he wanted me to file a lawsuit over the dog bite. Winning would help him promote his business further. I thanked my lucky stars for the divorce. Most of his television commercials poked fun at himself, but I knew the real story.

His overabundant ego had driven me out of the marriage. I'd blamed myself for several years, until realizing I needed to give up lingering guilt. I'd found true happiness with Jay Kirby.

We shared goals, values about family and friends, and plenty of laughter.

At the blaring honks behind my car, I restarted the engine and crawled past the jackknifed truck in a sudden downpour that pelted my windshield. Rosie and Sugar Bear hated thunder, which rumbled overhead. Poor babies. They needed special Velcro shirts to keep calm in the worst spring weather. After parking in the lot, I raced into the house. Peeled off my dripping jacket and checked the dogs' crates.

No dogs. They had to be hiding, probably upstairs in my bedroom. I tiptoed past the kitchen to the family room where Dad stretched out in a recliner. He snored along with my dogs on his lap. At a tap on my shoulder, I nearly jumped out of my skin and whirled around.

"Oh, sorry," Mom whispered. "I didn't mean to scare you. Mark Branson arranged to get Alex released over an hour ago! He didn't get much sleep in that nasty jail cell."

Her eyes looked clear instead of rimmed with red, and she flashed her usual bright smile. Mom wore a sleek pantsuit with heels, and her auburn hair was styled in a classic chignon. A big change from last night, when she'd been super stressed. I couldn't blame her, given how fast Detective Hunter had arrested Dad. We'd all been shocked. Rosie lifted her head and gazed at me with contentment, her tail wagging.

"Such spoiled doggies." I scratched behind her ears. Sugar Bear yawned, stretched her little body, and then accepted a few strokes over her curly hair. "But I love you both."

"I hope Alex sleeps for a long time." Mom beckoned me to the kitchen, filled the electric kettle, then fetched tea and sugar. "I do have news to share about the case."

"Oh? I'm all ears." I perched on a stool at the island and watched her check the cabinets. "We have a box of Girl Scout cookies in the freezer."

"Eve told me you had errands, so sit down and relax."

I quickly explained about the freeway accident while she arranged the frozen Thin Mints on a plate and poured hot water into a ceramic teapot. Impatient, dying to hear what Mark Branson said, I had to bite my tongue. Mom loved doing things her way. She fussed with pretty placemats, cut-glass teacups, napkins, and spoons. By the time she brought over our tea and strained it, I wanted to tear my hair out by the roots.

"Mom! If you don't tell me, I'm gonna scream."

"Okay, okay. It's good news." She smiled. "The coroner called Mark Branson back this morning. Teddy Hartman was killed between four and six o'clock yesterday, give or take a half hour either way."

"That's great! Dad was with Gil Thompson then—uh, except for when he visited the restroom," I added, crestfallen. "We don't know yet what time that was."

"At least I can sleep easier tonight." Mom blew out a deep breath. "So you haven't found anyone who saw him at Riverside?"

"Not yet. Mark gave me a list of people."

"I don't know why you have to do Detective Hunter's job."

"If it clears Dad as the prime suspect, I will."

I wondered if the estimated time of death affected Lucy Hartman's or Andrew Kane's alibis. Lucy said they'd dropped off Kane at his car in Silver Hollow after leaving the park. She could be lying. After all, her husband didn't trust her enough to add her to his bank accounts. Who knows what other problems they had in their marriage? I knew well enough how Teddy Hartman treated women. Badly.

A spouse usually had the best motive, given how they'd gain both money and freedom. Lucy may have wanted to throw suspicion in another direction, obvious or not, and set up Dad to take the blame. Her dog Sparky might have been the only witness, too.

I had to find other people who'd been at the park. Fast.

Chapter 11

At ten o'clock the next morning, I parked in front of Blake's Pharmacy. I'd texted Ben to confirm if Larry Sykes was working today. As for Reuben Johnson and his dogs, I'd have to stop by the Sunshine Café and track down his sister. My fingers ached at the memory of the little Morkie's savage bite. Would I ever forget? But I needed to restock my elastic bandage supply. I'd used up the last roll after my shower earlier this morning.

Around one aisle's end cap, I ran into Digger's brother. Larry held a wide broom and squinted at me through thick glasses. One earpiece had been taped to keep it in place. He wore a pale blue coat over his plaid shirt and navy pants.

"Hi, Larry. I'm glad to see you." I held up my wrapped hand with a smile. "Can you tell me which aisle carries this type of bandage?"

He studied my face first. "You run the teddy bear shop, huh."

"That's right. I manage it for my parents."

"My brother is friends with your sister," Larry stated in his flat voice.

"Yes, they went to school together."

He blinked a few times and then nodded. "I can show you the bandages."

I followed him. Larry must have needed to establish my relationship with Digger before he could focus on the search. He shuffled along with an odd gait. Larry was a head taller than his brother, who swaggered around the village and enjoyed giving out traffic and parking tickets to visitors. Even residents had little chance to escape, unless Officer Sykes gave them a break.

"Here they are." Larry pointed to a shelf. "All sizes of bandages."

"Those are for minor cuts on your fingers or knee. See, this type stretches," I said and demonstrated the wrap. "I need more to wrap around my hand and protect it."

"Huh." He moved down the aisle, where ankle, knee, and wrist braces hung from metal hooks. "You mean these."

I plucked up a package. "Exactly, thank you."

Larry held up a different one. "This has little clips."

"Yes, very handy, but I'd rather use the sticky wrap. Thanks, Larry."

"Your grandpa gave me a teddy bear." He stared at me. "I was five years old."

"That's sweet. Do you still have it?" I asked.

"I sleep with it."

"That's great. I'm Sasha Silverman, by the way." I held out my hand, but Larry didn't take it. His eyes slid over to Ben at the cash register, who was checking out a customer. "How are the Tigers doing so far this year?"

"Won four, lost nine," he said promptly. "They're playing Cleveland tonight."

"I heard they beat the Chicago White Sox."

He nodded. "All three games. That's a sweep."

Larry abruptly walked off and grabbed the broom he'd left down the aisle. He pushed it with care, making sure to pick up every bit of dirt or stray bit of dust. I hadn't gotten a chance to ask him if he'd seen Dad at the park. The Tigers' sweep of Chicago must have reminded him that he was neglecting his job. I headed to the back counter and waited my turn. Ben finally finished with the previous customers and fetched my prescription.

"Hey, Sasha. Anything else today?"

I held out my credit card. "Just this bandage roll."

"Any questions for the pharmacist?" Ben winked, flashing his dazzling smile. "Sorry, but I always have to ask in case."

I smiled. "I'm good. I bet Wendy's been crazy busy at Fresh Grounds."

"For sure. She wants to open her own bakery after Mary Kate returns to work. Not sure where yet, but I'm going to help her with start-up costs."

"I hope she succeeds, but the Thompsons will miss her." I took the bag he stapled and then handed to me. "Thanks so much."

"So I heard about another murder at Riverside Park." Ben raised his eyebrows. "The guy who opened the pet store with his wife."

"Yes, Teddy Hartman."

"How come the cops arrested your dad? No way would he murder anyone."

"Thanks, Ben. Did you happen to visit Riverside Park on Sunday?"

"Nope—"

"I was at the park." Larry Sykes leaned on his broom. "With Ryan."

"That's right," I said, glad he'd joined the conversation without being asked directly. "My boyfriend, Jay Kirby, told me he saw you both there."

"Ryan is my friend. He let me skateboard." He sounded proud of that, so I smiled again.

"Did you see Mr. Thompson, Larry? Or my dad, Alex Silverman?"

"Uh-huh. And big dogs, too. They barked a lot."

"Whose dogs? Reuben Johnson's?"

Larry nodded. "They stopped barking. He told them to stop, and they did."

Ben leaned over, his elbows on the counter. "But what were Mr. Silverman and Mr. Thompson doing at the park, Larry?"

"Throwing axes. They said it was too dangerous for me. Huh."

"That's true," I said. "Larry, did you see either my dad or Mr. Thompson leave at any point when they practiced?"

"Mr. Silverman did."

"Where did he go?"

"To the restroom," Larry said. "Ryan let me ride his skateboard that far. He said to go and come right back."

"So you saw my dad go into the restroom?" I asked. "Near the park entrance?"

"Yeah. He came out again, too."

"Where did he go after that? Down the road, out of the park?"

Larry thought for a moment. "No. He stopped to talk to people."

Frustrated, I wondered how to ask what time that had been, and who he'd seen. "Did you know any of the people my dad talked to that afternoon?"

"No."

"Larry, was Mr. Thompson with him?" Ben asked.

"Nope."

I had a sudden inspiration. "Did you happen to hear the village bells? I always count them when I do, and that tells me what time it is."

"I do that." Larry nodded, his eyes wide. "It rang five times."

Relief flooded me. I couldn't wait to relay that information to Mark Branson. I wanted to hug Larry but held myself back. That might scare the poor guy. Digger once told Maddie that his brother didn't like to be touched and rarely accepted affection from family members.

"If a police detective asks, will you tell him what you told me?" I planned to send Greg Mason, who'd be far more sensitive to Larry's needs and not dismiss him outright as a witness. "Would that be okay?"

Larry looked skeptical, but Ben nodded. "I'll help Larry with any questions, Sasha."

"That's great. I appreciate this so much."

I headed outside, tossed my prescription bag into the back seat, and then composed a text to Detective Mason. I wanted someone at the county level, more reliable than Phil Hunter, to know what I'd discovered. Besides, Mason had asked for updates.

I also decided to thank Larry by getting him and Ryan tickets to a Tigers home game in June. Digger could get his own ticket if he chose to tag along. Too cold now for a baseball game, in my opinion. My stomach rumbled. Hmm, almost noon. Since I'd skipped breakfast, I had a hankering for La Mesa. Maybe I could verify Larry's story with Ryan Martinez, who might be working today at his parents' restaurant. That would go a long way to convince Phil Hunter.

I'd forgotten to ask Maddie about setting up a Guilty Pleasures Gossip Club meeting, and how hosting it at ChocoLair was a brilliant idea. Joelynn Owens's shop was right next door to La Mesa, so I sent another text to my sister. I resisted going there first, since my stomach demanded at least one puffy-shell taco. Mmm. Pete Martinez served his delicious tacos and burritos with fresh salsa—all made on the premises.

I parked my car around the corner. Its wintergreen color stood out against La Mesa's whitewashed brick building and its charming red-tiled roof with a festive Christmas vibe. An outdoor patio out front held half a dozen ironwork tables and chairs, a new addition for the Mexican carryout restaurant, although no one chose to eat outside today. But once summer arrived, the patio would be packed.

Jay and I had hopes that Pete Martinez would enclose it for year-round interior space. La Mesa had only a line of five booths inside, far too small for night dining on weekends. Local residents usually ordered carryout. The weed-filled lot between La Mesa and the church parking lot was an eyesore, and expanding the restaurant would be a great investment. Pete could add on to the patio, as well. But I didn't know if he had such an ambitious plan in the works.

I pulled open the elaborately carved wooden door. Lacey Gordon sat in a booth with the same guy who'd walked three pit bull mixes at Riverside. So that was Reuben Johnson. Bearded and dark-haired, Reuben had the build of a football tackle. Tattooed, muscular arms bulged below a short-sleeved T-shirt. With his mud-spattered jeans and heavy boots, he looked as scary as his dogs.

Lacey sent a cheery wave in my direction. I waved back and then checked the menu while Pete Martinez waited behind the counter.

"Two chicken burritos and a root beer," I said. "Is Ryan working, by any chance?"

"Nope. He starts around six, and closes at nine for me."

"Okay, thanks. I wanted to ask him a few questions about Riverside Park." I took a pen and a slip of paper from my handbag and jotted down my cell, Maddie's, and our landline. "Whenever he gets some free time, can he call? I'd appreciate it."

"I'll tell him."

Pete turned to grill my order, so I wandered over to the bulletin board. A straw sombrero hung above it. Postcards of Puerto Vallarta and Cancun, a Day of the Dead skeleton, and other items had been tacked to the cork surface.

"Hey, Sasha," Lacey called out, and beckoned me over. "Got a minute?"

"Sure."

I walked over to the booth. We'd both served as dance judges at the Oktobear Fest last fall, and I knew Lacey worked at a local insurance company. She wore a wool blazer and bright red top over jeans, semi-casual, but with gorgeous gold necklaces and earrings.

"I heard you were bitten by a dog."

I held up my hand. "Afraid so. Lucy Hartman's Morkie."

"Little dogs are the worst offenders," Reuben said, shaking his head. "They're excitable. If you don't notice the warning signs, watch out."

"My poodle can be like that. She's nipped at the cat," I admitted. "Sugar Bear gets Rosie worked up, too. Would you help me train her out of that?"

Reuben pulled a business card from his pocket. "Call anytime. I'm free evenings, and I'd like to observe you with the dogs at home. See how they interact with the cat, too."

"He worked wonders with our Buddy, the Lhasa Apso dog we rescued," Lacey said. "Sounds like Lucy Hartman needs some training for her Morkie."

"If you see her, you can pass this along." Reuben dug another card out and then added, "I'm a certified trainer and keep reasonable rates. Not everyone around here can afford what a dog trainer in Ann Arbor would charge."

I took the second card, although I wanted to avoid Lucy Hartman. "Thanks."

"Reuben said he saw your dad practicing axe throwing at Riverside Park on Sunday," Lacey offered. "Along with Gil Thompson."

"Did you happen to see Ryan and Larry Sykes?" I asked him.

"Yup. Skateboarding." Reuben wiped his mustache and beard with a napkin. "I heard about Alex Silverman's arrest, but he didn't kill that pet store owner. Most lawyers are skanks, but not your dad." He leaned against the booth's cracked leather cushion. "He and Gil looked like professionals, though, tossing those hatchets. They didn't miss a single throw."

"But Dad went to the restroom."

"Yeah, and I saw Gil walking toward the trees—the road's that way. He left those sharp axes lying on the ground for anyone to pick up. I kept watch with my dogs. Didn't want Larry or any young kids getting hurt with them."

"Gil Thompson walked to the road?" I asked. "He never mentioned it."

"He was gone like twenty or thirty minutes. Came back before your dad returned," Reuben said. "I walked my dogs back and forth on the soccer field. A few young kids headed over to check out those wooden targets, but I sent 'em off."

I stared up at the clunky light fixture overhead, wondering how Gil Thompson failed to explain his absence. The bell at the counter clanged. Startled, I twisted around to see Pete bag up my order and place it near the cash register.

"Do you remember what time Dad left for the restroom?"

"Around five, I'd say, or thereabouts," Reuben said. "I checked my watch."

That confirmed what Larry told me. Two witnesses, enough for Phil Hunter to clear my dad as the prime suspect. Greg Mason once mentioned that old-fashioned legwork was vital in an investigation. Funny how his colleague in Homicide was averse to that methodical approach. But why had Gil Thompson gone toward the road during that time? What if he'd seen Hartman, perhaps by chance, killed him, and then hid the body under the shrubbery—and then pretended to discover it with my father? I'd have to confront him to learn the truth.

"Thanks. You've been a big help," I said to Reuben, who nodded.

I paid for my lunch and walked past ChocoLair to my car. I devoured one burrito and left the second in the bag before I drove to the Sunshine Café. Gil Thompson often met friends for breakfast, including Uncle Ross and my dad. Some days he remained all morning to read the newspapers in a back booth. Would he have eliminated Teddy Hartman, his rival for the SHEBA leadership, with a hatchet? A grisly death.

Garrett's uncle only helped on occasion at Fresh Grounds. He seemed like such a big teddy bear, always laughing and joking with customers. It was crazy to think he'd stoop to murder. But someone had. And Teddy Hartman's killer deserved justice.

I found Gil Thompson hunched over a table inside the Sunshine Café, newspapers scattered around him. My father sat across from him. Dad's hair looked a little grayer, but he didn't seem worse for wear after his brief stay in jail. Alex Silverman had a cheerful smile while he listened to Gil, who waved his hands while he talked.

Before I could walk in their direction, Lenore Russell greeted me. "Hi, Sasha." She wiped her hands on her apron, her waist-length dark ponytail swinging down her back. "You stop in for lunch? Or did your mom need Alex for something?"

I caught her quick wink. My mother was known in the village for sending Dad on errands and she liked to keep tabs on where he spent most of his time. "No, Mrs. Russell, and I already had lunch. But I'll take an iced tea."

"Coming right up. By now, Sasha, you ought to call me Lenore."

"Uh, okay. Sure."

She refilled a customer's coffee cup and returned to the kitchen. I'd called her Mrs. Russell for years, and felt uncomfortable being on a first name basis with her or anyone of my parents' generation. I walked toward the restaurant's back booth but hesitated. Maybe I'd learn something by eavesdropping on Gil Thompson's conversation with Dad.

". . . drove on past, angrier than a maddened hornet." Thompson chuckled. "You should have seen the look on his face. What a hoot."

"I'm surprised he didn't try to run you down." My father waved me over to join them. "Hello, Sasha. You here to have lunch with your old man?"

"No, sorry. I haven't had much chance to ask how you're doing," I said, "since your overnight stay in jail. I expect Hunter gave you a hard time with questions."

"Nothing worse than facing a cantankerous judge." Dad turned sober. "He grilled me hard, but I can't blame him. We found Hartman's body stuffed under that shrub, after all. Only because we had to search for one of Gil's hatchets—the one time he missed the target, and it sailed that way. Hunted around the woods for it, and finally found it."

"Too bad we checked the road," Gil said, "since that's what got us into trouble. Next time, let someone else find the corpse."

"Hope there isn't a next time," Dad said. "Been enough of that around here."

"Were there any bloodstains on the ground under Hartman?" I asked.

Gil Thompson rubbed his jaw. "Actually, I didn't notice. Did you, Alex?"

"No, which means he probably wasn't killed there. The light was fading by that time. That's why we had trouble seeing the target. Should have quit practicing earlier."

Lenore Russell brought over my iced tea, so I slid beside Dad on the seat and waited for her to leave. Then I folded my hands on the table and pointed a finger at Gil Thompson. He seemed surprised by that.

"Why didn't you mention walking out to the road while Dad visited the restroom? You didn't tell Detective Hunter about that."

Gil's cheeks reddened. "He never asked. But I was telling Alex just now about seeing Hartman drive past me. He didn't look happy."

"Was his wife in the car? Or their lawyer, Andrew Kane?"

"I only noticed him, and that little dog with its head hanging out the back window. I was stretching my legs," he added, sounding defensive. "I stood next to some birch trees, across from a sign that showed the squiggly road ahead."

"That's the exact spot where we found Hartman's body," Dad said. "Too much of a coincidence, Gil. The killer must have seen you there."

"So? You're the one Hunter suspected of murder, not me."

"Did you see any other cars after Hartman passed you?" I asked.

Gil nodded. "A black Cadillac Escalade. Tinted windows, very fancy. Had to be around eighty-five thousand bucks for such a premium package on that baby. Don't usually see those kinds of fancy cars around Silver Hollow."

My father tapped the table with a finger. "Did you notice what the driver looked like? Or catch the license plate number?"

"All I remember is that a big guy was behind the wheel."

I barely controlled my excitement. "That means Detective Hunter can track down who might own one around here, or rented that kind of Cadillac."

"Sounds easy, Sasha," Dad said, shaking his head, "but it isn't in reality."

"That detective doesn't seem convinced he's wrong," Gil said. "I doubt he'd bother to take on that kind of hard work. There's got to be hundreds of people driving a Cadillac around Ann Arbor and the metro Detroit area."

"It's worth a try," I said. "Someone followed Hartman and killed him, before he met Kevin Whittaker at Quinn's Pub. He told me Hartman never showed up."

Dad nodded. "Whittaker is credible, so that must be true."

"How do you know him, Dad?" I asked.

"We both attended several trade shows over the years. I heard Whittaker was interested in taking over Bears of the Heart long before Hartman sold it." He turned to Gil Thompson. "Looks like the murderer wanted to frame one of us, whichever sticks. Me because of that so-called business rivalry, and you because Hartman took over the SHEBA leadership."

"But I never confronted him over his dirty trick," Gil scoffed. "I saw him, what, maybe three times since he opened that pet shop."

"I never saw him around the village until last Saturday's

Teddy Bear Trot. I should have walked away, instead of letting things get out of hand."

"Guess we better tell Chief Russell, then," Gil said glumly. "Lenore said he's back from vacation. I'll go to the station and see what he thinks about this whole mess."

"I hope he agrees that Hunter jumped the gun in arresting you so quick, Dad," I said. "It's not the first time, either, according to Detective Mason."

They couldn't argue with that.

Chapter 12

On Wednesday afternoon, I drove out to Richardson's Farms. They were last on the list of shops Aunt Eve had given me earlier that morning to check inventory of our bears, collect unsold ones, or deliver more. I was frustrated that Mason hadn't replied about Larry Sykes yet, although Mark Branson had texted back after contacting Reuben Johnson. He didn't have any news of Hunter's investigation, however.

Orange barrels lined the gravel road to the farm and orchard, but work hadn't started on resurfacing. Whenever I couldn't avoid a pothole, the entire car shuddered. Vibrations tingled up my fingers to my wrists and arms. For years, crews had filled holes with tar, but patches never lasted. The material merely dried up and crumbled. Small stones and tar bits rattled inside my Aveo's wheel wells. The sound was maddening.

I muttered a curse and finally turned into Richardson's parking lot. Two vans from the Silver Birches Retirement Home sat near the front. I walked past seniors in warm coats, some using canes or walkers, who strolled the open areas with displays of trees, shrubs, annuals and perennials, tools, bags of dirt, and mulch. Several reminisced about their gardens from long ago. Two younger women examined ceramic pots of all sizes, whimsical metal artwork, statues of bunnies or turtles, birdbaths, and garden trellises.

I headed inside the long, low building where pies, coffee cakes, and doughnuts lined the shelves. Jams and jellies, apples, dried fruit, and plenty of kitchen gadgets were also for sale, along with aprons, oven mitts, and placemats. Our teddy bears, dressed in denim overalls, gingham dresses, and straw hats, sat in a separate display. I set a large box with more of the eight-inch bears on the counter and inhaled tantalizing scents of cinnamon and yeast.

Maybe one doughnut wouldn't hurt.

Emma Richardson waved a greeting. "Hi, Sasha. We sold all of your Silver Bears except the display ones. Want me to send the money we owe you online to your bank?"

"Aunt Eve wants a check, the old-fashioned way. Oh, and I'll take half a dozen cinnamon sugar doughnuts to go."

"Can't resist, huh?" With a laugh, she filled a bag and then fetched a check from their office. "I'm glad you brought more. Kids and adults love them."

"The shop's reopening Friday, if nothing else happens to delay it."

"We want to keep a dozen or so of your bears on hand all year," Emma said. "Some of our customers won't go to Silver Hollow. Too far, so they say."

"Really? It's what, two or three miles west."

Emma shrugged. "A straight shot, and easy to find if they use GPS."

"True enough." I glanced around the store. "So where does Kristen Bloom hold her goat yoga class? In the barn?"

"Yeah, but dress warm if you do sign up for the evening lessons." Emma lowered her voice. "So it's true you were bitten by a dog, given your bandage. Are you okay? Then we heard the owner was killed on Sunday, out by Riverside Park."

I nodded, although I preferred not to relate the details. "I'm not surprised the news has traveled this far from the village."

"Mom told me how Teddy Hartman took over leadership of SHEBA weeks ago. She didn't like him one bit. He kept insulting your parents, and pushing people to visit his K-9 and Kitty Korner pet store."

"His wife might have a better chance running it without him, from what I hear," I said. "Lucy Hartman's renting the shop that used to be Silver Scoop. Right next to the bakery."

Emma swiped a few sugar crystals from the counter with a cloth. "I met both of them right after they moved to Silver Hollow. They waltzed in here and pressured Mom to sell Lucy's homemade dog biscuits. Her husband even talked to Dad, but he didn't budge."

"I'm sure the Hartmans heard how busy you are in the spring, summer, and fall seasons. They probably wanted to take advantage of that."

"We don't have room to stock another perishable item. Dad doesn't like pushy people, either—" Emma looked disappointed when the bells jangled over the door and customers entered the shop. "Well, thanks for bringing in more bears."

"Sasha! I'm glad I ran into you." Amy Evans, the Highland Fling's committee chair, joined us at the counter. "I planned to stop and tell you the latest news."

"What's up?" I asked, dreading her answer. Amy loved trading juicy gossip with Digger Sykes, and I could see Emma's eyes light up to hear more gossip.

"I'm sorry your dad was arrested. Everyone in Silver Hollow knows he would never kill Teddy Hartman, despite their longtime business rivalry."

"Actually, there never was much of a—"

"No one would blame Alex Silverman if he actually did kill the guy," she breezed on, ignoring me. "Teddy Hartman was trouble from the start and caused friction among the SHEBA members. I'm glad Gil Thompson's taking over as leader now."

"That doesn't surprise me," I said.

"Hartman didn't know beans about Silver Hollow's history or how things are run around here," Emma said. "Not like Gil Thompson."

"True," Amy said. "You missed the Highland Fling committee meetings, Sasha, when Hartman showed up and tried taking over. He was unreal."

"Are you canceling the Highland Fling because of his murder?"

"No way!" Amy looked surprised at Emma's question. "The body wasn't found in the park, after all. We did cancel the axe-throwing competition, of course, but not the caber toss and hammer throw. We added a Hurl the Haggis contest, which will be a blast."

"Water balloons might be better, and less messy," I said.

"That wouldn't be as fun, Sasha. In order to be a contestant, people have to buy their own haggis at Jackson's Market and bring it to the park," she explained. "Didn't your boyfriend come up with the idea?"

"Yeah, but I wasn't sure if you'd agree with Jay's suggestion." I folded the check Emma gave me and stuck it in my purse. "I thought you might reschedule the Highland Fling for late May or early June."

"I can't do that to the vendors. They're committed to other events on their calendar. I'm not sure the police investigation will affect the Fling, anyway. You know what they say. The show must go on!" With that, Amy headed off to survey the jam butters.

Emma reached under the counter and retrieved a clip-

board, which she handed to me. "If you're interested in sign-
ing up for goat yoga, Kristen has three sessions. Thursday
night at seven o'clock here, eight on Saturday and Sunday
mornings at her place. Which would you prefer?"

"Thursday." I quickly printed my name on the first blank
space. Maddie's name was at the top. "I like to sleep in a little
on the weekend."

"Sure. Pay Kristen at the first class you attend," Emma
said. "Bring a mat, and wear your most comfortable clothes.
Don't go barefoot. Most people wear socks. The goats aren't
house-trained, so watch out. I mean barn-trained."

"I guess not," I said with a laugh. "Thanks."

Doughnut bag in hand, along with a lid-topped cup of
warm cider, I headed to my car. It sounded a bit callous, con-
tinuing with the Highland Fling after a gruesome murder, but
Amy and her committee had worked hard to plan the event.
Publicity had been churning out radio spots and on social
media since early March, too. Amy was right—the "show"
would go on.

On my way back to Silver Hollow, I pulled into the Legal
Eagles' small parking lot. The incredible carved eagle that Jay
had crafted last year hovered over their wooden sign closer to
the road. Its huge gray wings spread wide, and talons reached
out to catch invisible prey. A fierce expression glowed in its
glassy golden eyes. Each feather on the wings looked realistic,
created with Jay's wood-burning tool and other hand tools.

Flynn Hanson's TV commercials had boosted the Legal
Eagles' presence in the region. Despite my ex-husband's departure to start his own firm in Ann Arbor, Mark Branson and
Mike Blake still raked in plenty of business. They gave gener-
ous donations to various community projects, too. The
lawyers used a red-brick Queen Anne-style former residence
for their office, with lovely etched glass windows and a carved
oak door.

The Legal Eagle fiberglass statue, designed by artist Jim Perry for last fall's Parade of Bears during Oktobear Fest, stood on the wide porch. After being stored all winter, the bear's painted three-piece suit and wing-tip shoes remained pristine. A gold chain looped across the vest, and wire-rimmed spectacles perched on the bear's nose. The tan leather briefcase attached to one paw did have a few scratches, however.

Mark Branson answered my knock and welcomed me inside. "Thanks for coming in, Sasha. I do have a few updates on your dad's case."

In the large front room, two leather-topped desks faced each other from opposite sides. Mike Blake sat behind one, a phone cradled against his shoulder, pen in hand, his chair swiveling while he talked with a client. A tall bird-of-paradise plant with gorgeous orange flowers stood beside a snake plant and several armchairs, which acted as a privacy screen to shield one corner for consultations.

"Have a seat, Sasha—excuse me," Mark said when his phone rang.

He spoke briefly and jotted a few notes while I noted the glass-fronted cabinets that lined the walls. Huge research books filled them—no doubt references for law cases and rulings. The deep bay window, flanked by lush green draperies, gave the room an open feel. Several low wooden cabinets in one alcove held more books, folders, and papers. Mike's desk was piled high and threatened to spill sideways, while Mark's had a sense of order.

Mike ended his call and nodded to me. "Sorry to hear about your dad, Sasha. Sounds like his alibi is solid, though, if you found several witnesses."

Mark set his phone down. "Let's powwow in our 'conference' room, if you can call it that. You brought doughnuts?"

"I couldn't resist picking them up at Richardson's. Help

yourself." I edged around the snake plant, but its tall leaves stabbed me. "Oops. Sorry about that."

"A client gave that plant to Flynn, but he left it behind."

"I wonder if they meant something by that," I joked.

"Maybe so," Mark said with a laugh. "Mike's wife brought in the bird-of-paradise that someone sent after their daughter was born. I had a Boston fern that Wyatt gave me, but it died before our relationship ended. A sign of trouble, I guess. Have a seat. Coffee?"

"Sure, thanks."

He brought over two cups once I chose a leather chair near the fireplace inlaid with Pewabic pottery tiles. A cool breeze ruffled the lace curtains at a side window. I had trouble relaxing, though. Mike snagged a doughnut but hurried back to answer his ringing phone.

"How are you holding up?" Mark asked.

"I didn't sleep that well last night," I admitted, "even though Dad's free."

"Less to worry about now because the county prosecutor delayed the court arraignment. Lack of evidence. He didn't buy Detective Hunter's probable cause argument."

"That's great news. I figured you might want to learn what I heard from Larry Sykes and Reuben Johnson," I said, "so that's why I stopped in."

"Fire away," Mark said and opened his notebook.

I related everything from the other day and added the exchange between Lucy Hartman and her brother at the newspaper office. "That's important, isn't it?"

"It's not much use to us, though. So her husband dropped Andrew Kane off in Silver Hollow Sunday after leaving Riverside," Mark repeated, "because he either made phone calls or had a client to meet—I'll check that out. And ask the Hartmans' neighbors if they went home after that, or not. You said Kevin Whittaker is Lucy's brother."

I nodded. "He bought Bears of the Heart last year and is helping Lucy with the pet store now that her husband's gone. Teddy didn't put her name on their bank accounts, and she hasn't found his will. Why isn't Hunter investigating her for the murder and a motive?"

"He might be." Mark wrote more notes and then sighed. "I'd like to know why Teddy Hartman sold Bears of the Heart in the first place."

Once again I explained last year's Keepsake Contest, Hartman's jealousy, and his blatant attempt to copy our wizard bear by imitating a Disney design. Mark had heard most of the story about the pedophiles using Hartman's Benny Bears to secretly videotape children.

"Gil Thompson also saw Teddy Hartman on Sunday afternoon," I said, "driving his car. A black Cadillac followed him, too. Is it possible the driver, whoever it is, saw Gil and then chose to leave the body in that exact spot? Framing him, or Dad. It wasn't far from where they practiced axe throwing."

Mark looked skeptical. "Sounds like a long shot, but we can't rule it out yet. I haven't gotten a copy of the coroner's full autopsy report, but there was a skull contusion besides the wound in his back."

"So maybe the axe didn't kill him," I said. "Were there any signs that Teddy Hartman tried to defend himself?"

"It's possible the killer knocked Hartman out from behind. Dumping the body under the bushes on that stretch of road provided good cover, since few people drive through there. And less of a chance being seen by passing cars." Mark frowned. "There's another possibility, Sasha. Remember the 'long, slow death march,' as Alex named the fraud case, tied to the Las Vegas mob underworld?"

"Sure, but that didn't involve Hartman—"

"Unless someone bent on revenge sent that Cadillac driver

to frame Alex for murder. I'd rather be wrong, and cross it off as unfounded, than be caught by surprise."

I shrugged. "That was so long ago, though. And Dad ended his prosecuting career due to that particular case."

"So I understand. Thanks for the information," Mark said and ushered me to the door. "No more worries, okay? Focus on reopening the Silver Bear Shop."

I returned to my car, reassured that Mark was staying on top of things. His advice seemed sound. I had plenty of work to do by Friday. Maybe tomorrow night's goat yoga class would take the edge off my stress.

I needed to relax.

Chapter 13

"Oh boy." I rolled to one side, then shifted back into the plank pose. When my hand began to throb, I lowered myself to the floor. Little hooves suddenly thudded on my back. "Hey, get off!"

"Sasha, it's only a baby goat," Kristen Bloom said. "They don't weigh more than five or six pounds. Besides, it's good resistance training."

I groaned, though, when a second baby goat in flannel pajamas jumped on my spine. The first hopped off, bleating a protest, and wandered away. It skipped happily around my sister Maddie, whose short dark hair swung over her eyes.

"This is so much fun!"

"Sure. Real fun."

She ignored my sarcasm. So much for relaxing, too. My back muscles tingled from the pressure, but the goat jumped off me and butted heads with a black-and-white one. Bleating, they both hopped sideways in opposite directions. Another baby goat jumped on the chair that an older woman used to support herself. I had to laugh at their antics, despite the pain. They were awful cute and most of the yoga class enjoyed watching them.

Kristen directed her students, about half a dozen of us, to lie on our mats and position our arms. I remained flat, since I wasn't about to put any stress on my healing fingers. Another goat leaped and twisted, frantic, then skipped away.

"Let's transition to upward dog," Kristen directed.

Unfortunately, the black-and-white goat hopped onto my back and kept me from joining in the upward dog. Maybe that was a good thing. I drummed my fingers on my mat.

"He likes you," my sister called out.

"Ha. Go away, Billy," I said, but the goat only bleated. "Get off. Now."

"You ought to be able to handle the next position, Sasha." Kristen shooed the goat off me, although it butted against her legs and almost knocked her sideways. "Whoa, he's grown awful big for a baby. Can we send this one outside?"

Emma Richardson rose from her mat and herded the black-and-white toward an open doorway. I sneezed, since the goats had kicked up a dust cloud from scattered hay and straw. My eyes itched like crazy. I'd have to take a non-drowsy allergy pill before the next class.

"Remember, it's better to learn and perfect the simpler positions than attempt the harder ones and fail," Kristen said. "Sasha skipped the chaturanga earlier, which is quite difficult for a beginner. So from upward dog, we'll head straight into downward dog. Sasha, since you're new at this, lean against the wall in a half position."

I sighed and moved forward to obey, stretching out with my hands on the rough wood, and hoping to avoid getting a splinter. I did feel better already, despite my calf muscles and hamstrings protesting the deeper lunges. It might be good in the long run.

"—this transition, from upward to downward dog, will

benefit your back, your arms and shoulders, and of course, your core," Kristen continued on. "As well as your chest. Oh, Debbie, don't stretch that far. You might pull a muscle."

"I think I already did," Debbie complained. "*Ow*."

I contemplated the barn wall. I'd spent all day inhaling fresh paint fumes while putting the shop back in order—display bears back on the shelves, accessory racks rolled into place, and the Plexiglas boxes for our specialty bears hung in the rotunda's circular stairs up to the loft. I'd arranged bears in military or sports uniforms, German lederhosen, Japanese kimonos, hula skirts, and the like in our new "museum" area, along with bears dressed as Bear-lock Holmes, President A-bear-ham Lincoln, Shakesbear, Queen Eliza-bear, and the Three Muske-bears.

Then I retrieved the tot-sized furniture for the loft's playroom, set all the books back in the crates, and put Mr. Silver, our huge bear, in his usual spot. He looked great after being re-stuffed. Last of all, I hung Grandpa T.R. Silverman's photo in its place of honor. Joan Kendall had brought the barrel with our smallest bears back to the polished front counter while I'd been busy upstairs. Everything looked perfect for our reopening tomorrow morning.

"Let's position into the half warrior—stretch your bent knee forward. Yes, like that." Kristen demonstrated for the class. "Arms straight up, and stretch."

I nearly lost my balance and readjusted my stance. The stretch felt great. I was so looking forward to regular business hours again. We'd advertised a twenty-percent-off sale, which meant the weekend would be one of our busiest. I didn't have much trouble recruiting Joan Kendall and Chevonne Lang to help in the shop. Two tours were also booked for tomorrow.

"All right, class," Kristen said. "Let's try the second warrior pose, both arms stretched opposite each other. Good, good. I see this is easier for you, Sasha."

I almost laughed, since the baby goats kept wandering around and between my legs. Maddie, having practiced yoga for a few years, quickly transitioned to reverse warrior after that. By the time Kristen announced the last two positions, I'd given up and petted the smallest baby goat on the straw-littered barn floor.

"Meh to you, too, little guy." I fetched my shoes, coat, and purse when the rest of the class finally finished. "See you next time."

"I hope you had fun, Sasha," Kristen called out. "Don't run off, okay?"

With a sigh, I waited. I'd planned to check the shop one last time tonight, in case I forgot anything—our logo bags, or a receipt book. Now that would have to wait until morning. Maddie rolled up her mat while she chatted with Debbie Davison. Kristen answered questions from a woman with blue-black hair. Petite and slim in a pink leotard and matching tights, she looked familiar. I suddenly remembered her as Jen Chan's mother. Jen worked part-time in the Silver Bear Factory, one of our newest hires.

"I have to miss next week's session," Mrs. Chan said. "I'm on the afternoon shift at the hospital. How about if my daughter comes in my place? Jen might enjoy it."

"No problem," Kristen said.

"Maddie and I will have to miss in two weeks. We're setting up our booth for the Highland Fling on that Thursday night," I told her, and pulled two twenty-dollar bills out of my pocket. "Here's my fee for the rest of the month."

Kristen glanced at my faded T-shirt and sweatpants in disapproval. "You'd be more comfortable in leggings or yoga tights. By the way, I wanted to ask if you know when the road from Silver Hollow out this way will be paved."

"No idea."

"But I thought your mom and the council signed a contract with the road commission to get it done this spring. The potholes are horrible," Kristen complained. "I'll need a front-end alignment for my car, since I'm driving out here every week."

When I shrugged, she walked away in a tiff. Her dad, the previous mayor, never got around to approving the project. Poor Mom, getting the blame for Cal Bloom's procrastination. Maddie pushed aside a baby goat and headed my way, still listening to Debbie Davison. She was describing the house she'd recently bought, and my ears pricked up with interest.

"—plenty of room for my beehives. It's north of that little cemetery, right off Miller Road," she added. "Nice and quiet. The house has only two bedrooms, but a big kitchen and a shed off the garage. I do all my honey extraction and bottling there."

"Sounds great," Maddie said. "Eric told me he bought up the rest of your honey for the mead he's making to sell at the Highland Fling."

"How many hives do you have now?" I asked Debbie.

"A dozen, but this year I'm splitting them and buying more. My dad decided to become a business partner, so I can hire staff to help me at every stage. That should push me over the sales threshold and meet licensing requirements. I'll be able to extract a lot more honey this fall and then expand distribution."

Maddie nodded. "Tell Sasha about your business name."

"Clover Hill Honey Farm," Debbie said, beaming with pride. "I have an extraction machine, so that will speed harvesting."

"That sounds exciting. Keep us on your wholesale list," I said. "Your honey is a big seller at our shop, especially in those adorable ceramic pots."

"Did Cissy and Gus enjoy their honeymoon?" Maddie asked.

"Yeah, until she got sun poisoning. Cissy looks like a lobster." Debbie shifted her rolled-up yoga mat. "Already pregnant, too. I figured they'd wait a few months or a year."

"Oh, great," my sister groaned. "Mom's always competed with your mom. Now she's gonna badger us to get married and give her grandkids. No wonder she's dropping hints lately about the pitter-patter of little feet."

"Cissy said her biological clock was ticking too loud, but she wants to open another boutique. Probably in Plymouth." Debbie snorted. "You'd think she might take a year to relax and enjoy setting up their new house and all. My mom hints that if Cissy found a man and is starting a family, why can't I—but why? I'm happy enough being single."

"Exactly," Maddie said. "Getting married and having kids is not the end-all, be-all of life. I've worked too hard to juggle my career with three times the work."

While I agreed in spirit, I was closer to taking the plunge into marriage again. Jay had recently hinted about choosing wedding rings, too. Maybe next year. After February's murder at Cissy and Gus's wedding rehearsal, I still hesitated about making plans.

Debbie headed to the door. "Gotta run, ladies. See you around."

Mrs. Chan inched over to join us. "Mind if I ask you a question, Sasha?"

"Sure," I said. "We're thrilled that your daughter's the best at sewing our teddy bear eyes without any trouble."

"That's nice." The older woman cleared her throat, sounding nervous. "But I'm worried about Jen working at the factory. Last year, your uncle was suspected of murdering that sales rep, and now your dad's been arrested—"

"He's innocent," Maddie cut in, but Mrs. Chan held up a hand.

"I know you believe that, and I'd feel the same way about my husband or son. I only want to make sure Jen isn't in any danger."

"We understand your concern, of course," I said, "but Dad was once a prosecuting attorney for the Eastern District of Michigan. He respects the law. And the police released him from jail, so he may no longer be a suspect."

Mrs. Chan seemed to relax. "I didn't know Mr. Silverman was an attorney. Maybe Jen's right and I shouldn't have worried. Although yesterday, I stopped at the K-9 and Kitty Korner pet shop for some cat food. I'm sorry the owner's husband was killed, of course, but I don't think I'll shop there again."

"Why? What happened?" I asked, curious.

"Mrs. Hartman isn't the most pleasant woman. I felt so awkward, witnessing how she treated two men in the store. Telling one that he couldn't dictate to her like when they were children, and then she fired the other—her lawyer, from what I guessed. I left as fast as I could. Maybe I shouldn't have listened to her gossip."

"Gossip?"

"She claimed your father is a cold-blooded killer, although the two men tried to hush her," Mrs. Chan said and then sighed. "I'm never going back."

Once she departed, I pulled on my jacket. "Wow. Lucy Hartman lied to me about not believing that Dad was guilty."

Maddie nodded. "She lost a potential customer, too."

Bright lights in the gravel parking lot gave enough illumination to avoid most ruts and larger rocks. I fumbled for my car keys. "I'm glad you talked me into goat yoga."

"In spite of all the excuses you gave me today, trying to skip it."

My Aveo's starter protested but finally turned over. I

drove to the road, passing the Richardsons' white-frame farm house glowing with lights. The cozy scene looked similar to one of my mother's favorite Thomas Kinkade paintings.

"By the way, remember how the Hartmans accused Dad of posting bad website reviews for Bears of the Heart?" Maddie asked. "I read them out of curiosity, but they had tons of spelling and grammar mistakes. Mom and Dad are both perfectionists on that score."

"No kidding." I sighed in relief when the worst of the potholes ended and we reached the paved section of road. "Maybe a disgruntled customer wrote those reviews."

"I printed them out—"

"Good. I'd like to read them tonight."

No matter how late I stayed up last night, or how much sleep I needed for tomorrow's reopening, my curiosity ran on overtime. Word choice and sentence structure might give hints to whether a man or woman had written them.

The killer may have left them as a warning, too.

Chapter 14

On Friday afternoon, Joan Kendall handed change to a customer and pushed the cash register closed. "Have a wonderful day."

"Don't forget your credit card!" Chevonne Lang handed it to the woman at the second register we'd set up due to the crush of visitors. "Thanks for coming in today."

Both women plucked up their logo bags, chatting about their purchases, and passed me on the way out. I'd just finished the last tour of the factory. The Cub Scouts behaved very well until we arrived at the shop to choose the smallest size bears. Their leaders quickly herded them out to the vans—all fourteen, once they'd counted heads—and promised to pick up the stuffed bears on Monday. Weary, I slipped the check beneath the cash register drawer.

Reading all the printed reviews from Bears of the Heart's website hadn't been a wise decision, after all. I couldn't discern any pattern. Now my brain was slow and my eyes blurry. Three cups of coffee hadn't helped. How would I get through the rest of the day?

"What a madhouse," I said in a low voice.

Joan smiled. "And I thought the factory was loud," she whispered, watching several other mothers attempting to corral their boisterous children. "Shouldn't they be in school?"

"Half day today," Chevonne Lang said. "Kids can be awfully cute, until those Cub Scouts started throwing the bears around."

"Yeah, I bet the leader didn't expect that." I greeted an older couple who entered the shop and turned back to my staff. "What time is it? I'm starving, and I've got to let the dogs out at some point. Aunt Eve's swamped with month-end reports."

Joan shooed me toward the hallway. "Go now. You may not get another chance."

I glanced at Chevonne, who flashed her dazzling smile. "It's okay, Sasha. Joan was a big help when I rang up the first customer and overcharged by ten bucks."

"And then she insulted you about not being smart." Joan's anger was clear. "I mean, you caught the mistake right away before she paid. Why can't people be kind?"

"Believe me, I've heard a lot worse."

"If any other customer acts like that, show them the door," I said firmly. "Our business, our rules, and we won't tolerate bad behavior. Someone called me a ditzy blond my first day as manager. Dad insisted that the customer apologize or shop elsewhere."

"That's cool. I love how your teddy bears are based on actual breeds in the wild. Anyone can buy a cheap purple or pink one," Chevonne said. "Yours are so unique."

"Made in America, too. Not overseas," Joan added. "Go let your dogs out, Sasha, and grab a bite to eat."

"Okay. Thanks, both of you."

I headed to the shop's back half, our living quarters. Rosie and Sugar Bear jumped off the window seat and rushed outside to the yard. "Poor babies! Crossing your legs the whole time, huh? Wonder if Maddie ate all the bagels—"

The landline phone rang, so I grabbed it. "Mary Kate! How are you?"

"So tired," my best friend moaned. "Noah still isn't sleeping through the night. He wakes every two hours to nurse, and I forgot how hard that was with Julie. She's jealous of all the time I spend with the baby, and Garrett's working long hours. He's not much help."

"I saw him this morning. He yawned the whole time he made my double shot latte. Poor guy," I said, trying not to laugh. "That kept me going for our reopening."

"That's right, you're back to work in the shop! Hey, I called to get the scoop on the latest murder. Your dad's such a straight arrow. Nobody I know believes he's guilty."

"I hope they can identify the killer's fingerprints at the scene."

"Here's a bit of news," Mary Kate said. "Uncle Gil told us last night that Teddy Hartman paid for ads that several SHEBA business owners always take out in the *Silver Hollow Herald*. In return for not objecting to him becoming the leader, that is."

"He bribed them? Wow, that's crazy."

"My brother Mark said he wasn't surprised—no, Julie, don't touch that! It's hot," Mary Kate added. "Anyway, Maddie texted me about the Guilty Pleasures Gossip Club meeting next week. ChocoLair sounds perfect!"

"I can't wait—"

"Sorry, gotta run!"

Mary Kate hung up to comfort Julie, who wailed in the background. Clearly, my friend needed a juicy gossip session. I wolfed down a small yogurt, let the dogs back inside, and hunted in the fridge for some fruit. Rosie hopped onto the window seat and sprawled in comfort. Onyx snoozed on her tower's highest level, so I didn't have to deal with any cat-dog war.

Sugar Bear trotted halfway up the stairs with her ball, dropped it, and gave chase when the ball bounced down the steps. At a loud knock on the door, she rushed over with several sharp yaps. Rosie whined and scratched, since Jay stood on the porch. Buster, his gorgeous Lab-husky mix, panted at his feet. But his tail swished madly.

"I'm here to take the crew for a long walk at the dog park," Jay said. "I needed a break from that wolverine carving."

"Thanks!" I rushed to fetch their leashes and harnesses, then hugged him tight. "You're a real lifesaver."

"I've been neglecting Buster." Jay ruffled his dog's thick fur. "Isn't that right, boy?"

"You'll have to carry Sugar when she gets tired. She won't last," I warned him, but he unzipped the hidden pocket sewn into his sweatshirt.

"Bought this hoodie at the new pet shop. Pretty handy, I'd say."

"Really? So you must have seen Lucy Hartman."

Jay shook his head. "Her brother was holding down the fort. Decent guy, although he had no clue if she stocked anything like this. We searched the store together. Whittaker even checked the back storeroom. Found a bunch of boxes with some Benny Bears and all kinds of junk. Sports trophies, tools, ropes, fishing gear. You name it."

"Make sure to close the gate when you leave. Remember how Cissy's dog always jumped the fence, and I want to discourage any stray dogs coming in our yard."

"Picket fences might be quaint, but they're not practical." Jay tugged on Buster's leash, since his dog circled Sugar Bear in a far more friendlier manner than she wanted. She growled a warning. "Hey, mister, none of that."

I scooped her up and plopped my little poodle inside his

sweatshirt's pocket. "Better avoid any trouble from the start." I kissed him hard. "Thanks again."

Jay headed out with Rosie and Buster in tandem. At least those two enjoyed walking together, while Sugar Bear's feisty manner was more of a challenge. I rushed back into the kitchen when the landline phone rang again.

"I need a big favor," Maddie said, frantic. "Run over to the antique shop and pick up a vintage poster—it's for a graphics layout."

"Can't Abby text or email the image?"

"She did, but it's too blurry. I'd send Asia, but she's on deadline with another project, and Zoe's delivering a rush job to a client in Jackson. I've got something else to finish or I'd go myself. Abby's alone, and she can't leave to come here."

"Yeah, the village is hopping today."

"Spring fever, I guess. People are getting ready for the weekend, too."

Instead of walking, which might take too long, I drove to Church Street. The antique shop always displayed interesting items on the sidewalk in front of their bay window. A red Schwinn bicycle, free of rust, had an attached basket filled with white geraniums and overflowing mint. Next to that, several porcelain dolls sat in the vintage red wagon. I admired the gold and pale green upholstered chair that perched atop a squat walnut cabinet.

The set of long metal tubes chimed overhead when I entered the shop. I loved browsing here whenever I had a chance. Estate sale finds crammed ironwork or wooden shelves—teacups, china, flatware, furs, hats, gloves, ceramic bowls and other kitchen items, records, comic books, and other toys. Clothing hung on a rack, and jewelry sparkled beneath glass counters. I plucked a classic Steiff bear from a small basket.

"How darling. I should buy this and display it at our shop."

Abby Pozniak fastened her dark brown hair into a ponytail. "That's what you said the last time you were here."

"But it's so cute. We have a 'museum' area now up in the loft."

"Take it, then. Five bucks. You came for the poster, I bet. How's the reopening?"

"Crazy busy." I eyed her T-shirt. "'Not all who wander are lost'—isn't that from *Lord of the Rings*? Cool."

"Some guy in Ann Arbor sold me this, and a *Game of Thrones* one with a huge dragon." Abby handed over a skinny tube. "Mads already paid me."

"How's business here?"

"Slow over winter, but today's made up for it. We're having our annual spring sidewalk sale on the same weekend as the Highland Fling. Might as well piggyback on that, plus all the promotion the committee's done." She leaned on the polished walnut counter. "I'm glad the cops released your dad. Anything new happening with the investigation?"

I shrugged. "I haven't heard anything."

"Guess what I heard—Lucy Hartman couldn't unlock her shop door in back. She was so upset, kicking and screaming, because it's a keyless entry and she couldn't remember the code. Vivian Grant had to punch in the numbers for her."

"That's crazy. So how did Vivian know the code?"

"Lucy's brother texted it to Lucy, but she kept getting it wrong and totally lost it. So when Vivian arrived to open the bakery, she had to punch in the numbers for Lucy."

"She was that upset, huh. What day was this?" I asked.

"Monday, the day after her husband was killed," Abby said. "I heard the story about how their dog bit you at the Teddy Bear Trot. Vivian told me another interesting story, how Lucy Hartman blew a gasket over her husband's insurance policy. He'd already cashed it out."

"I wonder what Teddy needed the money for—"

"Didn't he lose out on opening a bed-and-breakfast?"

"Yeah, his loan was denied. Maybe Hartman had to pay start-up costs for their pet shop," I mused. "Lucy must be strapped for cash, since I heard he wouldn't put her name on his bank accounts. I'm wondering if she fired that lawyer. I haven't seen him around this week."

"Your mom snagged the best booth at Riverside Park for the Silver Bear Shop, by the way," Abby said. "The one closest to the pavilion. Everyone will see you first, but you won't be able to think straight with all those bagpipes wailing."

"I won't mind. Thanks again."

I headed back to the shop. At some point, I'd have to find time to visit the Pretty in Pink bakery. Maybe ordering Aunt Eve's birthday cake would be a good excuse. Vivian Grant might share some insights about Lucy Hartman.

And maybe a theory or two about her husband's murder.

Chapter 15

After checking with Joan and Chevonne, I walked across Theodore Lane with my sister's poster. Tyler and Mary Walsh's cottage had a riot of tulips and clumps of iris in their yard, also surrounded by a picket fence. I'd always wanted to live in a Cape Cod, its door and shutters painted green, and I admired the house every day. Birds trilled above me, and a butterfly wandered over the bright azalea bush I passed. The warm sunshine cheered my spirits.

So did all the *Peanuts* paraphernalia in Maddie's office at Silver Moon. She'd collected mugs, file folders, Snoopy bobbleheads, and many other items. Eric Dyer had given Maddie a framed and signed book cover proof for *Speak Softly, and Carry a Beagle*, showing Sally holding Snoopy, last Christmas. My sister had danced around the tree in absolute joy and hung the artwork beside her worktable.

"Thanks, Sash." Maddie slid the poster out of its cardboard tube and spread it flat, eyeing the border and image. "I really needed to see these details up close."

Asia Gibson rushed over from her desk and squealed in

excitement. "I love the 1920s vibe. We're doing a whole series for the Flynn Wins ad campaign, using sepia tones, with
him and his fiancée in vintage clothing. She looks like a flap-
per, in fact. Very sultry, with fringe on her dress and a long
pearl necklace."

That didn't surprise me, given Flynn's flair for drama.
He'd once asked me to appear in a commercial, but I turned
him down flat. I perched on a tall stool to watch Maddie
sketch out a few ideas for the ad. When the door opened
again, a gust of fresh air swept into the large room. We all
grabbed loose papers before they flew in every direction.

"Traffic was wild, to say the least. So glad I'm out of that."
Zoe Fisher, her turquoise and pink hair gelled into spikes,
tossed her purse on a chair and then leaned over Maddie's
table. "You almost done with Hanson's Law Firm ad? He's so
full of himself."

"I can attest to that." Rather than dwell on my ex-husband,
I changed the subject. "Has anyone visited the K-9 and Kitty
Korner shop, by any chance?"

Zoe waved a hand. "I did, the day after they opened.
What a mess! So disorganized, and the Hartmans fought like
crazy over how to stock the shelves or display stuff at the register. Like World War Three, I tell ya. And Lucy can curse
like a drunken sailor."

"That bad?"

"Yeah, and Teddy Hartman looked ready to wallop her.
He stopped when I walked in to check out a new collar for
my French bulldog," Zoe said. "His wife grabbed a bunch of
trophies off the counter and then dumped them in the back
room. I guess her husband thought they looked too cheap.
She was not happy, let me tell you."

"Trophies?" I suddenly recalled Jay mentioning those earlier. "What kind? Like tennis, golf, or bowling?"

"Not if you play with an axe instead of a ball."

I nearly fell off the stool. "Are you serious?"

"Yep," Zoe said. "Engraved with Lucy Hartman's name, too. First place, from what I saw, before she stuffed them into that box."

"Shut up!" Maddie glanced at me in amazement. "That ought to put Lucy as number one on Detective Hunter's suspect list."

"Mine, for sure," I said. "I'd better let Mark Branson know. Mind if we tell him to call you, Zoe? He may need a statement."

"Sure." She pushed a turquoise strand of hair behind one ear. "If she did kill her husband, I bet Lucy dumped those trophies in the trash by now."

I hoped not. They'd certainly give weight to a motive for murder. Unfortunately, my call went to Mark Branson's voice mail. Since Maddie and her staff had a deadline to meet, I walked over to visit the Kilted Scot boutique. Jay had carved their large sign out front with Celtic-style letters. No doubt the commission for Molly, the MacRaes' little Scottish terrier, would be more difficult. The boutique's exterior was a close match to our two-story Victorian style, with its wrap-around porch, turret, and bay windows.

Gavin and Bonnie had painted the outside trim a bright red and draped plaid swags over the porch railings. They'd hired a landscape company to rip out the bushes, but had yet to plant anything new. But lush green ground cover lined the curved walkway to the porch.

"The heather will bloom one day, I hope! Come inside, Sasha," Bonnie called out from the front door. "I've got something for you."

Puzzled, I walked into the shop. Gavin waited on a couple, who admired several lengths of wool fabric. They listened to him explain the difference between tartans and plaids and then watched when he demonstrated how to wrap one length as a kilt. He draped another over his shoulders and secured it with an ornate burnished brooch.

"Three-inch pin, and lethal if push comes to shove," Gavin said, his eyes twinkling. "Traditional Penannular in make, brass, with a wolf's head. We feature a different clan every month, don't you know. During the time of Robert the Bruce, Ewan Ban MacPherson had three sons, so sometimes the clan is also called the Clan of Three Brothers . . ."

Bonnie led me through the front room with built-in oak shelves. The shop's new layout was well organized, with clothing on one side and a variety of other items for sale opposite. Walls had been taken out to open two other rooms, probably the former dining room and library, which added display space for fabrics, tweed capes, wool blankets, tartan handbags, caps and tams, ties, and adorable baby clothes.

"We call these jumpers," a young woman said, laying out soft sweaters in several colors for an older customer. "Go ahead, you can feel how it's the finest cashmere wool."

"That's my girl, Sophie," Bonnie whispered with pride.

I noticed jewelry set out on velvet-lined trays or in glass boxes—earrings, necklaces, even fancy tiaras. A tall bookshelf displayed photo books of Scotland, Ireland, Wales, and England. Other cabinets held bottles of imported whisky, tins of tea and coffee, glassware, stoneware, canned haggis, and other foodstuffs. Beyond that, a heavenly scent drew me into the kitchen like a moth to the flame.

"Just out of the oven, these are. Thought you'd like a sample." Bonnie's cheeks looked rosy from the kitchen's heat. "We'll be sellin' these chocolate-dipped fingers at the Highland Fling. That's Belgian chocolate, on the best shortbread you've ever tasted."

I loved her lilting accent as much as the delicious sight of those cookies. "I'm such a fiend," I said, breathing deep. "Are you sure?"

"Give me an honest opinion. Are they too crumbly?"

"No way. Mmm." I nearly swooned, tasting sweet dark chocolate and rich, buttery shortbread that melted on my tongue. "I don't care how much you charge for these, Bonnie. You won't be able to bake them fast enough."

"You think so? Take these scones for your tea or supper. They're best eaten right away," she advised, handing me a wrapped package. "This kitchen is a dream."

I knew that Barbara Davison had long ago installed commercial grade appliances and expanded the room to take up the entire back of the house. Granite counters, maple cabinets, and a wide island added to the kitchen's appeal.

"So you're baking everything here, and transporting it to Riverside Park?" I asked.

"No, I've rented a portable oven. Like the ones they use on *The Great British Baking Show*," Bonnie added. "I'd rather be on hand, and sell everything fresh."

"That sounds great. I bet people will love to stand around watching you work, too. Thanks for these." I took the scones with a twinge of guilt. "I should have asked for your input on our teddy bear kilts."

"I saw one, and the wee pleats are perfect. But I'd like to ask—what might be the rate for wages here? I need someone with baking experience."

"I'm not sure. Aunt Eve takes care of payroll for us, but you could ask Winona Martinez. She works at La Mesa, her parents' restaurant," I added. "She may not be available for that weekend, but you could always ask."

"Back home, the living wage minimum is voluntary and changes every November. It also depends on a worker's age."

"It's mandatory here." I licked chocolate off my fingers. "By the way, did that detective question Gavin about how Jay almost hit Teddy Hartman with the hammer?"

"You mean the doaty bloke with the fishy stare? So rude,

walkin' off before my Gavin finished tellin' him it was a pure accident! He went to the station, next day, and a young man wrote up a report."

"Tell Gavin thanks for that. Every little bit helps."

I returned to the shop and helped close for the day. If only Greg Mason would take over the investigation from Hunter. Joan, Chevonne, and I devoured the scones, which proved as delicious as the shortbread. After they headed home, I checked on my dogs. Both Rosie and Sugar Bear lay curled together in one crate. Jay must have worn them both out at the dog park, so that meant I could de-stress with a bike ride around Silver Hollow.

Daylight savings put off darkness for several more hours, and the exercise and fresh air helped after such a busy day. I circled the village a few times, glad I'd donned a heavier jacket, and then walked down Main Street. Fresh Grounds remained open. I glimpsed Mark Branson sitting at a corner table with another man, so I set my bike into the iron rack out front and walked inside. An outgoing customer passed by with a cup and a bag. Gil Thompson locked the door behind the guy with a wide grin.

"We're closing in five minutes, Sasha. Or are you gonna question me again?" he teased. "You didn't seem convinced by my alibi, after all."

"That's not funny, Uncle Gil." Behind the counter, Garrett dumped used espresso beans from the metal portafilter into the trash with a loud *thunk*, then wiped the steamer wand, machine base, and counter. "Murder's not a joke."

"No, but that lazy Detective Hunter isn't doing much investigating. I bet she'll nail the killer again. Just watch. We all want to breathe easier."

"Did you want anything, Sasha?" Garrett asked.

I sensed he'd already cashed out and shook my head. "I'm good."

Garrett raised an eyebrow when I glanced toward Mark, as if understanding my desire to eavesdrop. Once I filled a plastic cup with water, I crept to the booth closest to the back table. Both men wore tailored business attire, with a touch of flair— Kevin Whittaker's red bow tie, and Mark's flamboyant purple shirt, pink tie, and pocket handkerchief. I wasn't facing them, but their voices carried to my ears.

"—so gullible. They paid Teddy to adjust the Benny Bear pattern," Whittaker was saying. "I'd have asked them why they wanted a front seam without the double-stitching. Talk about a red flag, but Teddy claimed he didn't know they inserted a video camera inside."

"Did he mention the criminal case when you bought the company?"

"Not a word."

"And your sister didn't know?"

Whittaker cleared his throat. "He never told her anything. Teddy knew that I'd taken on companies in trouble before, either bankrupt or reorganizing after a Chapter 11 filing. My team assesses whether a business can be salvaged," he added. "Bears of the Heart still had a decent reputation and a solid customer base. So I bought him out. Then my assistant heard about the pedophile investigation a week after, way too late to back out."

Mark didn't speak for several minutes, so I assumed he was taking notes. "When did Hartman stop making the Benny Bear?"

"I'm not sure. Lucy did say that Teddy recommended the Silver Bear Shop to customers who wanted bears with a front seam."

"That's odd, since they're a competitor."

"I'd say."

I wasn't surprised. Maybe Teddy Hartman had learned why the group wanted his Benny Bear for voyeurism and stopped production. Maybe he sent them our way in hopes of getting us in trouble, but that failed. And maybe Hartman moved to Silver Hollow, got himself appointed as head of SHEBA, spread rumors about Mom being a corrupt mayor, and planned to make a lot more trouble for us. Until his murder.

"So Mrs. Hartman had good reason not to trust her husband."

Kevin Whittaker tapped on the tabletop, a staccato sound, before he continued. "Lucy begged me to fly out here and look over the account books, too. She suspected that the money from selling Bears of the Heart had vanished. Teddy claimed he paid off his creditors, but Lucy is still fielding calls from them."

"Was your sister unhappy that the bed-and-breakfast deal fell through?" Mark asked.

"Not really. Lucy didn't want to clean or make breakfast for guests. The two of them fought a lot over that. Listen, Mr. Branson, I told that detective all this information. If you need anything else, call me. But I've got to close the shop for my sister tonight."

"Thanks for meeting me today."

Chairs scraped across the floor. Whittaker brushed past my table without a glance. His confident manner reminded me of my dad, in fact. Garrett locked the door after his departure. With a smile, Mark slid into the booth across from me.

"That was interesting."

"Did Whittaker ever mention how Lucy took the news of her husband's death?" I asked him. "Badly, or not surprised?"

"Hysterical, yes. He drove her to the morgue to identify the body, and the attendant confirmed that when I called to check."

"Don't you think it's plausible that Lucy killed him? For abusing her, for keeping secrets, and all the money issues?" I held up a finger before Mark could reply. "And I doubt if Detective Hunter is aware that Lucy won several axe-throwing contests. Jay saw her trophies at the shop, and so did one of Maddie's employees. She may have thrown them out, though."

"Hang on a minute." Mark scribbled fast in his notebook. He scanned the pages from his interview with Kevin Whittaker and then met my gaze. "Where were these trophies?"

"Zoe Fisher visited the K-9 and Kitty Korner after it opened." I explained the whole story while Mark jotted more notes. "Jay saw them in the back room, though, recently. Seems odd that Lucy would pretend to be an amateur at Riverside Park."

"Not really. She may have wanted to keep her skill secret, given how Alex and Gil were stiff competition. I've seen YouTube videos of them both. I guess Garrett recorded them at the last tournament they entered."

"I had no idea," I said with a laugh. "Anyway, Amy Evans canceled the axe-throwing event because of the murder."

"Not the caber toss and hammer throw, I hope."

"No, and they're putting on a Hurl the Haggis contest. Messy, but fun. I bet it'll be the most popular event at the Highland Fling."

Mark turned serious. "Detective Hunter is still fixated on Alex, unfortunately. He's like a rat caught in an escape-proof maze and refuses to admit he's wrong. I've faxed over statements from Reuben Johnson and a transcript of my interview with Larry Sykes and Ryan Martinez. Despite how tight your dad's alibi is, Hunter won't concede. You'd think he'd concentrate on the other suspects, who have gaping holes in their alibis."

"What other suspects?" I asked.

"For one, Andrew Kane did call several clients but I'm still trying to access his cell phone information and pin down the location. I haven't gotten far in checking Lucy Hartman's movements after she left Riverside Park, either."

"How about that driver of that black Cadillac? Too bad Mr. Thompson didn't catch the license plate number."

"I traced the Vegas mobster that Kane defended, but he died in prison." Mark slid out of the booth and stood. "The hostile witness who gave your dad so much trouble is in a Florida nursing home, with dementia. So the 'long, slow death march' link is broken. It was a long shot, anyway. We'll just have to keep digging and hope that Hunter comes around."

"The Hartmans fought a lot, from what I've heard," I said. "That's another reason Lucy may have wanted him dead."

"I can research whether she filed a domestic abuse complaint against her husband, back east, but don't count on it. Not many women do."

"If only Detective Hunter would do his job. Or give up and turn over the investigation to Detective Mason. Do you think he might?" I asked. "I've texted Mason all the information I've learned so far, but haven't heard back from him yet."

"I'm sure they both have other cases. That's common for all detectives, in small towns or big cities. There's only so much they can do." Mark squeezed my shoulder. "Don't get discouraged, Sasha. Your dad will be completely cleared in the long run. You'll see, so be patient."

That was easy for him to say.

Chapter 16

Saturday proved to be busier at the shop, with customers pouring in to pick up their pre-orders of kilted bears. And Sunday's usual routine of church and family dinner meant little time to spend alone with Jay. While he'd asked me to keep him company while he finished the wolverine, I knew my presence would have distracted him. I spent the late afternoon and evening reading and relaxing with Rosie and Sugar Bear, who snuggled close on the sofa.

Monday and Tuesday rushed by, with more customers than usual and several more tours of the factory, which were boosted in popularity by Maddie's social media posts. No doubt the upcoming Highland Fling helped as well.

We'd also placed ads with sale notices and special discounts. Photos from the Bears for the Cure cancer fundraiser held in March had garnered thousands of likes on Facebook and Instagram. Maddie crowed in delight over her success, since it also boosted Silver Moon.

By Wednesday, customer visits slacked off. I craved relaxing at the Guilty Pleasures Gossip Club meeting that night, held at ChocoLair, but a large senior group booked a late tour. While Renee Truman covered the shop, Maddie and I each led a dozen people through the factory. I'd never be able to handle such a large group without losing my voice, so I appreciated her help. And our staff wasn't overwhelmed while sewing the tartan bears.

Afterward, Aunt Eve flagged me down when I passed the office. "I'm missing that check from Richardson's Farms—Sasha, wait! Where are you going?"

"To find it," I called back to her, and searched until I found it in my purse's inner pocket. Check in hand, I raced to Aunt Eve's desk. A dull pounding, louder than a sledgehammer, started up outside. "I've been hearing that noise all afternoon. What's going on?"

My aunt had to yell an answer. "They're working on the project to open Theodore Lane to Main Street." One finger in her ear, she waved the check. "Emma said she'd given you this, only I couldn't find the deposit in the spreadsheet."

"Sorry, I forgot all about it."

She smiled and unlocked the Smart Safe mounted under her desk, her mid-calf floral skirt swirling, placed the check inside along with a stack of bills. Once she re-locked it, Aunt Eve turned back to me.

"Maybe it's time for online bank transfers, although I don't like all this sophisticated technology. I prefer old-fashioned checks and paper receipts."

I repressed a laugh. Aunt Eve loved vintage everything. Gold clips held her creamy cardigan sweater in place over her blouse, and her reading glasses hung from a chain around her neck. She leaned her elbows on the polished desk and raised an eyebrow.

"So, Sasha. About our combined birthday party—"

"Hold on," I interrupted. "You're the star, remember. Maddie's planned everything with Mom's help, and all your friends have been invited."

"But why can't you share the spotlight?"

"I suppose I have to, if you insist."

"I don't mind sharing," she said, looking delighted. "I wanted to order a cake, but the bakery said Maddie already did."

"Oh, that's great." I sighed, since I'd planned to use that excuse to talk to Vivian Grant. "Are any of your friends unable to come? Mom said some haven't called yet to RSVP."

"I'll talk to them." Aunt Eve handed me a blueprint. "I hired Jen Chan to fix the garden beds since you've been so busy. Write down whatever shrubs, trees, or flowers we want, and then she can design the best landscape. She'll buy everything and plant them, too. Jen will be here soon, but I've got to ask Ross something over at the factory."

The incessant pounding outside drowned out her clacking high heels. My head pounded by the time Jen Chan breezed into the shop half an hour later. Her long black hair was held back with butterfly pins, and she wore a floral jacket over her white sweater and distressed jeans. Jen had on ankle-high hiking boots, as if preparing for a mountain trek. She smiled at me, perfectly confident, and set a thick binder on the shop's front counter.

"I appreciate being hired for this job," Jen said. "I finished my forty hours from MSU's Master Gardener program, but haven't gotten my certification yet."

"No problem." I waved the landscape blueprint. "It looks like a tornado went through our flower bed, and I'm not sure what survived."

"Your iris won't bloom this year, but they should revive. I'll have to replace the tulip bulbs. They're goners. Read the fine print in that painting contract, because they might have a guarantee about paying for any damages."

"Aunt Eve can check that out."

She flipped open her binder. "I'm sure you want to replace the hydrangeas, of course, but I'd suggest dwarf ones that won't grow higher than the porch railing. I can add fertilizer if you want blue or pink, or I could mix them up—that would be pretty."

"Whatever looks best against the shop's front," I said, "although Mom likes the huge bush in the yard with white snowballs."

Jen laughed. "That one needs plenty of room. What about teddy bear sunflowers at each corner of the house? They're brighter yellow and not as tall as regular sunflowers. Alyssum will work as ground cover, maybe in white." She pointed to another photo in her binder. "I suggest two containers on either side of the porch steps, with coleus, mini petunias that you won't have to deadhead, and trailing sweet potato vines. I can get ceramic or resin—"

"I trust you," I interrupted, since two customers had entered the shop. "Do whatever you think is best, okay? Take out any shrubs if you need more room, and send a detailed bill to Aunt Eve. Supplies, flowers, and labor, straight to her for payment."

"All right." Jen waited until the older women began browsing through the accessory racks, and leaned close to whisper. "Sorry about what my mom said at goat yoga. She worries all the time like I'm a little kid. I handled worse things at college."

"My mom's the same way."

"And your dad's a big teddy bear at heart, too. Thanks again."

Jen closed the binder and headed outside. I left Renee in

charge of closing the shop and greeted my dogs, who seemed eager for a walk. A text from Jay pinged my phone. He'd nearly finished the wolverine, and planned to deliver it tomorrow. Fantastic.

"Ready, girls? Let's get this done."

I fastened the buckles of their harnesses, clipped the coupler on their leashes, and headed outside. They shied in fear at the huge wheeled machine on the street with alternating hydraulic hammers. The noise was deafening. It had managed to break all the concrete around the curve of Theodore Lane. Behind the machine, workers in orange vests raked the pieces free from the iron fretwork below. What a mess.

An excavator collected the largest pieces and fed them into another machine that pounded them into bits. Several trucks blocked the lane past the foot of our driveway.

"It's okay, Sugar." I picked her up when she shivered, refusing to budge, and urged Rosie to continue toward Kermit Street. "Come on, girl."

Our parking lot was crammed with cars due to the road repairs. Visitors to the Queen Bess Tea Room and the Kilted Scot boutique might be inconvenienced for a short time, but the crew worked faster than our painters.

After a quick trot around the Village Green, my dogs curled up back home on their fluffy bed. I barely had time to change, freshen my makeup, and brush out my hair. Maddie had already left for ChocoLair. I hurried over on foot, sat across from my sister at the pub table, and sighed in relief. My cousin's wife and best friend, Elle Cooper, handed me a glass of white wine.

"What a day. Where's Mary Kate?"

"Still on her way," Maddie said, "and then we can party hearty."

We chatted for another twenty minutes with Joelynn Owens, the shop's owner, and then broke into applause when

Mary Kate walked into the shop. She wiped a tear away, her auburn hair gleaming, and did a pirouette to show off her slinky blue dress and strappy heels.

"Mama llama, ain't no drama," Maddie sang out. "Not here, anyway."

"That sounds wonderful." Mary Kate collapsed on a stool at the pub table. "I had to read *Llama Llama Mad at Mama* five times before Julie agreed to nap this afternoon. She only slept for ten minutes, if that."

"How goes the potty training?" Elle failed to hide a broad smile. "Remember, they don't go to kindergarten in diapers."

"Ugh, don't ask. Julie won't give up her binky, either." Mary Kate rubbed her eyes. "And then Noah woke up, of course, and wanted to nurse. Hand over that tray of chocolate, right now. Uh, I mean, please send it my way. I'm so used to being bossy now."

"Now?" I teased her. "Maddie didn't leave much for anyone else."

"There's plenty more to sample, don't worry."

With a laugh, Joelynn handed out white plates, festive floral napkins, and plastic glasses. My sister opened another bottle of wine from Eric Dyer's brewery and winery, but Mary Kate declined with a sad sigh.

"I'll have to settle for water."

"Your husband needs to buy you a spa package," Joelynn said. "Doesn't Luxe have some kind of massage with a mani and pedi combo?"

"They do," Elle said with a mischievous smile, "and here's a gift certificate for the new mom! Early birthday present."

I vaguely remembered Maddie texting me about pitching in for that, so I'd have to pay her back for my share. Mary Kate clasped the envelope against her chest.

"Wow, thanks! I can't wait to make an appointment."

Maddie laughed. "If you need company, let us know."

"Garrett better finish clearing out that extra bedroom. He promised to do it before the baby arrived," Elle said. "Why do men need so much junk? Matt has loads of boxes in our basement, and it drives me nuts."

"Noah will need his own room eventually," Maddie said, "so call us when the time comes, and we'll pack up all of Garrett's stuff."

"He would kill me if I touched a single pile," Mary Kate said in frustration. She snatched a chocolate. "But I'm not here to complain. I only want to relax."

"You should try goat yoga," I joked. Everyone but Maddie groaned.

"It's actually fun." She brought out several tiny bottles. "I have two types of nonalcoholic wine for you, Mary Kate. There's chardonnay and rosé, plus sparkling cider."

"Cider is too acidic for my stomach, but I'll take the rosé." Mary Kate moaned with ecstasy while eating a truffle. "Mmm. Hazelnut, right?"

"Yes. That's an espresso, this is a raspberry, and the last one's dark chocolate sea salt," Joelynn pointed out. "The one with dark and milk chocolate together is called a 'Side-By-Side' on the order list. All my specialty chocolates are available in a gift box, of course. Choose six different ones for a personal truffle stash."

"I'll sacrifice myself for a truffle." I bit into the square. "Heaven on earth, for real! I'm gonna buy Mom a box for Mother's Day."

Maddie waved. "I already ordered one, but she won't mind getting two. You know how she loves truffles. Like Mom always says, if she can't eat it or smell it, she doesn't want it. No clothes, no books, just candy and flowers."

"Give me a book any day," Elle said, "although I'm biased."

"Being a bookseller, of course," Mary Kate said, and snatched a caramel. "I'm the same way. I wish I had time to read, but I'm exhausted when the kids are finally asleep."

"I hear ya lately. Totally exhausted, and I can barely keep awake at the shop. Even with lattes from your coffee shop." I bit into a shiny chocolate sphere. "Mmm, malt balls."

"I have a question about your mom's art gallery show Friday night," Joelynn said. "She's having that Jim Perry guy come in, right? The one who makes weird sculptures. I saw his work when I went to New York City to visit an aunt."

"He got his start in Detroit, though," I said, "and taught college classes."

"Cool. I didn't know that."

Joelynn wiped chocolate from her fingers with a napkin. She'd let her dark curly hair go natural instead of straightening it; a riotous mass fell over her shoulders beneath a black and gold head scarf. Gold hoops bobbed at her earlobes, and both wrists had multiple bracelets. Her slacks matched the black gold-banded jacket loaded with fringe. I envied her fashion sense. My usual jeans and a tweedy blue sweater seemed drab in comparison. I'd forgotten jewelry, too.

"Ooh, chocolate-covered potato chips!" Elle swooped on the tray that Mia Donovan, Joelynn's part-time assistant, brought to the table. "And nuts, right?"

"Coated cashews and almonds. They are totally lit." Mia slid the tray closer to everyone else. "These are turtles, with caramel and pecans. We also made—er, Joelynn made these cordials. Mandarin orange, rum, amaretto, and crème brûlée."

"Wow." I swooned at the explosion of orange and chocolate in my mouth.

"But we're not here to just eat chocolate," Maddie said, snatching another truffle. "This is the Guilty Pleasures Gossip

Club, after all. Does anyone have news about Teddy Hartman's murder? I mean, anything. It's been ten days."

"Detective Hunter is MIA," Elle said. "Especially the inaction part. Get it?"

I ignored that lame joke. "I heard he's busy with other cases."

"Tell us everything that happened, Sasha, from the beginning at the Teddy Bear Trot," Mary Kate said and poured another small bottle of nonalcoholic wine. "I've been so out of the loop, I don't know much."

I couldn't reply at first, since I'd popped a chocolate-coated sandwich cookie into my mouth. Maddie answered for me, crunching a few chocolate-covered coffee beans while giving a rundown of that weekend. First my dog bite, then what happened the next day at Riverside Park. Joelynn had not heard the complete story either and peppered us both with questions. She shook her dark curls over one shoulder and took a sip of wine.

"That detective sounds like a total jerk. Like, grab the easiest solution and don't bother with anything else."

"You're talking about Phil Hunter, right?" Mia piped up. "My mom knows about him. He investigated a friend of hers in Ypsilanti. Detective Hunter planted evidence, and the drug case got tossed out of court."

"Whoa. Add corrupt as his middle name," Joelynn said.

"When was this? Your mom hasn't left Silver Hollow since she started working at the Queen Bess Tea Room," Elle said. "It couldn't be recent."

"I'm not sure." Mia shrugged. "Gary, my stepdad, worked with a guy who was accused of selling drugs. Only he didn't do it. The guy, not Gary, my stepdad. They both worked at the Rawsonville auto plant before he left. The guy, not—"

"Gary, your stepdad," Maddie and Elle chimed in.

"Yeah. So Hunter planted drugs in the guy's gym bag, only someone claimed to see him do it. Another dealer, only nobody believed him," Mia said. "Wild."

"So he got away with it?" Mary Kate asked.

"I'm not surprised Hunter would pull that kind of trick," I said. "I bet he'll never solve Hartman's murder and the case will go cold."

"Maybe Hunter doesn't care." My sister drained her glass of wine. "A shame, because as much as I didn't like Teddy Hartman, nobody should get away with murder."

"That's true," Joelynn said. "Less than half of all murderers are caught. I heard that once, either on TV or the radio."

"I heard Lucy and Teddy Hartman fought like crazy," I said. "Could be he abused her, and she decided to get back at him. For good."

"Who told you they fought?" Maddie asked.

"Garrett. He overhears a lot at Fresh Grounds."

"Hey, that's right." Elle pointed a toffee at Mary Kate. "I ordered coffee—it's so convenient right next door. Wendy was telling Garrett that she was at Pretty in Pink, and how Vivian had overheard the Hartmans arguing. They'd just opened their store, but the inventory supplies were delayed. Lucy expected Teddy to call the vendor, and he yelled at her to do it, that she couldn't boss him around. Vivian also saw a big bruise on Lucy's cheek later on."

"And then Teddy ends up dead." Maddie gave a low whistle. "Maybe I should text Digger and ask if Lucy filed a complaint."

"Mark Branson is checking into that already," I said. "I'll ask Vivian whether she saw or heard anything the day of the murder when I pick up Aunt Eve's birthday cake."

"She might not talk to you," Elle said. "Wendy told me

that Lucy threatened her. She's scared of that woman and won't go near the pet shop."

"I bet Lucy said she'd sue her." Maddie snorted in disgust. "Lucy throws that around like birdseed. She wanted to sue Sasha, me, my parents—"

"Not a lawsuit," Elle interrupted. "Lucy shook an axe in Vivian's face. Remember that her husband ended up with one in his back? Shades of Lizzie Borden."

Chapter 17

"Lizzie Borden, ha. I wouldn't think Vivian Grant would scare that easy." Maddie yawned wide and poured another cup of coffee. "Why didn't she complain to the police if Lucy threatened her?"

"I don't know, but I'd like to find out what happened." I capped my travel mug full of coffee and then let Rosie and Sugar Bear back into the house. "I texted Detective Mason to meet me at the bakery this morning."

"Wish I hadn't eaten so much chocolate last night." Maddie yawned again. "I feel as bloated as a beached whale. I thought the bakery doesn't open until nine or ten."

"They open at six. We prefer going to Fresh Grounds, but Jay told me his brother and other Quick Mix factory workers buy doughnuts from Pretty in Pink. Aunt Eve said she'll cover for me at the shop. I don't know how long this will take."

"I still say it's a lost cause." Maddie rubbed her face. "If Vivian Grant didn't file a police report by now, she's not gonna tell you."

"Doesn't hurt to ask. Besides, if Lucy did kill her husband, she shouldn't get a free pass." I snatched up my purse and a light jacket. "You're the one who said so last night. Or don't you remember—that you hated Hartman, but he deserved justice."

"I know." She yawned again. "Good luck. Hope it works for you."

I didn't confess that I was so tired I wanted to crawl back into bed and sleep the whole morning. I'd even left my peanut-butter slathered bagel behind after one bite. This trip to Pretty in Pink had better be worth it.

After parking in Ham Heaven's lot, I walked quickly away from the scents of ham, bacon, and coffee and past the K-9 and Kitty Korner shop. A light glowed through the front window. Lucy must already be prepping for opening, but what about her dog? A frantic but muffled yapping answered that question. My hand ached in memory so I rushed toward the bakery's propped-open door.

Pretty in Pink's scalloped and striped awning ruffled in the early breeze. Inside, a line snaked around the interior. I backed away and stood beside a large cement planter by the street's curb, filled with a mass of pink and white tulips. A parade of customers left the bakery with flat white boxes sealed with pink stickers. People kept arriving, too. I checked my phone—eight fifteen, so Detective Mason was late. At least my queasy stomach had settled.

I joined the line inside. Two workers quickly filled boxes from trays behind the glass counters or fetched reserved boxes from a shelf. The crowd dwindled. Muted floral wallpaper stretched behind a white ironwork table and two matching chairs in the corner. The vertical bakery case beside me held large boxes with decorated cakes. Notes with scribbled names were taped on their sides. None had Silverman written on them, however.

Pretty in Pink had a reputation for decadent French buttercream. Aunt Eve loved their cakes, although she rarely ate pastry or chocolate. Another long counter with a glass front showed assorted pies, cupcakes, tortes, fruit tarts, and éclairs.

"Can I help you?" the young woman behind the counter asked brightly.

"Actually, I'm here to talk to Mrs. Grant. If she's available."

"I'll fetch her, just a minute."

She slipped through the back room's door. I knew that both Mary Kate and Elle had worked at the bakery long ago. They'd related the tale of a nasty food fight between Vivian and the wife of Will Taylor, who once worked as a sales representative for the Silver Bear Shop & Factory. The two women trashed the place—unbelievable, given its current tranquil atmosphere. I breathed a sigh of relief when Greg Mason finally sauntered through the door.

"Glad you could make it, detective."

Mason saluted me with his index finger, then pushed up his wire-rimmed glasses. He had bags under his eyes from lack of sleep and held a nondescript cardboard coffee cup. Not from Fresh Grounds, but a popular chain that I never visited. Too bitter, in my opinion.

Mason gestured to a doughnut in the case once the worker returned. "Boston cream, please. Want anything, Ms. Silverman?"

When I shook my head, the young woman handed over the doughnut wrapped in wax paper. He tossed several dollar bills on the counter. "Keep the change."

"Thanks!" She plunked the leftover coins into the small TIPS can by the register and disappeared into the back room.

"So what's this about?" Mason took a huge bite of doughnut, chewed, and swallowed before he spoke again. "You said the owner of this place might have information."

"Actually—"

The back door swung open. The young woman emerged with Vivian Grant as well before I could continue. The bakery's owner wiped her hands on a pink ruffled apron. Her frizzy dark hair was captured in a net behind her head, and she looked warily at us both.

"May I help you?"

"I'm Sasha Silverman—"

"I know who you are," Vivian interrupted with a smile. "We're decorating the cake your sister ordered. A Beatles theme, right? It won't be ready until Saturday."

Detective Mason brought out his official badge. "Ma'am, I have a few questions—" He grabbed a stray napkin from the counter and wiped his mouth. "My colleague, Detective Hunter, is investigating the murder of Mr. Hartman. He's unavailable today, so that's why I'm here. If you have a few spare minutes, that is."

Her bright smile faded. "I suppose I have no choice."

"You do, ma'am, but the police will appreciate any help you can give them to solve this case. Any assistance at all."

"Like what?"

"Conversations you overheard, or any odd behavior you witnessed from either Teddy or Lucy Hartman," I said, unable to stop myself. "Like at the SHEBA meetings, or doing business right next door to their pet shop. Did you talk to them at any point?"

Annoyed, Vivian shot a telling glance at her employee, who fled to the back room once more. "Not really. I didn't know the Hartmans that well. I heard Alex Silverman was arrested and then released—"

"Mr. Silverman is not our only suspect," Mason interrupted smoothly. "Other witnesses have told us that the Hartmans argued often. Can you verify that?"

She crossed her arms over her chest. "I heard them yelling at each other, sure. We raise our voices in here, too, if things get busy or stressful."

"But what did they argue about?" I asked, impatient.

"I'm short on time today, Ms. Silverman, so allow me to direct the questions." Mason had deftly taken over, which I didn't mind since Vivian was acting so defensive. He took out a slim silver pen and his small black notebook from an inner coat pocket. "So you never spoke to either of the Hartmans at SHEBA meetings?"

"Not beyond the usual hello and good-bye."

"But you heard Mr. Hartman discussing Alex Silverman, or the Silver Bear Shop?"

Vivian nodded. "Everyone knew about their business rivalry."

I bit my lip, wishing Mason hadn't flashed me a warning sign. He jotted a note and then waited for her to continue. Vivian squirmed a little under his direct gaze.

"He also insulted Mayor Silverman, and accused her of corruption, that sort of thing. None of us paid that much attention, though. Teddy Hartman enjoyed bullying people, even his wife. I refused his offer to pay for an ad in the local paper—in exchange for letting him take over as SHEBA president. Pretty bold of him, really."

"You said Hartman bullied his wife?" Mason asked. "In what way?"

Vivian looked uncomfortable at that question. She glanced at the door and rubbed her hands together, clearly unhappy. He waited her out, flipping to a fresh page, until she cleared her throat. Had Teddy Hartman threatened her, too?

Vivian leaned against the counter, elbows supporting her torso, hands clasped. "The walls between our shops are paper thin. Teddy Hartman constantly yelled at his wife—putting her down and accusing her of flirting with other men. He didn't strike me as a jealous type, but you never know. That one man hangs around the store an awful lot."

"Andrew Kane, their lawyer?" I asked, unable to resist.

"I don't know who he is. But Teddy smacked her around," she said. "I saw Lucy had a big bruise on her face near her eye. She couldn't cover all of it with makeup. I offered to drive her to a nearby women's shelter, but then Lucy threatened me. She said she'd sue me for slander if I ever told anyone."

Mason kept his eyes on his notebook, still jotting in tiny print. "About seeing the bruise, or that her husband abused her?"

Vivian frowned. "She didn't say which, but—I got the message. Loud and clear."

"Did you ever witness Mrs. Hartman fighting back against her husband?"

"Yes. She flung a set of keys at his head, right outside their shop."

"When was this?"

"Uh." Vivian seemed reluctant to explain. "Lucy yelled at him, on Saturday morning. The day before her husband's murder. She pushed him right out the front door and screamed at him. That kind of ridiculous behavior scares customers away. Mine, too."

Mason waited, patient, and then glanced up from his notebook. "Did you happen to see them the next day, by any chance?"

"I'm not open on Sundays, so no." Vivian folded her arms over her chest. "But I left my shop door open on that Saturday, because it can get so warm in here. I heard Lucy yelling and then saw her whip Teddy Hartman with a dog leash!"

"What time was this? Morning or afternoon?"

"Almost six o'clock, when I locked the door. I had to wait

for a customer who was late picking up a birthday cake for a party that night."

"So how did Mr. Hartman react to his wife's beating?" Mason asked.

"He laughed, if you can believe it. Grabbed for the leash, but I heard her, clear as day. She told him that if he didn't start treating her better, she'd bury an axe in him."

When I gasped aloud, Mason ignored me. "Is that when you offered to help? To drive her to a women's shelter."

"Yes, because I—I know what it's like," Vivian said, her hand at her throat. "But Lucy turned me down flat. And then threatened me a few days later."

"Exactly what did she say, Mrs. Grant?"

Vivian licked her lips, eyes darting to the street once more. "When I came to open my shop on Tuesday morning, I found Lucy standing by my back door. I told Lucy I was sorry to hear about her husband's death—she looked angry, though, and told me not to say anything. To anyone." Her hands trembled when she patted the hairnet behind her head. "Then Lucy showed me the axe, or hatchet. The kind used to chop firewood."

"Can you describe it?" Mason asked, not looking up from his notebook.

"Well, the handle was curved at one end. It had a sharp blade. She shouldn't go around threatening people! I'm so scared, I'm going to retire early."

"Did you report the incident to the police?"

Vivian shook her head. "I suppose I should have. I protested, of course, but she claimed free speech. That seemed excessive in my mind."

"Yes, ma'am. It's a criminal offense to threaten someone with bodily harm, but without a secondary witness to the incident, the police cannot take action. If it happens again, please call 9-1-1." Mason closed his notebook. "Thank you for this information, Mrs. Grant."

He quickly ushered me out of the Pretty in Pink bakery before I could pose my own questions. But that didn't matter in the long run. I was ecstatic after hearing Vivian's story and almost danced around him on the sidewalk.

"Wow. Is it common for a wife to abuse her husband?"

"More than you think," Mason said wryly, "although a bigger percentage of domestic abuse victims are women. More than eighty percent end up as homicide victims, too."

That sobered me, fast. "So Lucy can't use 'free speech' as an excuse for threatening to bury an axe in her husband."

"Mrs. Grant did witness that, so no. Along with physical evidence like a text or email, which can be recovered and used as evidence," Mason said. "I'll pass on all this information to Detective Hunter."

"Tell him that Lucy won trophies for axe throwing, too."

"That's not direct evidence of her planning to follow up on the threats, however."

I sighed. "Did the autopsy report ever come in?"

He nodded. "Hartman suffered a contusion to his right temple. A brain bleed may have caused his death, and possible asphyxiation."

That suddenly reminded me of the photos Phil Hunter showed me at the police station. "So maybe he was strangled? I saw a thin line around his neck in a crime scene shot, but Hunter said that could be just a shadow."

Mason shrugged. "I'll look into that. No DNA evidence under his fingernails, and no other defensive wounds. Hartman may have been caught by surprise—"

"Yeah, by someone he trusted," I cut in. "Like by his wife."

"Lucy's a petite woman, remember. Would she have enough strength to lift his body into a car, and then drag him out and leave him by the road? It's possible she has another man in her life. A lover, perhaps. Especially if Hartman expressed jealousy."

"Maybe if Lucy lifts weights, she'd be strong enough."

"Someone could be framing her, too."

Mason followed me past the K-9 and Kitty Korner. I caught a flash of movement behind the closed window blinds. Uneasy, I walked faster down Kermit Street, passing Amato's Pizza, all the way to Ham Heaven. The detective panted when he caught up to me.

"I bet Lucy listened to that whole conversation," I told him. "Vivian said the walls are paper thin between the shops. But why threaten her to keep quiet about Teddy's abuse?"

"I can't answer why husbands abuse their wives in the first place, or why women don't leave and file for divorce." He rubbed his jaw. "I'm sorry, Sasha, but without better evidence, Hartman's murderer may go free."

I recognized the bitterness in his tone. Being a homicide detective, Mason must have seen the consequences of abuse in his career. I divorced Flynn Hanson, but he'd never hit or threatened me. My experience was nothing like less fortunate victims.

"So they haven't found any fingerprints?"

"Nope. Only Hartman's DNA matched hair and blood at the scene. Hunter did learn that someone saw Lucy Hartman at the pet store with her dog on that Sunday, but the witness wasn't sure of the time. That's all he's gotten so far."

Once Mason headed to his SUV across the street, I returned to the shop. We may have gotten confirmation about Teddy and Lucy's strained marriage, and threats against a witness, but that was a small victory.

The rest of the day dragged, and I decided to skip goat yoga. I fell asleep on the couch, my dogs curled on my lap, and never heard Maddie return home. On Friday morning, I pasted a smile on my face for customers and grumbled to myself during a lunch time walk with Rosie and Sugar Bear. The Theodore Lane repaving project had progressed to the crew setting up wooden frames for the street, curbs, and sidewalks.

Maddie picked up a Thai carryout order on the way home from an errand to Ann Arbor. While she inhaled drunken noodles with egg, vegetables, and a spicy sauce, I picked at my chicken coconut curry. I hadn't recovered from yesterday's disappointment. Vivian Grant's story had sounded exciting, but it didn't really prove much. Like Mason said, without evidence, they'd never resolve the murder.

"Why aren't you eating?" Maddie pointed her chopsticks at my carton.

"I'm not that hungry, I guess."

"You will be later. Mom only ordered enough appetizers for the guests, since she didn't want a lot of leftovers. I wouldn't have minded."

I glared at my sister. "Why are you being so critical?"

"You're in a rare mood." Maddie raised her eyebrows and leaned back in her chair. "Something else is going on, Sasha. Did you and Jay fight?"

"Of course not. I haven't seen him much, since he's been so busy at the studio." I glanced at the clock. "We'd better hurry. Mom will be mad if we're late to the gallery show. She said to come before seven-thirty at the latest."

Upstairs in my room, I eyed my bed with longing but changed to a white blouse, black slacks, a tan wool blazer, and animal print leather flats. Mom had asked us both to "sparkle" tonight given the upscale crowd, but I was in no mood for it.

I added a few gold rope necklaces and pinned my hair back with matching clips. I kept my makeup toned down as well. Maddie would have to sparkle for the two of us.

My sister fit the bill, too, in a fluffy black tulle skirt spotted with red sequins. Her black lace stirrup tights ended above the red five-inch heels with ankle bows she had worn as a bridesmaid in Gus and Cissy's Valentine's-themed wedding; Maddie's plunging and sheer red blouse was racy enough to show off a black lace bra. She'd also streaked her pixie cut with purple, red, and blond highlights. She topped it all with a faded and patched denim jacket.

I didn't dare criticize her choices or the velvet clutch she carried. Instead, I dropped her off on Main Street and then parked in the narrow alley behind the Vintage Nouveau. Mom had wanted to save spaces for guests in the nearby lots and on the street. Light blazed through the gallery's front window. I helped Maddie and Dad in setting up two dozen chairs against the walls, away from any sculptures and low-hanging artwork.

The appetizers did look skimpy. Crab on toast points, shrimps wrapped in tiny lettuce leaves, fried wontons, tomato and cheese-crusted crostini, and miniature quiches lined a few trays. Jacob Evans, my mother's assistant, fanned the napkins beside plastic plates and poured out glasses of wine. Maddie lined up small bottles of water.

By nine o'clock, the gallery held wall-to-wall people in every niche. Jim Perry finally arrived, fashionably late, at half past. Mom wore a black lace cocktail dress and low heels. She chatted with the energetic artist, while fans pressed them from all sides. Perry, with his booming laugh, gladly signed napkins, books, or event flyers.

"This is great. Thanks so much—yes, I'm going to reinstall that sculpture . . ."

Mike Blake and Mark Branson had allowed the Legal Eagle Bear to be displayed tonight with Perry's other artwork, although the crew they'd hired to transport it had a difficult time. The briefcase had several fresh scratches, and there were nicks in the painted statue. I admired a seven-foot-tall pedestal with a colorful bust of Van Gogh, minus an ear, slated to be showcased at the Detroit Institute of Arts. Several people dropped money into the statue's remaining ear, and laughed when Van Gogh responded with a wise saying about art.

Perry chuckled. "Stick it in his ear—all donations go to charity."

I suddenly noticed Andrew Kane with Lucy Hartman and Kevin Whittaker in one corner of the gallery. Lucy's brother stabbed a finger at the lawyer, clearly angry, while she held up both hands as if trying to intervene. I turned away in pity. Lucy had enough problems besides Teddy's murder. Maddie waved me over to join her and Eric Dyer. I headed to intercept them, but felt a firm hand on my arm.

"Hey, Sasha. Glad I ran into you." Flynn Hanson quickly released me when I gave him a pointed stare. "You look tired."

My ex-husband's spiky blond hair resembled a porcupine. He'd loosened his tie but still wore a tailored suit and Italian loafers. His tanned face and neck hinted at a recent trip to Florida, or several sessions in a tanning bed.

"Thanks for coming to support Mom's gallery show," I said lightly, although I suspected he had another reason for showing up tonight.

"Sure." He flashed his trademark grin. "I guess you aren't filing a dog bite lawsuit after all. You never called me back."

"Why do you care?"

"You had a legit claim."

"At least you're not pretending concern over whether I

recovered. Or about Dad being arrested for murder despite being innocent."

He seemed taken aback. "Damn, you're touchy tonight. I've got plenty of cases to win, but it's your loss. I could have gotten you a big settlement."

"Sorry you lost a hefty cut of that, you mean. Your career comes first, as always."

"You don't have to get nasty about it—"

"I'm stating a fact, Flynn." I was tired of hearing his usual phrase, and how he pushed the blame back on me. "I don't like taking advantage of people. I'm happy with my life, especially without you in it. In fact, why haven't you ever apologized for what happened long ago? You're the one who ruined our marriage."

He laughed that off, as if I were joking. "Oh, come on."

"I'm serious. You should apologize." I waited, but Flynn shook his head. "We're not friends anymore, you ought to know that by now. And you don't really care about my mother or her gallery. So why did you come tonight?"

"I was in the neighborhood." He reached for my arm, but I stepped back. "I really was worried about you being bitten by that dog—"

"Right, sure you were. So long, Flynn."

I walked away, my heart pounding, but relieved that I'd finally found the courage to stand up to him. Ann Arbor wasn't far enough from Silver Hollow. Maybe he finally got the message and would stay far away from me and my family. Dizzy from a headache, the room's raucous laughter, babble of voices, and the crush of people, I slipped out the front door. The chill air helped clear my head.

"Too much for you, too?" Andrew Kane crushed a cigarette under his boot heel and stuck his hands in his leather jacket. "Perry's a creative genius but has a weird take on some things. Like the congressional piece with the tipped scales of justice."

"And the falling dollar." I rubbed the bridge of my nose. "I heard Lucy Hartman fired you. Is that true?"

"So far, she's fired me twice and keeps hiring me back." He grinned. "Who knows how long before she does it again. I heard Hanson isn't filing a lawsuit for you over Sparky."

"You talked to him, I take it. What do you remember about the tax fraud case that my dad prosecuted, against the Las Vegas mobster?"

"Not much, except how Alex grilled that hostile witness like a T-bone steak until he was charred on both sides. Then he fried the mobster with a ton of evidence. Died in jail, I think, and is probably roasting in hell now."

"Do you prefer defending criminals?"

"It's a job," Kane said with a weary sigh. "Someone's gotta do it. I'm getting plenty of hell from Lucy over representing the pedophiles who bought Benny Bears. Open-and-shut case, the way they stuffed spy cameras in them. Innocent until proven guilty, of course."

Several people emerged from the gallery, chatting about the show's success, while Kane leaned against the brick wall to give them more room. Another couple walked out and scuttled in the opposite direction. At last they'd gone out of earshot.

"Do you think they killed Hartman, or hired someone to do it?" I asked.

"Why bother? They're gutless cowards, preying on little kids. Not smart enough to cover their tracks online, for God's sake. Besides, Teddy didn't care what they used the Benny Bears for and sold 'em at a higher price—he refused to give them a discount."

"I heard a rumor that Teddy was jealous of Lucy's flirting. With you, maybe?"

"No way," Kane shot back. "I never get involved with clients."

The lawyer pushed himself off the wall and headed back inside. I pondered his quick and vehement denial. Was he telling the truth? That seemed suspicious, given the earlier argument that I'd observed between Kevin Whittaker and Kane. Lucy looked upset. Maybe her brother wasn't happy if the lawyer had gotten romantically involved with the new widow. That wouldn't look good for either one of them.

Jay walked out of the gallery and drew me into his arms for a big bear hug. "I've been looking everywhere for you inside. Big crowd tonight."

"A great turnout." I kissed him. "Did you finish the wolverine?"

"Done and delivered. The pub owners are ecstatic," Jay said. "They're installing it this weekend. My stuff might not be world famous like Perry's, but I got paid in full."

"Wonderful. Now you can carve that little Scottie dog for the MacRaes."

He nuzzled my ear. "I feel like celebrating, so how about we head somewhere for a burger and beer? Not Quinn's, like Chelsea or Ann Arbor. Unless you have to help clean up after the gallery show."

"Nope. Mom hired that out, but where's your truck?"

"I walked over from your parking lot, since I couldn't find a spot anywhere near."

"My car's in the back alley. Let's cut through the gallery, though." We threaded our way between and around smaller groups inside while I filled Jay in on our preparations for the Highland Fling. "One week away," I said. "I can't wait to see if our kilted bears sell out. We already shipped over a hundred out of state, or to people who can't attend next week."

"Remember we talked about wearing matching kilts? Did

you order the Gordon—" Jay stopped so suddenly past the outer door, I bumped into his back. "Is that your car?"

I gasped, hands over my mouth, and sagged against him. My sweet little Chevy Aveo, with its beautiful wintergreen paint job, had been sprayed with weird symbols, swastikas, and skulls all over the hood, doors, and trunk. One word stood out. DEATH.

Definitely a threat.

Chapter 18

Aerosol cans littered the gravel lot, from what I could see from the light spilling from the open back door. I called the police, numb with shock. Jay circled the car to survey the damage and took cell phone photos from various angles. The vandals had scratched and gouged the driver's door with a key or tool, deep enough to show the primer. Who would do such a thing? My poor Chevy, so dependable. And so beyond salvaging.

I'd bought the car off a used lot, so a complete repaint job was bound to cost more than its Blue Book value. My insurance company might total it, given its age. Jay grabbed my arm when I reached for one of the paint cans.

"Don't touch anything, Sasha. Fingerprints, remember?"

"Oh yeah, you're right."

Flustered, I straightened and shielded my eyes from the patrol car's flashing blue and red lights. No siren blared, at least, when it drove into the alley. My parents, Maddie, and Eric Dyer emerged from the gallery's back door, no doubt attracted by the lights. Officer Bill Hillerman emerged from the car and raised his eyebrows when he spied my Chevy. He ducked back into the cruiser and re-emerged with plastic gloves and large zippered bags.

"Stay back, everyone, until I've collected evidence."

"I've already taken photos," Jay said, waving his phone.

"Email them to the department in a zip file. That way I can attach them to the final report," Hillerman said. "Anyone see anything?"

"No." I glanced between Officer Hillerman and Jay, wiping away a few tears for my poor car. "What do all those crazy symbols mean?"

"They're gang-related, I'd say." Dad examined one painted mark.

More people streamed out of the gallery show and murmured together in groups. Jacob Evans and Kevin Whittaker stood among them, but I didn't see Andrew Kane or Lucy Hartman. Officer Hillerman finally finished his notes of the damage.

"They may look like gang signs, Mr. Silverman, but Silver Hollow doesn't have any local groups," the policeman said. "Punks, yeah. We've seen kids writing graffiti at the schools, but never on any cars in the neighborhoods around here."

"And only on your car, not the buildings back here," Maddie said. "Doesn't that seem suspicious? You'd think they'd spread it around."

Hillerman agreed. "Another thing—no crude swear words. I saw plenty of gangs writing messages like that when I walked a beat in Detroit."

"No windows back here, behind the building," Jay said. "Whoever did this had plenty of time to do all this without worrying about any witnesses. Pretty dark back here, too, with the street lights so far away."

"Clever," Kevin Whittaker said. "They must have left some fingerprints."

"Not if they wore gloves," Dad said. "Too bad they didn't leave them behind."

"But the alley isn't that remote." I glanced toward Main Street. "Don't you think one or two pedestrians walking past could have seen them spray-painting the car?"

"Maybe. We'll put out a notice for anyone with information to come forward," Hillerman said. "Might help if you offer a reward."

"It's bad enough that Silver Hollow has had several murders." Mom's tone dripped with disgust. "And now vandalism! Didn't a car have its tires slashed in front of the theater, back in February? I remember reading about that in the *Silver Hollow Herald*."

"Yep, but that case was solved. Vandals hit and run, working fast. I'd say this car was targeted deliberately, Sasha."

"I don't think any punks did this tonight." Eric Dyer pointed near my car's tire. "One clear boot print in the dirt. Left heel worn down. Kids usually wear sneakers or hiking boots with tread soles and distinctive patterns."

Hillerman shrugged. "Might be a partial print on this spray can." He stashed the evidence bag in the cruiser's back seat. "We'll run it through the database."

"I hope you catch them so they pay for this," Mom said.

"Your insurance company will want a copy of the report." He handed me a clipboard. "Sign here, and I'll put this on file at the station."

"Officer Hillerman is right, Sasha," my mother said. "Someone wanted to get revenge on you, although why is beyond me."

My head cleared. Who else but Lucy Hartman would have vandalized my car? She must have slipped out the gallery's back door while Andrew Kane distracted me out front. I turned to Kevin Whittaker.

"I wonder if your sister did this."

"Why would you accuse Lucy?" His voice icy, he stared at me in surprise.

"She overheard me talking to Detective Mason the other day. All about how her husband abused her—"

"No way is that true. Lucy would've told me about it, and I'd have slapped him with a restraining order. She's never been in trouble with the law before."

"Oh? Her dog Sparky bit several people, and she settled out of court," Maddie said, one hand on her hip. "Or don't you call that trouble with the police?"

He rocked back on his heels. "I advised her to do that. Pretty stupid, a pet shop owner who can't control her dog. Lucy ought to get a cat or a parrot in a cage."

"Let's hope her store succeeds," Dad said, his tone diplomatic. "People here had to drive too far out from Silver Hollow for pet food and cat litter."

"She won't take my advice about stocking more essentials. Lucy keeps ordering fancy hair bows or Halloween costumes." Whittaker changed the subject. "I've heard rumors that the homicide detective may not solve my brother-in-law's murder. Lucy deserves closure. She wants to hold a memorial service back east."

Officer Hillerman looked uneasy. "Contact the county sheriff's office, sir, if you'd like any current information."

Several loud beeps startled me. The tow truck from Randy's Garage pulled into the alley, spewing dirt and gravel. We watched Barry Brown, Randy's brother, load up the Aveo and then drive off with it. Jay slid an arm around my waist. No doubt I'd never see my car again.

The policeman nodded in sympathy. "We'll let you know by Monday or Tuesday if we do get a lead on that partial fingerprint."

"I know you didn't have comprehensive insurance," Dad said, "but I'll check if there's any deals for a replacement. Remember how you needed new brakes and a muffler a few months ago. And the transmission gave you fits."

"I know," I said sadly. "Guess it was past time to replace it."

My parents returned inside the gallery, although Maddie and Eric remained behind. Kevin Whittaker and the other curious onlookers headed off to their cars. Maddie linked arms with me while we walked home, Eric and Jay following behind us. I wasn't up to conversation but heard the guys talking in low tones. My sister soon dropped back to join their discussion, but I surged ahead and pondered the vandalism. The dog bite. Hartman's murder.

I knew Kevin Whittaker was wrong about Lucy. She'd threatened Vivian Grant with a hatchet, after all, and I could visualize her glee while she spray-painted my car. Nobody else in Silver Hollow had a tendency to toss threats around.

"Sasha, wait up!"

I turned to see Jay trotting across Theodore Lane. Maddie and Eric lingered near Silver Moon, still chatting, while Jay and I walked to the Silver Bear Shop's back porch. At Sugar Bear's sharp barks, Rosie joined in with a few plaintive whines.

"Are you okay? You can borrow my truck if you need to, since I'll be working on that Scottie dog for the MacRaes' mailbox for a while."

"Thanks," I said and kissed him. "I appreciate it."

"Promise me you'll be careful, Sasha."

"What do you mean?"

Jay planted his hands on my shoulders, a wry smile on his face. "Don't go off sleuthing without someone tagging along with you. Me, Maddie, your dad. Anyone will do."

I laughed. "Okay. I promise."

"She'll be too busy to do any sleuthing," Maddie said, walking over to us. "Tomorrow's the birthday party, and then next week we're back to work until Thursday night. That's when we have to prep the Highland Fling vendor booth."

"By the way, I ordered my Gordon kilt," I said, "but I refuse to enter the Kilted 5K or the Hurl the Haggis contest."

"Poor sport." Jay kissed me. "See you tomorrow."

He drove out of the parking lot. I waved and headed inside. Sharing Aunt Eve's Beatles-themed party tomorrow wasn't thrilling, but Mom convinced me to be a good sport. Yawning wide, I was so glad to fall into bed and overslept on Saturday morning. After checking the alarm clock, I realized I'd set it to PM and not AM. I rushed to get ready for work and take the dogs out before feeding them. Five minutes before opening, Aunt Eve carried an oblong box into the shop and plopped it on the counter.

"Jay dropped this off this morning. I was so surprised to see him! He said you should open it right away. I bet it's a dozen roses."

"It doesn't have the label from Mary's Flowers, though."

I cut the string, lifted the lid, and dug through shredded paper. Inside, a hard piece of wood was wrapped in Styrofoam. "It might be a carving," I said and found a note.

Part one, and happy birthday. Love you. J

I revealed a small bear cub lying on its belly, legs crossed behind him, one elbow resting flat, paw on his chin, with an open book before him. I knew exactly where to put this wonderful carving—atop my overflowing bookcase in my bedroom.

"I've never seen anything so cute," my aunt said. "Unique, too."

"I love it!" I admired the detailed fur and sweet expression.

"I remember the bear holding a lantern that he gave you

for Christmas, and that's just as precious," she said. "Call him, I'll man the fort. Take your time."

Wordlessly, I pulled out my new cell phone and hit speed dial. "It's adorable, thanks so much!"

"You almost found it under the canvas covering when you visited my studio," Jay said with a laugh. "I had to hide it away after that."

"So it wasn't a commission after all? You sneaky devil."

"It's hard to fool you, Sasha Silverman. I'll see you at the party tonight, okay? Making progress on the Scottie dog, so I want to finish."

After texting Jay a string of hearts, I spent the day in a wonderful mood. Chatting with customers and wrapping purchases didn't feel like work. Feeling loved and appreciated by Jay felt so different than during my brief and unhappy marriage. So what if he preferred comics over classic literature? He loved sharing classic movies, or romantic chick flicks like *The Princess Bride* and *The Guernsey Literary and Potato Peel Pie Society*.

Despite the staff's heavy workload, I'd designed a kilted bear with the Gordon tartan fabric for Jay as a special order. Joan insisted on sewing it, too, after hours so that Flora wouldn't interfere. I planned to give it to him on the last day of the Highland Fling. Along with a warm sweatshirt hoodie, one sleeve in the Gordon tartan fabric, along with a modern clan crest.

Saturday's birthday party proved to be a blast for Aunt Eve and her friends. With Zoe Fisher's and Asia Gibson's help, Maddie and I hung old vinyl albums from the ceiling in Mom's gallery and printed copies of Beatles album covers mounted on cardstock. Posters of the Fab Four hung on the walls, and colorful streamers criss-crossed the tables. We set out a cardboard figure of Paul McCartney in one corner along with feather boas, sunglasses, and other props.

"Maybe Aunt Eve will update her wardrobe," I said, tying a balloon to a chair. "I'm only wearing this tie-dye shirt and fringed vest because you forced me. Ratty bell bottoms, too. You got the cool go-go boots and hot pants."

"Trust me, they're not comfortable. Aunt Eve will wear her usual fifties crinoline, and maybe a rhinestone-studded sweater," Maddie said. "Wanna bet ten bucks? No, twenty!"

"You're on."

Asia hooted with laughter. "I can't bend over in this mini-skirt," she said, "but it was my mom's favorite along with those go-go boots. She kept them in the original box for years."

"And those frayed jeans were hip, Sasha," Zoe said and pushed up her fake granny glasses. "My mom loved 'em. Here comes your uncle and aunt now."

Maddie grudgingly slapped a twenty-dollar bill in my outstretched hand when Aunt Eve showed up in a sleeveless V-neck peach satin gown. A matching bow perched at the waist, and white gloves extended past her elbows. Uncle Ross wore a tux with a peach cummerbund. He looked naked without his sailor's cap, his gray hair thinner than ever, and grumbled under his breath about having to dress for the party.

"Your aunt's channeling Jackie Kennedy, I guess," Zoe whispered. "Her pearls look amazing with that dress."

My parents followed Aunt Eve and Uncle Ross into the gallery. Mom's navy dress had a velvet bodice, quite modern, with a sash tied at one side, and she wore her auburn hair in loose curls. Dad tugged his tux's tight bow tie at his neck.

"It's only a few hours waddling like a penguin, Ross."

The rest of the guests soon arrived, dressed to the nines as well. They mingled and chatted, drinks in hand, before the caterers set out the platters of burgers, hot dogs, fries, and milkshakes. Embarrassed, Maddie clearly hadn't expected people would wear formal clothing.

"I'm sorry, Aunt Eve! I should have consulted you about the menu—"

"It's so much fun. Like my prom long ago, except for the marvelous decorations. You girls outdid yourselves, thank you! I'm thrilled."

Zoe and Asia beamed with pleasure at her compliment, then joined us at the buffet line's end. Aunt Eve dragged me to the gallery's center table before I could carry my plate to a back table. My face flamed when Uncle Ross whistled shrilly for everyone's attention.

"Thank you for coming tonight, everyone," Aunt Eve said. "And thanks to Sasha for sharing my celebration. Her birthday's next week, close enough, on May first."

I kissed her cheek and then fled to sit with Maddie, Zoe, and Asia. Jay and Eric had also arrived. "Burgers and dogs, my kind of party," Eric said and opened several bottles. "I hope you don't mind trying out my mead. Be honest, let me know if it's any good."

"So we're your guinea pigs?" Maddie teased him.

"I don't wanna get a bad name. Better find out now if it didn't ferment the right way." He sounded cheerful when he poured glasses all around. "Bottoms up."

I smelled it first and set it aside. "Nope, sorry. I can tell it's too acidic."

"Not bad," Jay pronounced, and finished his glass. "Top it up, bro."

At the next table, Dad devoured half of a hot dog in one gulp. "Don't you dare get mustard on your tux," Mom chided, since he couldn't speak.

"Lucky he dripped on the tablecloth instead," Aunt Eve said with a wink. "This dress is so old, and has weathered a few stains. I've had it dry-cleaned several times."

Everyone enjoyed the evening, dancing to Beatles music,

taking "selfies" dressed up in costume, with arms casually draped over the cardboard cutout. The Red Hat Society ladies pulled my aunt over for a group photo, in fact, before they gathered around to admire the beautiful three-layer cake. Pretty in Pink had done a fabulous job, decorating the layers with musical notes and the number 64 on top in rainbow-hued marzipan.

Molded fondant figures of each Beatle perched on the lowest tier's edge, along with a small yellow submarine and a VW bus. Maddie took several photos from multiple angles, and then staged another with Aunt Eve cutting the first piece. Uncle Ross stood behind her, frowning, until she elbowed him into a semblance of a smile.

"That is one cool cake," Zoe said, clearly amazed. "Did Vivian Grant decorate it?"

"She begged Wendy Clark to make those figures, the bus, and submarine," Maddie said. "Then she charged extra to cover the extra cost. But Mom didn't complain."

"It looks great, at least."

My sister slipped on the tile floor and grabbed me for balance. "Think I had too much mead. Guess who texted me a few hours ago? Digger Sykes."

"Why?" I glanced over at my parents, who leaned against Aunt Eve and Uncle Ross for a foursome photo. "Unless he's got some hot gossip."

"Nope." Her eyes twinkled with mischief, and she leaned to whisper in my ear. "Digger answered a phone call this morning from Detective Hunter, but the chief was in a meeting. He took a message. You'll never guess what he told me."

"So tell me."

"Hartman did have strangulation marks. The coroner's report said the brain bleed could have killed him, but the lack of oxygen also contributed. So maybe both."

"I knew it! That wasn't a shadow on the photo," I said, triumphant. "If they can identify any fingerprints on the hatchet, they'll solve the case."

"That's the bad news from Digger. Most prints on the handle were smeared," Maddie said, "and they failed to make a match on the only clear partial."

Zoe and Asia had inched our way, although I didn't realize they were listening to our conversation. "They found a fingerprint at the crime scene? Where?" Zoe asked.

"On the hatchet."

"Stuck in Hartman's back?" Asia looked impressed. "But what does that mean? I don't watch any cop shows on TV like you guys do."

"They ran it through the national database," Maddie said, "so it means the killer doesn't have a criminal record."

My hopes faded. "It also means we're back to square one."

Chapter 19

The streak of wonderful spring weather that blessed most of April ended the first day of May. Through a heavy downpour, Jay and I dashed into our favorite pub in Ann Arbor. After dinner of truffle fries, a burger for him, and a grilled chicken with brie sandwich for me, we rushed into an ice cream parlor and splurged on gelato. Soaking wet, we drove back home and snuggled with the dogs—including Jay's dog Buster—on the couch.

We enjoyed leftover cake from Aunt Eve's party while watching the latest episode of *The Crown*. I flipped the television off with a happy sigh and set aside my empty plate. Before I had a chance to stop her, Sugar Bear eagerly licked up the crumbs.

"Brat head." I ruffled her curly hair. She curled up once more on my lap.

"Ready for part two of your present?" Jay asked.

"You already gave me a present," I said, leaning against his shoulder. "I love my reading bear, and the lantern one by my bedside."

"Is the light enough? I could change it to a brighter LED bulb." He shifted me aside and stood, then pulled me to my feet. "Come on. Let's go check."

Puzzled, I followed him upstairs. The dogs rushed ahead of us. Rosie and Buster jumped on the bed, but Sugar Bear—who usually waited for me to lift her up—ran up a wooden ramp at the bed's foot. She wriggled between the other two dogs.

"That's new! Did you build it?" I kissed and hugged him in thanks. "Did you have to teach her to use it, or is this her first try?"

"I set it up this afternoon and Sugar loved running up and down. Happy birthday, again," Jay said and sat on the window seat. "No room for us on the bed, but turn the lantern on. I want to see how bright the light is for reading."

I pushed the switch, but nothing happened. "Oh, no. What's wrong with it?"

"Open the little door on the back side."

Suspicious that he'd fiddled with the lantern earlier, I obeyed and saw a tiny box inside the lantern. "If they're earrings, I can wear them with my new kilt—"

My heart stopped. I stared inside the box in shock. Jay plucked the diamond ring from the velvet and slid to one knee on the floor, holding it out, his eyes bright. Tears filled mine, and my breath caught in my throat.

"Sasha Silverman. Will you marry me?"

"Oh, Jay. Yes, yes. With all my heart."

I watched him slip the beautiful ring on my left hand, amazed that it felt so right. I hadn't worn a ring on that finger for so long. The gorgeous setting had carved white gold on the band in a leaf pattern; a central diamond, not huge but lovely, was surrounded by a halo of smaller gems. Jay pulled out a photo attached to a rough sketch. My sister's name was scrawled on the bottom, with notes in her nearly illegible handwriting.

"Maddie designed it?" I squealed at his nod. "I love it! And I love you."

He pulled me down onto his lap. "We don't have to set a wedding date now. Unless you have a time in mind, that is."

I stretched out my hand to admire the ring. "Maybe later this year in the fall. That's my favorite season, but you know that. When did you talk to Maddie about this?"

Jay shrugged. "Before Christmas, but then your ex ruined my plans by announcing his engagement. I thought Valentine's Day might work, but Gus and Cissy's wedding craziness put a wrench in that, with their best man knocked off—"

I smothered the rest of his sentence with one hand, to his surprise. "Don't remind me, please. How's the little Scottie dog carving coming along?"

"Not as easy as I thought." He shifted a little and nearly rolled me off his lap. "Gavin decided to replace the mailbox, but I'd already measured the old one. Good thing I'd ordered a bigger block of wood."

"Good thing you asked him."

"No kidding. Hope your birthday's been a lot of fun."

"Wonderful." I yawned wide and rested my head against his chest. "I'm beat. The next few days will be crazy. I've got to help finish all the tartan bears, hand-sewing the eyes and noses, because Jen Chan can't do them all. She worked so hard on the landscaping around here and did a great job, so I offered to help her."

"I've got to practice for the games, or I'll embarrass myself in front of the crowd. Maybe I shouldn't bother with the caber toss."

"Why? It looks easier than the hammer throw."

"You try tossing a telephone pole," he joked. "See how easy it is."

Jay moved the dogs off the bed, although they quickly rejoined us—Rosie and Sugar Bear between, with Buster at our feet. I fell asleep to the drumming rain overhead, all stress and worry fleeing, so grateful for our exciting future together.

Over the next few days, morning mist and fog alternated with thunderstorms. Local creeks rose above their banks, and more roads closed when the Huron River flooded farmland. Amy Evans sent frantic emails and texts, bemoaning what to do if the park also flooded. Most committee members exchanged a flurry of messages about filling sandbags, but the rain tapered off on Wednesday. Amy was relieved. We all agreed that attendance might fall below our expectations, but diehards always showed in any weather.

"Vendors along the riverbank will have to set up their tables in a mud pit," Maddie said on Thursday morning. "Good thing Mom chose our booth spot near the pavilion."

"Good thing all that rain wasn't snow, or worse, an ice storm. There'd be fallen branches all over the place." I filled my travel coffee mug. "Jay drove over to the park yesterday. The higher ground is dry, so that's one good thing."

"What's-her-name on TV, Flynn's fiancée, says the weekend will be dry."

"Cheryl Cummings? Yeah, I saw her forecast."

"So what did Mom say about your engagement?" Maddie asked. "She almost broke my eardrums, screaming with joy, when she called me."

I snorted a laugh. "Yeah, she and Dad are over the moon."

"They couldn't ask for a better son-in-law with Jay. Not like your ex—"

"Don't go there," I interrupted, but my sister only laughed.

"I've got even better news. A rumor's going around that a certain forecaster is in heavy negotiations for a news anchor job in Chicago." Maddie chuckled at my shock. "Oh, yeah, girl. Digger heard that, and then asked someone who knows one of the legal assistants at Flynn's law firm. That guy said Flynn's gonna open another office in Chicago when she gets it. When, not if. They're that certain Cheryl will be hired."

"Out of range forever," I said, smiling at the thought. "Gotta get to work."

"Hey, don't forget Uncle Ross wants to borrow Jay's truck to haul the tent stuff to the park tonight. He won't risk his precious car in all that mud. I hope it won't take too long setting up the booth. Eric and I have plans after."

Maddie headed across the street to Silver Moon. I had a full day ahead, checking all our inventory and packing it for the Highland Fling. Renee Truman wasn't available to cover for me at the shop this weekend; she had to study for upcoming college exams. Isabel French seemed reluctant to man the shop alone, but I compromised—she and Karen Anderson would take turns staffing the shop and our vendor booth. That way they wouldn't miss the fun.

Aunt Eve, my parents, and Maddie had also signed up for shifts at the booth. I planned to take photos along with my sister for social media posts. Being on the event committee, we were expected to help wherever needed, especially bathroom breaks for other vendors.

"Girls, time to go outside again." I crumbled a half-eaten piece of toast into small pieces, set it out on the bird feeder, and set my breakfast plate and knife in the sink. My dogs had wolfed their kibble but disappeared. "Where are you two lazybones? Rosie, Sugar!"

No dogs in their crates, a bad sign. Dad wasn't here taking a nap, and Onyx sat on the highest level of her cat tower, watchful and wary. Suddenly I spied a bit of torn tissue in the living room. A long trail of it led from the half bath and all the way up the steps. I followed in dread, knowing what I'd find. But which dog had gotten into mischief?

Rosie hid in the bedroom corner, face to the wall, with a torn and wet cardboard roll in her mouth. She dropped it in remorse. I found Sugar Bear in the bathroom, her newest dog toy ripped to shreds, but without a trace of guilt in her eyes. I repressed a laugh and gathered up the remains of both the tissue and the toy. They had to be bored stiff to get in this much trouble.

"Poor doggos. How about early camp?"

I shooed them out of the room, closed the door, and followed them downstairs. I also shut the half bath's door, just in case of more trouble. While they were outside on a second potty break, I called the Furry Friends Lodge, part of the Wags and Whiskers Pet Rescue.

"I booked a suite tomorrow, but can I bring my dogs today instead?" I asked, turning the Silver Bear Shop's CLOSED sign to OPEN. "I've bagged up their food, beds, and toys."

"Of course! We love Rosie and Sugar Bear," Jodie Richardson added. "They're so funny together, and so well behaved."

"Not today." I related Rosie's and Sugar Bear's naughty deeds, but she only laughed. "Add the TLC package and group playtime, today and Saturday. I'll pick them up Monday morning."

"Sure thing. Sounds like they need special attention."

I ended the call. That meant I had another task this afternoon, dropping off my pets, but that gave me a chance to check our booth's site at Riverside Park. Better be prepared for mud or worse. I needed transportation. I texted Maddie about borrowing her car and then sewed eyes on half a dozen tartan bears. Jen Chan finished the noses with embroidery thread, since I wasn't as confident in keep the stitches straight.

"I've got a crew coming tomorrow to get the landscaping finished," Jen said. "Hope that's okay with you, Sasha. The ground will dry up after that rain so I don't want to put it off for too much longer."

"That means I'd better rope off the front entrance." I added "make signs" to my list of tasks. "Customers will have to use the side door."

By mid-afternoon, the laminated signs now showed the way from the side door and past Aunt Eve's office to the shop's front. I headed across the street to Silver Moon. Maddie hadn't gotten back to me about using her car yet.

My sister shook her head. "Sorry, Sash, I was charging my phone. I needed a new starter, but I thought the repair shop would call by now. Guess they're still working on it."

My heart sank. "Great. The insurance company hasn't okayed a rental yet, and I need to take Rosie and Sugar Bear to the kennel."

"Aunt Eve can take you, I bet. I'll call her." Maddie snatched up her business phone, chatted for a few minutes, and gave me a thumbs-up signal. "She said no problem. Be outside and ready to go in five minutes."

I rushed back to the house. Both dogs snoozed on the window seat, but now Onyx had disappeared. I suspected she was in trouble, given the pitiful meows coming from the half bath, and found her stuck in the window blinds.

"I didn't know you were in here, poor kitty!"

Untangling her claws from the strings wasn't easy. With a yowl, the cat jumped free and streaked out of the small room like her tail was on fire. The blinds dangled on one side, and my attempts to fix it proved futile. A large tree shaded the window anyway. Most visitors to the shop probably wouldn't notice. I'd have to get Jay to fiddle with it or replace the whole thing. Some other time.

"What a day this is gonna be," I muttered. "Rosie, Sugar! Get your leashes."

They brought them eagerly, dragging the canvas leads and scraping the metal hardware across the tile behind them, and submitted to being harnessed without fuss. They both loved car rides. Out on the porch, I stared at Aunt Eve, who waited behind the wheel in the pale blue Thunderbird with its peacock leather interior. No way. Was she crazy? What if Uncle Ross found out she was driving me and my dogs using his precious vintage car?

He'd blow a gasket.

Chapter 20

Alarmed, I jerked open the Thunderbird's back door. "Aunt Eve, are you sure about this? What if the dogs scratch the leather seat—"

"Get in, Sasha! Before Ross sees us." She cranked up the window. "It's only a car, for pity's sake. But what he doesn't know won't hurt him."

I used Rosie's favorite blanket to cover the seat and arm rests. My teddy bear dog loved to brace herself against the window and watch the scenery outside. Sugar Bear squirmed to do the same, but I buckled my seat belt and hugged her tight. In her excitement, she'd claw up the chrome and leather both. I nearly lost my grip when Aunt Eve turned the corner fast onto Kermit Street. Poor Rosie ended up on the floor and rolled onto her stomach with a whimper.

"Poor baby! We'll be there soon," I said. "Be patient, Sugar. You'll have plenty of time to play with your friends at day care."

Pedestrians and other drivers ogled us, openly admiring the car's chrome bumpers and white leather top. It certainly deserved my dad's nickname of "Rattle Trap," given how it jounced over the rutted road to Wags and Whiskers. I cringed at every stone's ding after hitting the undercarriage. Uncle Ross would be livid if he noticed any dents.

"Aunt Eve, take it easy!"

"What's that? I can't hear you over this engine."

She swerved to avoid a pothole. Her gold bracelets jangled when she turned into the large, two-story complex, less than a mile from Richardson's Farms. Aunt Eve pulled her kitten-heeled shoe back on; I hadn't noticed her driving with bare feet. I led the dogs inside. My aunt followed with the bags I'd packed with their paraphernalia. I breathed easier once the reception staff accepted Rosie's and Sugar Bear's leashes.

The dogs wagged their tails and accepted treats. Jodie Richardson had established the pet rescue shelter along with her husband, Phil—Tim's older brother. They'd soon expanded to add day care rooms and overnight boarding in kennels surrounding an oasis with trees, greenery, and a soothing fountain. Monitors showed the small dog corral, where Rosie and Sugar Bear barked a welcome to their four-legged friends. Jodie handed me a clipboard with forms.

"This is a lifesaver." I slid my credit card over the counter. "We'll be swamped until Sunday night, when the Highland Fling ends."

"A lot of people have brought their pets in," she said. "I've got a booth to take donations and sell our calendars. Homemade dog treats, too."

"I'll be sure to stop by—oh. Wait a sec." Puzzled, I pointed to a little Morkie on the monitor, alone in a separate corral. "Isn't that Lucy Hartman's dog, Sparky?"

"Yeah, she surrendered him." Jodie nodded at my shock. "He's scared out of his wits. We're handing him over to Reuben Johnson for fostering. I hope he's able to train that dog not to bite. He's been successful with other dogs."

"Why didn't she hire Reuben as a trainer instead of giving him up?" I asked.

"Didn't want to bother, so she said. It's time consuming, and a lot end up dumping the dogs on the road or in a field. It's a shame."

"That's true. Thanks again, Jodie. I'll pick them up Monday morning."

Aunt Eve had already gone back out to the car in the parking lot. "The Blue Bomb has a lot of horsepower. Can you feel that?" She revved the engine and headed back to Silver Hollow. "Ross is such a baby about this car. The pickup is amazing."

"He lets you call it the 'Blue Bomb'?"

"Better than 'Old Rattle Trap,' like your dad calls it." She thumped the steering wheel. "I'd rather drive an old sixty-four Mustang Fastback, but we can't afford another vintage car. I'm gonna lease an SUV or a pickup with plenty of room to haul stuff around."

We took several detours to avoid huge puddles and muddy ruts. Finally Aunt Eve drove sedately into Riverside Park, but she parked shy of the gravel. A small crew swarmed around the newly built pavilion. Its massive posts and trusses supported a high-pitched roof; all four sides were open to the air. Electricians on ladders installed lighting beneath the ceiling, while other workers nailed down the last shingles on the roof.

"That looks fantastic!" Aunt Eve shielded her eyes from the sun, her headscarf flapping, and walked over to join Amy Evans. "Wow."

"Isn't it great?" Amy beamed in excitement. "We considered putting on a metal roof, but that was way too expensive at sixty by thirty-five feet. As it is, with the lights and outlets for the musicians' amplifiers, this cost over twenty thousand bucks. We're lucky we got a big donation to cover half of it."

"It's bound to last a long time and come in handy for other events."

"That's right." Amy sounded proud. "We're still collecting community donations, too."

I turned at the sound of spinning tires to see Jay's truck, its rear wheels churning mud. Uncle Ross cursed a blue streak, seeing his car with spatters on the fenders and paint, so Aunt Eve rushed over to explain. Maddie jumped down from the truck's passenger side and joined me to push the back end. At a signal, my uncle managed to drive forward. My sister and I ended up spattered to the waist, however.

Thick goo dripped down my jeans past my ankles. My shoes were coated, but at least my feet didn't squelch while I walked to Silver Bear's booth. The afternoon's sunshine vanished behind a bank of clouds overhead. I huddled in my sweatshirt, glad for its warmth.

"Let's get this show on the road," Uncle Ross growled.

Most booths, constructed of metal scaffolding, had canvas or thin sheeting material for coverings. Several leaned haphazardly due to sinking in the wet ground. A blacktop walkway stretched from the pavilion to the riverfront and then back around in an enclosed loop, with booths on either side. Ours was marked on the outer ring. Deon Walsh scattered a large bale of straw around our tables to help soak up dampness from the surrounding grass and mud.

We soon ran into a problem. "Damn, it hasn't dried out enough." Uncle Ross slid his cap back from his sweaty forehead. "The poles are sinking too deep under this canvas tarp."

Aunt Eve shook a finger. "I told you we needed a new tent with polyester material, but you wouldn't listen. These poles are bent up and rusted, too."

"And I told you a new tent is too expensive," he shot back.

"This one looks old and dirty, Ross. Especially since we

have double the space than the regular-sized booths," she said. "Our displays will suffer."

"You're too particular. This will be fine once the poles hold—"

The rest of us stood back while they argued for several minutes. Tim and Deon, our shipping clerks, shifted from side to side in silence while Maddie examined the dirt streaks along the canvas folds. After a few minutes, I stuck my fingers in my mouth and gave a shrill whistle.

"Forget saving money. We need a decent-looking booth given what's happened over the last few weeks. It's my fault for dropping the ball. I didn't realize this tent material wasn't serviceable before now."

Uncle Ross frowned. "It's good enough—"

"It's ready for the trash," Aunt Eve said, hands on her hips.

"Both of you, calm down. I'll see if I can find something last minute," I said. "If not, we'll be stuck with this over the weekend."

I checked my phone for a Wi-Fi signal, trawled several online sources for available stock, and called a supply store. They agreed to deliver two ten-by-twenty-foot canopy tents tonight, texting me if that was possible, or else early tomorrow morning. We'd eat the cost, but the tent fabric was lighter and waterproof with walls that rolled up for greater light exposure, or down in case of rain. That would provide some protection, at least.

"I'd rather make sure we're covered if the weather reports are wrong," I said, "given how we can't sell wet teddy bears. We need a new sign, too."

Maddie called Silver Moon. Asia Gibson and Zoe Fisher promised to design and laminate a banner with our logo and bring it tonight. Somehow we'd figure out how to hang it from the new tent, even if I had to use Uncle Ross's duct tape.

"Aunt Eve's right," I told him. "This canvas material is dingy, and look at how warped these posts have gotten. No wonder they won't support the weight."

He grumbled while helping Tim and Deon position the tables and fasten coverings over them. I checked NOAA's weather graphs. Tomorrow's sunshine and sixty-eight degrees would be followed by a cloudy Saturday, with colder temperatures and a slight chance of showers. Sunday's forecast was iffy. If a storm threatened, plenty of vendors would break down the tents and leave early.

Since we couldn't do much else now, Aunt Eve, Maddie, and I slowly wandered over the park grounds. Many vendors in muddier areas laid plywood to cover the worst spots and then scattered gravel or hay. Few complained. Some came prepared with large fans or heaters plugged into electric or battery-powered generators. The deluge had affected everyone.

"I hope the park dries out better by tomorrow," Amy Evans moaned. "We didn't think about bringing in heaters— those vendors told me they're used to conditions of all kinds. Even snow in May. Can you believe it?"

A woman with two dark braids caught my eye. Lucy Hartman, hands on her hips, in jeans as filthy as her boots, surveyed her marked area. She looked furious. She marched over to confront Amy Evans, who stood in the loop's inner center.

"Why is that Wags and Whiskers rescue group only a few booths away from mine? Did you notice they're selling home-baked dog treats, the same as me? Leashes and collars, even calendars, too. The least you could do is put them over by the river."

"They signed up before you did, Mrs. Hartman, and their charity work is important here in Silver Hollow." Amy checked her clipboard. "If you're interested, we do have an open spot on the riverbank, right next to a popular food vendor—"

"I'm not gonna move, they should! It's a mud pit over there."

"Make the best of things, then. Excuse me."

Amy headed off to solve another problem. Lucy stalked toward her single tent, where Andrew Kane waited. He ignored her ranting while they hung garlands printed with tiny paws, banners with cartoon dogs and cats, plus colorful ribbons. Kane ripped strips of duct tape for Lucy after she spread plastic coverings over her table.

"Kind of makes you wonder," Aunt Eve said, one eyebrow raised. "That man hangs around her an awful lot, so maybe they are in a relationship. And if so, did it start before her husband was killed?"

I shrugged. "Andrew Kane claims he doesn't get involved with clients."

But he'd been far too quick to insist on that, in my mind. Dusk soon settled over the park. Most people left, including my aunt and uncle, who insisted on driving straight to the nearest self-serve car wash. Asia Gibson had already dropped off the new banner and headed home. Maddie and I waited for the deliverymen with the new tents, walking to keep warm and using our phone flashlights. We both shivered in the chill wind.

"What is it, forty degrees?" my sister asked, jumping up and down.

"Fifty-five. Wish I'd worn my winter coat. Here, use this." I peeled my hoodie off, since I'd dressed in layers. "I've got a short-sleeve shirt over a long sleeve, and this fleece jacket over them. By the way, I love this engagement ring. Thanks for designing it."

"Y-y-you're welcome. Jay wanted something with f-flowers in the band."

"It's gorgeous. How's it going with you and Eric? Are you two getting serious or staying friends? With or without benefits."

Maddie didn't answer at first while she adjusted the sweatshirt sleeves. "I don't want to get married at all. Mom and I had a huge argument over that a few days ago. She's not talking to me, or haven't you noticed?"

"No, but why wouldn't she understand?"

"Because she thinks a double wedding would be perfect," she said with a sigh. "Your engagement opened up that idea in her head, like in *Pride and Prejudice*. Mom's been sending me photos from that BBC version in texts and emails, even though she's giving me the silent treatment. Remember how she was so geeked to watch it with us when we were teens?"

"Good movie, but—"

"It's not reality. I told her that, but it doesn't matter." Maddie sighed again. "My life is mine. I'm not gonna bow to her pressure. You didn't, for years."

I nodded. "Do what's best for you, Mads. Jay and I will support you, no matter what."

"Good. I hope Mom doesn't push you into another huge wedding. Unless that's what you want, of course. But ask your friend Laura to be maid of honor, because I jinxed you the first time. Seriously."

"You did not. I should have listened to you and called it off."

"Let's blame Mom."

Maddie started giggling and then burst into laughter. I joined in, letting stress roll off my shoulders when we leaned against each other. I was so lucky to have a sister. We'd been through so much together over the years.

"How about being our witness when we elope? No way do I want Mom going crazy over a wedding dress again, a reception, flowers—"

"Too late, she's already planning," Maddie said with a laugh, "the minute she saw your ring. Dad hasn't been able to convince her to wait."

I waved a hand, unable to deal, and was relieved when a truck finally drove into the park. Two young men carried the tent equipment over; quick and efficient, they set up the metal poles, hung the white coverings, showed us how to roll up the sides and strap them into place, and even figured out a way to attach our new sign. My sister and I climbed into Jay's truck, too tired to unload the boxes, while several vendors chatted outside their small campers.

"No way would I spend a weekend in one of those," I said.

Maddie snickered. "Guess you don't want to live in a tiny house."

"Bite your tongue."

"I've actually considered buying a Winnebago and working remotely, if I could get a good internet connection. I hate being stuck at my desk over the summer. Do you realize we haven't had a real vacation in years? Weekends on Mackinac Island don't count. I could drive to a few national parks, soak up the scenery. Even for a few weeks."

I shrugged, though. "You know I'm more into hotels with room service. Jay did promise to take me to New England in the fall. Or Vancouver—but yeah. We want a simple wedding, and dinner with family and friends. Nothing big."

"Good luck dodging Mom's big plans for you."

Friday morning, I stumbled into the shower and got dressed. Bleary-eyed, I let Maddie drive Jay's truck to Fresh Grounds. After a fortifying latte and an egg-and-cheese bagel, with a bag of pastries for later, we headed to Riverside Park. Thankfully, the Highland Fling wouldn't hold the official opening ceremony until four o'clock.

"I hope my dogs are okay," I said and checked my phone. "The live feed doesn't start until ten, so remind me to log on in half an hour. Sugar Bear can get a little hyper, but maybe she's worn out after having so many dogs to play with yesterday."

Maddie parked in the lot's front. "Relax, they're fine."

I listened to a voice mail from Aunt Eve, who'd promised to check on the shop several times today. All in all, I only had to worry about our kilted and tartan bears selling at the booth. Pre-orders had been filled, and I hoped we didn't end up with a surplus of unsold teddies.

"You can always hold a special sale, or let the MacRaes sell them at their boutique," Maddie said. "Or think about adding a miniature set of bagpipes."

"Ha. Ha," I said sourly. "Uncle Ross would have a heart attack."

We walked past the pavilion, where people swarmed like angry bees to set up a sound board for the stage and wire huge speakers. Musicians lugged their cases and equipment from vans in the parking lot. Amy Evans waved us down at our booth.

"I'm so sorry, Sasha." She wrung her hands, clearly upset, and pushed aside the polyester fabric that hid our booth's interior. "I called the cops already."

Maddie and I stared in shock. A puddle of red stained the white plastic covering of one rectangular folding table. Dried streaks trailed over the edge to the straw below. A length of corded firewood sat in the table's center.

With a red-stained hatchet stuck in its middle.

Chapter 21

"That can't be real blood." I prodded a dried streak on the plastic table covering. "It's gotta be fake. Ketchup, or slime?"

Maddie bent to swipe the straw below and then examined her finger. "Still damp. I bet it's some kind of gel with red food coloring."

"What the hell—" Uncle Ross had arrived and plucked up the hatchet before I could stop him. "Stupid punks. Probably the same idiots who spray-painted your car."

"You think so?" I asked. "Maybe."

Amy waved off the small crowd of curious onlookers, who slowly returned to their own booths. "I got here around nine this morning, but didn't notice until someone saw a big splash of red on the walk outside your booth. That's when I checked inside the tent."

"I don't think punks did this, Uncle Ross," Maddie said. "The hatchet is supposed to remind people about Dad being arrested for Hartman's murder."

"But he's innocent, right?" Amy asked. "I'm surprised

Chief Russell hasn't had a press conference, though, or talked to the local TV or radio stations."

Uncle Ross nodded. "Only the cops know that Alex has a solid alibi."

"And Detective Hunter hasn't been trying hard to catch the real killer, either."

A cruiser with flashing lights arrived in the parking lot. This time, Digger Sykes climbed out from behind the wheel. He sauntered over but looked surprised when he saw the table, with the hatchet Uncle Ross had put back into place in the length of firewood.

"Is that blood?"

"Some kind of red gel," Maddie said, arms folded over her chest.

Digger pulled out his cell phone and snapped several photos from multiple angles. "So no witnesses? Anyone who might have seen something odd, footprints or whatever."

Amy Evans stepped forward. "A few vendors stayed here overnight in their campers," she said. "I hired a security guard for tonight and tomorrow, because I didn't expect problems like this last night. Someone noticed the red stain on the blacktop over there, and then called me over to check out the booth."

"I'd say whoever did it snuck into the park long after midnight, after the vendors were asleep," Uncle Ross said. "Wouldn't take long to set up this little scene."

"Hey, that's a shoe print," Maddie said. "Look at that outline, over there, with the red stuff on the edge. No treads, either, like the prints we found in the alley when your car was vandalized. It could be the same jerk, Sasha."

"Sounds logical to me." Digger hooked a thumb toward the campers. "I'll ask around, but that's not a lot to go on. I doubt we'll figure out who did it."

"We've got work to do," Uncle Ross said. "Let's clean up

this mess and get the booth set up. There's Tim and Deon now. Did you bring the doughnuts?"

"How can you think of food after this?" my sister asked, clearly frustrated.

Maddie stomped off to Jay's truck. I decided to check on Lucy Hartman. I had a feeling she or Andrew Kane may have had a hand in this. My simmering anger spilled over into action. But I stopped in surprise to see her booth. The paw print banners hung in tatters. The trailing ribbons had been ripped down and trampled in the mud. I noted similar footprints, without treads like sneakers or hiking boots would leave. Lucy, her face tear-streaked, waved a hand.

"Look at this mess! I can't replace those banners before the opening ceremony," she wailed. "I special ordered them from an online shop. They aren't sold in stores around here, and my ribbons are totally ruined!"

"Any other booths trashed besides yours?" I asked, suspicious.

"Right next to mine, except they already cleaned up."

I stared at the empty booth beside hers, devoid of tables or evidence of any vandalism. Whoever rented the booth had merely erected the metal tent structure. Some red slime gleamed on the ground when the sunshine hit it, but I wasn't convinced of her story. Lucy wandered around her booth, collecting trash, sniffling the entire time.

"Who would do this—oh! What if it was Teddy's murderer?"

She clutched her chest, breathing hard. Despite the damage, her gushing emotions had to be faked. Amy Evans would have mentioned Lucy being a victim, too, unless she failed to tell the committee chair—unbelievable given her complaints yesterday.

"I don't have extra tablecloths, either." Lucy wiped her wet cheeks with the back of her hand. "Andrew's busy today, and Kevin has a virtual call for Bears of the Heart for the next few hours. He said he can't skip it. What am I going to do?"

"We have extra plastic cloths," I said reluctantly. "We had to order a new tent and the company sent along a few extra coverings. Our booth was vandalized, too, but we only have to replace one."

"Really?" Lucy stared at me in surprise. "Thanks! How bad was it at your booth?"

"See for yourself."

I led the way back along the blacktop walk. A pile of boxes were stacked on the ground near our booth's tables. Uncle Ross, Deon, and Tim carried more from Jay's truck, but they hadn't cleaned up the damaged table yet. Lucy gasped in horror at the red slime and the hatchet stuck on the cord of firewood. Her face looked pale when she finally spoke.

"That's exactly like the axe they found in Teddy's—"

Lucy broke down in heavy sobs. This time her shock seemed genuine. Then again, the last few murderers I'd encountered had completely fooled me. I couldn't trust my judgment right now, so I busied myself rummaging under the tables for the extra plastic coverings.

"Here's a few, go ahead and take them."

I handed her the packages along with several tissues from my purse. Lucy wiped her face, although tears continued to streak her cheeks. She looked guilty when Uncle Ross stomped to the booth and dumped a load of merchandise before he returned to the truck. Deon and Tim did the same and followed him back to the parking lot.

"Maybe I shouldn't take these, Sasha." Lucy held them out. "I mean, I haven't been that nice to you and your family, and take advantage—"

"When bad things happen, people in a small town help each other out," I said and noted her look of disbelief. "The

community in Silver Hollow is like one big family. We look
out for each other, and share in the work to make life better."

"Uh—that's nice. I feel bad that Teddy made so much
trouble since we moved here." She sank onto a nearby folding
chair in dejection. "Things have gone wrong since the minute
he put an offer on that house for his crazy bed-and-breakfast
idea. I didn't want to do that. He couldn't get the loan, and
fought with me over the pet store."

"Why did you give up Sparky?" I asked out of curiosity.

"He tried to bite the landlord." Weeping again, Lucy
swiped her face with her sleeve. "He's impossible to control,
he's so possessive! He wouldn't let anyone get near me. I even
hired a dog psychologist back home, but that failed."

"Maybe Reuben Johnson can give you training tips."

She shook her head. "I don't know, I bet your business
has never been in trouble before. Not like Bears of the Heart.
Teddy had that Disney lawsuit to deal with, and those creeps
who wanted the Benny Bear—it's so unfair!"

I suspected she'd resent me worse if I disagreed. No business was perfect. The Silver Bear Shop & Factory had faced
plenty of trying situations—sewing machine repairs, mishaps
with the stuffing machine spewing fiber, and our sales rep's
murder.

"—pet store will ever survive," Lucy continued. "Andrew
warned me that location is everything. It's crazy being next to
the bakery, and no customers come through my door. Kevin
said I'm in a terrible spot in the village."

"You could use that drive-through window in the back,
after people order online. That's a great option for busy customers who just want essentials."

"Maybe it worked for ice cream, but how am I going to
shove a big bag of dog food through that tiny opening? Or
buckets of cat litter—"

"Oh, my heavens! What's going on, Sasha?"

Flora Zimmerman's sudden arrival surprised me. She set down a box onto our table and stared at the hatchet; I hadn't expected her, since she wasn't on the list to help out at the booth. Flora's reading glasses hung from a silver chain around her neck, along with her usual array of turquoise necklaces. Before I could explain, Lucy spilled the entire story of the vandalism with a heavy emphasis on her booth's damaged banners, ribbons, and tablecloth.

"I don't know how I'll get through this weekend!"

"That's terrible." Flora patted her frosted bob. "Come along with me, Mrs. Hartman, and I'll help you put everything to rights. You can tell me the whole story about your poor husband, too. I'm all ears."

Maddie's jaw dropped in surprise, her arms full of boxes. I shook my head in warning while Flora linked arms with Lucy and walked away. "What just happened?" my sister asked.

I laughed. "A gift horse, actually—they're both out of our hair. It's almost two o'clock, and we don't have much time before the opening ceremony. Is this all the merchandise, or is there more?"

"Deon and Tim are bringing the racks."

We rushed to clean up, replace the ruined tablecloth, and decorate the tent with streamers in a variety of colors. I wasn't pleased that Flora lacked patience with Joan and Isabel but had taken Lucy Hartman under her wing. Maddie and I spread the old tent canvas over a patch of straw-strewn mud between our booth and the next, which offered pottery in unique designs and lovely glazes and patterns. The young artist thanked us in relief.

"Maddie, Sasha!" Aunt Eve arrived with our costumes in plastic bags. "I picked these up from Bonnie MacRae's shop. You should see the crowd waiting at the park entrance already! There's a long line of cars for at least a mile down the road."

"Elle texted me that schools had another half day, so that could be why," Maddie said. On her tiptoes, she adjusted the laminated banner. "Is this more centered now?"

"A little more to the left," I said. "Just a tad more—"

"Good enough," Uncle Ross growled, stalking our way. "Now get into those kilts, girls. The Fling may open early, and they're testing the PA system right now."

With that, we rushed to the public restroom by the pavilion where a short line snaked to the women's door. Musicians milled around the stage. I waved at Emily Abbott, who waved back and plugged in her electric guitar. Her Goth makeup and waist-length black hair, braided down her back, complemented her red and black kilt, black shirt, and black leather boots. Her band colleagues had numerous tattoos, outlandish spiked and dyed hair, and grungy clothes.

"Ouch!" I winced when a passerby dug their elbow into my ribs, and inched closer to the door. "I hope this skirt fits. I had to guess the size off a European chart."

"The kilt buckles are adjustable," Maddie reassured me. "I hope that guy with flaming bagpipes is coming—"

"The Unipiper from Portland?" I squealed with excitement and followed my sister inside the restroom at last. "Riding a unicycle, and the pipes spout flames while he plays?"

"Yup. Amy wasn't sure he could fly out this weekend." She whipped off her cardigan and wrap dress to reveal biker shorts and a white T-shirt. "You wore shorts, right? See how easy the kilt buckles, and there you go. I'm ready. Wanna borrow my sweater?"

I held up a gym bag. "I've got shorts, a sweater, and a jacket in here. After last night, I'm not gonna freeze again."

"Okay. See you back at the booth."

Maddie rushed off. Inside a stall, I stripped and buckled on the new kilt over my thin shorts, added a white blouse and knee-high socks, then tied my cardigan's sleeves around my waist. I avoided my reflection in the mirror above the restroom's sink. No doubt I resembled my mother during her Catholic high school days except for the red hair. With her tasseled leather loafers on my feet, no less. I felt ridiculous but headed outside.

"Alright, Sasha?" Trina Wentworth stood in a now-longer line of women outside the restroom. "Lookin' dishy, love."

"Thanks, I guess. The committee should have ordered porta-johns for the guys. That way women could use both sides of the restroom."

"Ooh, great idea for the ladies. Takes longer for us at the loo." Trina glanced backward, since more women joined the line behind her. " I helped Bonnie set up this morning. Now I've got to nick back to the Kilted Scot while they stay here."

"I take it you haven't scheduled any tea events, then."

Trina shook her blond head. "No. Bonnie's helping us next weekend. It's chockablock—full up, I mean, due to your Mothering Day. We celebrate that during Lent back home. I hear you're engaged, you must be chuffed!"

"Uh, yes, and thanks! Gotta run."

I suspected my mother had been spreading the news all around the village. Aunt Eve had been thrilled for me as well, telling all her friends, and joined Mom in discussions for a wedding shower. Even though I'd begged them not to—plus setting a day to shop for a wedding dress, a venue for the reception, and plenty more. Somehow I'd have to break it to them both that Jay and I didn't want any fuss. His mother agreed with us about a quiet ceremony and family dinner.

Why couldn't things be simple? I'd had a huge wedding the first time, and didn't want to repeat that. Too embarrassing, plus we didn't need to soak relatives for cash. Jay and I were established in household goods. We only needed time for a honeymoon, to get away and relax, enjoy new scenery. Jay had hinted at going up north, while I yearned for a sunny beach. Hmm. Compromising might be a problem.

Amy Evans stood near the pavilion, in a full-length tartan skirt, a green velvet vest, and dark sweater. Mud caked her short boots. My mother suddenly joined her, waving a hand in the direction of our booth. Her tartan beret matched her royal blue and yellow kilt, with a sash across her blouse, pinned at the shoulder with a Celtic brooch. When she caught sight of me and then beckoned, I walked over with gritted teeth.

"Sasha, don't you look nice," Mom said, surveying me up and down. "I take it you were at the restroom. Was it clean enough? I got on the park manager about that."

I nodded but turned to Amy. "The only problem is the huge line."

She held up a hand. "I know, and yes, I ordered porta-johns."

"Good idea." Mom waved again at our booth. "So ours wasn't the only one vandalized? You said you were hiring a security guard."

"For tonight and tomorrow," Amy said. "Nobody planned to set out their wares until today. Who knew there'd be a murder, for heaven's sake, right outside the park entrance? And then with all the rain we had, the mud, almost a flood over the riverbanks. I'm so afraid another shoe will drop."

"You're doing the best you can." Mom changed the subject. "I'll gladly act as a judge for any dance or music competition, but are you sure? You could ask April Rogers, the band teacher at the high school. She's more qualified. . . ."

When Jay rounded the corner of the pavilion, I hurried to meet him. His Gordon kilt in the same blue, green, and gray pattern was fuller and longer in the back than my tailored one.

A matching plaid over his shoulder, pinned with a silver brooch, felt scratchy over his linen shirt.

"What gives with more vandalism?" Jay shook his head. "Someone for sure is targeting your family. That's crazy."

"I know." I squeezed his upper arm muscle. "Ready for the caber toss?"

"Yeah, too bad it's not tonight. I had to move some heavy wood blocks, twenty-five pounds or more each, at the studio."

"Oh, there's Dad with Mark Branson."

We threaded our way through the growing crowd, which had swelled given the warmer weather. Apparently the food vendors had already opened for business, since people held bottles of Irn-Bru or cups of coffee, scones and shortbread, or even the usual cotton candy or corn dogs at county fairs. Kevin Whittaker, grumbling about the lack of parking, passed us by on the way to Lucy's booth. A glum Andrew Kane followed him.

What was bothering him? Ignoring them both, I snapped a few photos of Dad and Mark Branson, who both wore dark suits and flat caps that matched their tartan ties. Then I motioned Jay over for a group photo, and Mark took several of me, Jay, and Dad. At least my brand-new cell phone had plenty of digital storage.

"What, no kilt?" I asked Mark. "Mary Kate's gonna wear one."

"I'll let her. This hat is good enough for me," he said and then lowered his voice. "I heard about the vandalism at your booth with fake blood—"

The slow drone of bagpipes suddenly swelled in the distance and drowned out my reply. A group of men and women, young and old, soon marched into view in full Highland dress with kilts, stockings, polished black leather shoes, sporrans made of horsehair, and plaids crossed over their white shirts. They slowed to parade around the oval walkway, from the pavilion to the river and then back, bags under their arms, fingers busy on the chanter pipes, while they played many traditional Highland reels.

Many people joined me in taking photos of the bagpipers, admiring their precise movements and costumes, if not the shrill music. I managed several close-ups of an older man and a teen girl. Once the music died away, Amy Evans stepped onto the pavilion's stage.

"Welcome to our first annual Highland Fling!"

Only the people in front heard her, since the microphone failed to pick up her voice. Amy signaled the sound tech at the stage's back, waited for a volume adjustment, and then boomed out the same greeting. Everyone applauded wildly until she held up both hands.

"First of all, please be aware of the wet and muddy ground conditions. The river's banks may give way, so stay on the paths and blacktop." She held up a flyer, folded open to show the map. "Remember that shuttle buses are available to return you to your cars in distant parking lots. Check the schedule. They'll operate until ten p.m. tonight and tomorrow."

Mom leaned over and whispered in her ear. Amy raised the microphone again. "We also have a first aid station set up behind the restroom building, in case anyone falls or slips in the mud. And yes, that is possible. One of the band members can demonstrate."

A guitarist stepped forward and lifted one side of his kilt to show a streak of mud all the way up his muscular thigh. Several women in the audience whistled and cheered. He winked and rejoined the band. Amy continued her announcements and directions, pointing out the number system to various vendors. Before she could introduce my mother, though, everyone winced at a burst of shrill feedback.

The tech quickly adjusted the soundboard dials. "Sorry!"

Amy looked relieved. "I'd like to introduce our village mayor, Judith Silverman!"

Mom took the microphone amid another ear-splitting whine and waited until that awful feedback died away. "Good afternoon! Or should I say, *Fàilte?*"

That sounded like 'fault-cha' to my ears, but Bonnie MacRae whistled in approval.

"That's the limit of my Scottish Gaelic, I'm afraid," Mom said, "but welcome! We're excited to be here, and the weather is finally cooperating. What a marvelous tradition for Silver Hollow and the surrounding region, too. Enjoy, and lang may yer lum reek—translated as 'long may your chimney smoke.' In other words, live long and be well!"

Everyone applauded. I rushed back to our Silver Bear booth, hoping Maddie wasn't mad that I'd observed the ceremony. She and Flora handled customers, most of them parents with excited kids in tow. While Maddie made change from cash or swiped credit cards using a mobile reader on her phone, Flora retrieved kilted bears from the shelves and bagged purchases. The line dwindled after I joined them to help.

"Internet access is spotty," my sister complained. "I might have Aunt Eve bring those old-fashioned credit card impression things, and run transactions through that way."

"That might help." I retrieved several tartan bears and set them on a shelf next to the kilted ones. A young woman eyed the boxes behind me. "Can I help you?"

"Do you have a pair of wedding bears? My grandmother's getting remarried in June, and she loves teddy bears. I want to surprise her."

"Wonderful, and congratulations to her and your family." I lifted the box onto the table. "We have a choice of bride bears, with either pink posies, yellow, or purple."

"Purple, since the groom has a matching vest. Sweet."

"Thanks, we thought so."

I cringed at a burst of loud music from the band's huge speakers on stage. Flora decided to head back to the factory, given the noise level. For the next hour and a half, I had to exchange shouts with Maddie and other customers to be heard. My voice soon grew hoarse, and my head pounded from the booming bass. The loud music affected every vendor close to the pavilion, but we made the best of conditions. At last the band took a break for dinner.

"Dad said he'd bring over something," Maddie said. "I'm starving."

"I packed peanut butter crackers for emergencies." I wolfed down a package and shared the last water bottle to wash them down. "Jay didn't answer my text either, so I have no idea where he's been all this time."

A harpist took the stage next, rolling her gorgeous instrument out from the side and then tuning a few strings. I unpacked more kilted bears, listening to the soothing music and grateful the evening was drawing to a close.

"What time does this thing end again?"

"Eight." Maddie sank onto a folding chair. "It's been fun, and not too bad for the first day. Wanna bet tomorrow will be nuts?"

"People will be too busy eating and watching the games to buy much," I joked.

Emily Abbott trudged over to our front table. She tugged one fishnet stocking beneath her red and black kilt, biting her lip, and then pointed at the kilted bears. "Can I just order a kilt? I'd like one for my Hairy Bear, even if it costs extra."

"Sure, we can sew one for you."

"How fast, though?"

"A week, maybe two," I said, "because some of our staff are covering the shop while I'm here. Sorry about that. I doubt it could be sooner than next Wednesday."

"That's fine. I like to change my outfits when we play at Quinn's," Emily said. "I think the next Scottish Sunday is late in the month."

"Scottish Sunday?" Maddie raised an eyebrow. "With bagpipes?"

"Nah, but Danny plays a tin whistle. We had a gig on St. Patrick's Day weekend down in Detroit, and that's really popular. Brian Quinn wants Scottish and Irish music once a month at the pub. Draws a lot of people." Emily lowered her voice. "We were playing the Sunday that pet shop guy was killed. Didn't your dad find the body around here somewhere?"

"Teddy Hartman, yes." My ears pricked up. "Did you ever meet him?"

"Once. I asked him for a part-time job in his store, but he blew me off. I can't pay all my bills without a second job, Hartman didn't like my tats and piercings, or my makeup. He didn't say that, but whatever." Emily shrugged. "I get that from a lot of people."

"Bonnie and Gavin MacRae might need help at the Kilted Scot. Their daughter will be heading back to Edinburgh soon," I added. "Tell them I sent you."

"Wow, thanks for the tip."

"Was there a homicide detective that Sunday night at the pub? Asking questions?"

She looked puzzled until I described Phil Hunter and then shook her head. "Nope. I'm sure I would have remembered him."

"Weird. I thought he'd have wanted to question people at the pub whether Hartman's brother-in-law showed up. That man, over there." I pointed to Kevin Whittaker. "Tall guy, white hair slicked back, red bow tie—"

"Yeah, I saw him." Emily made a face. "Kept staring at

me like I had two heads, and then he wanted to buy me a drink. Like, he's gotta be fifty or older. No thanks."

I suspected that Emily and Aunt Eve both received attention, wanted or unwanted, for their unique fashion styles. It puzzled me why the police detective never visited Quinn's Pub to check Whittaker's alibi.

As Bonnie MacRae would say, Hunter was a right scunner.

Chapter 22

After a chilly Saturday morning at the Highland Fling, the sun burned off a light fog long before noon. It had to be nearly eighty degrees, so I stripped off my cardigan and rolled up the sleeves of my white T-shirt. A ponytail kept the hair off my neck, at least. I couldn't complain, though, given how Jay dripped with sweat after he finished the Kilted 5K. His brother Nathan was among the last few joggers who staggered to cross the finish line.

"I need a shower. Come on, bro." Jay set off in a jog to his truck.

"Kill me now, Sasha," Nathan moaned and limped a few steps. "How is he still able to run like that? My feet are burning."

"Soak them for half an hour in Epsom salts. You'll feel better, trust me."

I backed away from our booth to take more photographs. This new phone was amazing. After snapping several shots from various angles, I took photos of the crowd, of the Fresh

Grounds booth and its long line, plus the pavilion and dance competition.

"I'm ready for lunch." Mom bagged up one of Jay's adorable carved teddy bears. Karen Anderson showed another customer a tartan bear with a bright blue bow. "Please get something for us to eat. Anything at all."

"Okay, three haggis plates with a side of ketchup."

She gave me a stink eye. "No, thanks. I'm sure you can find something else."

With a grin, I headed off to the vendor booths by the riverside, past the blacktop walkway and down the straw-strewn path. A few thick patches of mud remained, but they'd been marked with sticks and orange plastic strips. Besides sweets like cookies, muffins, and scones, the offerings varied from huge turkey drumsticks, bowls of lobster mac and cheese, smoked salmon, baskets of fried fish and chips. Lidded cups held potato and leek soup.

One man raved over his, while another ordered "neeps and tatties"—mashed turnips and potatoes—as a side with the haggis plate. I waited with several other curious observers when he took a first tentative bite of the haggis.

"Mmm, good stuff. Spicy, too."

"Told you so," the first guy said. "I had that last night. Still a bit livery, even without the sheep lungs, but an earthy taste."

"Give me lobster mac and cheese any day instead of that," one woman said, waving a plastic fork. "Total heaven!"

I moved on to greet Garrett and Mary Kate Thompson at the Fresh Grounds booth, in a shaded spot across the path from those lining the river. Besides their usual pastries, they offered frosted and sprinkled cupcakes topped with sugary pink unicorns. So cute. After waiting a few minutes in line, I placed a special delivery order for Monday afternoon.

"I want to reward our staff for working so hard on the

kilted and tartan bears," I said. "Wendy did a fabulous job helping out with the cake from Pretty in Pink."

"I'm trying to talk Wendy into staying with us," Mary Kate said, "but she's got her heart set on running her own bakery."

"Maybe she should buy out Pretty in Pink." I took a box with half a dozen cupcakes for now. "Vivian Grant might be thinking about early retirement."

"Whoa, really?" Mary Kate clapped her hands. "I'll text Wendy right now. If she stays in Silver Hollow, we can work together to expand our pastry offerings."

"We heard about the vandalism yesterday, Sasha," Garrett said. "That seems fishy to me, with only your booth and Lucy Hartman's getting hit."

"Tell me about it," I said. "She claimed the one next to her had damage—"

"No way," they both chimed in, and Mary Kate shook her head. "We know that vendor. Joe had car trouble and arrived this morning to set up his leather goods."

I mused on that, not surprised that Lucy had lied to me. It wasn't a coincidence for only two booths to be damaged. But I could have sworn her surprise was genuine when she saw the hatchet sticking up in that piece of firewood.

"Okay, guys. See you later."

Walking on, I recalled seeing the K-9 and Kitty Korner booth earlier, with Lucy and her brother Kevin Whittaker behind the table. The crowd streamed past without stopping long. Across the blacktop, five spots down, Jodie and Phil Richardson answered questions about the Wags and Whiskers rescue organization, handed out adoption applications, and discussed their day care and boarding packages. Lucy scowled at the people swarming around them.

At the Kilted Scot booth, Winona Martinez opened the

portable oven to retrieve trays of shortbread fingers. The fragrant scent drew a huge line who watched two other ladies dip cooled cookies into bowls of melted chocolate. Bonnie and Sophie MacRae filled orders of fresh-baked baps with fried eggs and either bacon or sausage patties. They also wrapped shortbread and scones in wax-paper squares for customers.

Gavin manned the adjoining tent, where people examined and bought tartan fabrics, blankets, hats, adorable stuffed animals, bundles of dried heather, and other items. I planned to head there later after lunch. I waited in line, impatient, until I finally reached the table.

"Three baps, a dozen fruit scones, same with the shortbread. I'll try an Irn-Bru, too," I said to Bonnie. "Business is booming."

"I'm gobsmacked," she said with a laugh. "It's certainly be'er than expected."

That came out as "sair-ten-ly" given Bonnie's thicker accent, which seemed to charm everyone around us. And I figured "be'er" meant "better," too. I loved listening to her and dug out the exact amount of money from my purse, which she appreciated given the line.

"One li'el orange skoosh fer ye. You were right about the shortbread, Sasha. I sent Trina to fetch more flour and caster sugar, oh, more'n an hour ago. She blatted into the market and bought the lot. I've had to hire on two of her tea room ladies to help."

I nodded, happy for her. "Can't make them fast enough, I see."

Bonnie flipped the bottle's tab top and handed it over, then bagged the food. "That's a braw kilt. That means lovely, by the way. People expect me to talk this way, o' course."

I laughed. "I love this kilt. I've gotten a lot of compli-

ments, in fact, and sent them over here to check out your se-
lection."

"You need the child's size sporran to go with the kilt instead of luggin' that big satchel around," she said and winked.
"Tell Gavin I said to give you a big discount."

"I will, and thanks."

My shoulder did ache from my heavy purse. I headed
away from the booth's line and devoured my delicious bap,
savoring the egg and crispy bacon. When I took a hefty swal-
low of the Irn-Bru, I coughed so hard that my eyes watered.
Dad hurried over along with Mark Branson. The lawyer
grabbed my bags while Dad pounded on my back.

"You okay, Sasha?" he asked.

"Yeah—I'm good. Oh, man. Too fizzy. Thanks."

I coughed again. The Irn-Bru tasted like pink bubblegum
and way too sweet. I liked coffee with cream and sugar, but
this sugary drink was over the top. I held the bottle to Mark,
who eyed it warily.

"So you don't like it?" he asked. "I was gonna order one."

"Better try it first." I traded him the bottle for my other
bags. "Sip it, though."

Mark obeyed, squinted a few times, then handed the Irn-
Bru to Dad. He finished it off and bought another. Bonnie
had been laughing the entire time. Despite how fast she filled
her customers' orders, she raised her voice to call my way.

"Your da's too sweet to murder anyone!"

"Tell that to Detective Hunter," I shouted back, "although he wouldn't listen before to you or Gavin. Which was
ridiculous—"

Dad hushed me and glanced at the crowd. "Given the
vandalism last night, Sasha, I'd advise keeping quiet about the
police."

"I have to agree," Mark said, although he didn't seem as

somber as my father. "Until the killer's caught, anyone might be listening and report back to them."

"I suppose you're right."

Once Dad headed off toward the soccer and baseball fields, and Mark strolled toward the pavilion, I decided to buy the sporran. Gavin MacRae held up a silver necklace for an interested customer so that its pendant winked in the sunlight.

"Real heather from the Highlands, forever preserved in resin," he said with a smile. Gavin turned to me after the woman walked off. "What can I help you with, Sasha?"

"A child's-size sporran, and I'd love one of those adorable stuffed animals. The one with a plaid scarf," I added, pointing to the cow labeled as a Scottish Highland Coo. "Or should I get one with the tartan cap between its little horns?"

"The one with the cap." Jay suddenly hugged me from behind, freshly showered and shaved, and smelling wonderful. "I bought the scarf one already."

"Matching kilts, and almost-matching coos?" I twisted to kiss him. Before Gavin rang up my purchase, I noted a basket filled with silver and red foil-wrapped rounds. "So what are these Tunnock's Tea Cakes like?"

"Biscuit base, meringue on top of that. What you Americans might call a 'whoopie pie,' maybe? Only covered in chocolate instead of topped with another biscuit."

"Ooh, I'll take half a dozen." I paid and glanced behind Jay, but no other customers waited in line. "Did my friend Emily Abbott stop by to talk to you? She wondered if you might need help this summer at the Kilted Scot."

"Already hired her," he said promptly. "Quite experienced, too, from what your mother said. Emily worked at the shop before Judith took over and opened her gallery."

"That's true."

"Her schedule works perfectly with ours. We won't need her until noon," Gavin said, "and Em sleeps late due to her pub gigs. She'll come in for the afternoons until closing. I'll be going back to Edinburgh with Sophie for a week, too. I'd rather Bonnie not work alone at the shop while I'm gone."

"Sounds wonderful for you all." I handed a foiled tea cake to Jay. "I've got to get back to the booth, okay? What time is the caber toss?"

"I'm not scheduled till after six for both events. Coming to witness my failure?"

"No way, you'll be great."

"Don't be surprised when I go down in flames."

Jay planted a kiss before I hurried off to deliver lunch for Mom and Karen. I'd been keeping an eye out for Detective Mason, too, in case he showed. He must have seen my text about the vandalism, but had not answered. He also hadn't updated me with news about Hunter or the investigation. If only their boss would transfer the case to Mason. I staffed the table while Mom and Karen ate their baps, although the crowd wandered past most of the time.

"Speak of the devil," I muttered.

Detective Hunter slowly meandered past the pavilion, his lean form half-hidden by the long trench coat he wore. Not as wrinkled as TV's Lieutenant Columbo, but I was surprised he didn't have a cigar stub in hand. Mom looked up from checking receipts.

"What's that, Sasha?"

"Oh, nothing."

"Isn't that the guy who used to date Kristen Bloom?" Karen Anderson ducked her head when Phil Hunter glanced our way. "I heard nasty things about him," she whispered. "Stuck her with the dinner check when Kristen broke up with him. Just walked off, and he was the one who ordered an expensive bottle of wine—eighty bucks."

"Did he?" I asked. "Not surprised, though."

"Yeah. Scumbag."

Mom tapped a finger on her pursed lips. "Karen and I have things under control here, Sasha. Why don't you go find out what detective's up to, hmm?"

"Good idea."

I followed the lanky detective at a safe distance. Hunter jarred the elbow of a juggler, no doubt on purpose, but the man only dropped one ball before deftly bending to snatch it from the ground. He resumed his dexterity while the crowd applauded. Men and women in black leather pants and gold shirts practiced fencing. Their choreography of quick steps and clashing weapons proved a feast for the eyes.

After taking several photos of the group, I joined another crowd—well behind Hunter—to watch a man discuss falconry. He wore a laced jerkin over woolen trousers, boots, and a hooded cape, while a gorgeous brown falcon gripped his leather glove. Detective Hunter soon stalked off but halted at the St. Andrews Society booth where members handed out flyers, answered genealogy questions, and explained Scotland's family crests and mottos.

"The Jacobean era? A huge mess," the man said. "Bonnie Prince Charlie managed to gain support of the clans, which eventually led to the battle of Culloden Moor . . ."

Somehow I'd lost sight of Hunter, given the growing crowd. How could that be? He was hard to miss, being so tall. I skirted another group watching a weaver demonstrate her loom, took a few quick photos, and left the rhythmic clacking behind. Hunter must have headed for the athletic events. Flags fluttered on tall poles beside the fields, and signs pointed the way to the caber toss and hammer throw events.

I checked my phone. Half an hour until Jay's turn, so I raced to find Jay, Nathan, and Charlie Volker. They stood talking with my dad, while Detective Hunter watched from afar. A team of teen boys and girls warned onlookers away from the competitors' open space. Others ran forward to measure distances when the logs fell onto the mud-streaked grass. Several judges sat at a table tracking results and consulting each other whenever necessary.

Hunter followed Dad when he walked off to observe the hammer throw event. I had a feeling the detective remained convinced of his guilt in Hartman's murder, and hoped some kind of evidence would prove him right. With a sigh, I hurried after them.

The baseball diamond wasn't muddy at all, almost hard as cement, with scattered gravel and stones. Hunter kept his distance until Dad joined Gil Thompson. Then he moved in to intercept the two. What now? I inched closer to overhear the conversation.

"—black car, is that correct? Following Mr. Hartman?"

"Yeah," Gil Thompson said to Hunter, who looked displeased. "I'm supposed to compete in this event, you know. Can't this wait until later?"

"Why didn't you mention that when I questioned you at the station?"

"Didn't think it was important, and you didn't ask."

"Right." His tone dripped annoyance. Hunter brought forth several small photographs from his pocket. "Do you recognize any of these men?"

Gil Thompson perused them half-heartedly, keeping a closer eye on the competitors. They spun the large mallets around their heads and then flung them into the field. An assistant called out distance numbers to an older woman, who jotted them in a notebook.

Hunter snapped his fingers in front of Gil's nose. "Pay attention, okay? Have you seen any of these men coming into your coffee shop or around Silver Hollow?"

"Do you know how many people visit my shop, Detective? Too many to recall."

"Look again."

With a sigh, Gil glanced at each one. "Nope. Not familiar."

"So none of them drove the Cadillac you happened to see and never told me about?"

"These photos are so blurry, I can't see their faces," he complained, waving them. "The guy driving that car sped by so fast, I didn't notice what he looked like."

"You didn't even try to catch the license plate, then."

"How was I supposed to know I should've written it down?"

"But you recognized it as a black Cadillac Escalade, the priciest model, with tinted windows. You'd think you'd have noticed the plate. A vanity, or out of state?"

"I didn't expect a murderer to drive past. Happy now?"

Detective Hunter bristled at Gil's sarcasm. "Fine. Anything else you conveniently forgot about that particular Sunday afternoon?"

"Hey, you were so focused on proving Alex's guilt. And he avoided Teddy Hartman, even staying away from the SHEBA meetings. The guy made a point of insulting Alex, Judith, and the Silver Bear Shop."

"Don't forget that Maddie Silverman punched him in the nose—"

"Hartman deserved that!"

"That's enough, Gil." Dad pushed himself between the two men, his voice firm. "My daughter was wrong to resort to violence, Detective, but Teddy Hartman shared some of the guilt due to his actions. It's moot now, though."

"Not until this murder is solved, Alex." Gil glared at Hunter. "Too bad you've wasted so much time, Detective. Whoever killed that jerk will get off scot-free."

"For your information, I have new evidence," Hunter interrupted, his tone cold.

That surprised me, and I pushed forward to look at the first photograph that Gil still held. The detective grabbed for the bunch, but I gasped aloud.

"I recognize this guy with the curled mustache! He's one of the men who wanted us to make a sitting teddy with a front seam like the Benny Bear. And this guy, too." I pointed to the second photo. "So what new evidence do you have, Detective?"

"That first guy owns a black Cadillac Escalade." Hunter sounded triumphant. "I'll be in touch if I have any further questions."

He walked across the field toward the parking lot, where more people climbed out of two shuttle buses. Gil Thompson stared after him, fists clenched. I wasn't satisfied. So what if one of the pedophiles drove a Cadillac? That didn't mean he'd followed Hartman. Unless Teddy was due to testify against the group—that seemed unlikely, though. Hunter should check into Lucy being involved with another man, who might have helped kill her husband.

"Dad, do you think the prosecutor would have called Teddy Hartman as a witness?" I asked.

"Mark Branson asked about that, but no. So that's a dead end."

"I heard Hunter's so incompetent, he planted drugs to arrest a dealer," Gil said. "That backfired on him big time."

My father raised an eyebrow. "Who told you that?"

"Mike Blake heard it from a lawyer friend of his. Small

world, Alex. You can't pull that kind of stuff and not get caught."

"Okay, you made your point. But you're up next."

Dad tugged Gil Thompson back into line with the rest of the hammer throw competitors. Someone handed him a long-handled mallet. Gil gripped the length of wood, flexed his meaty hands, but hesitated at the starting line with his gaze on the ground. He whirled the hammer around and around his head but stopped, as if finding it hard to focus.

"Give me a minute. Yeah, I'm all right, Alex. Back off," he growled at another man who stepped forward. "Let me get this over with, so be patient."

Halfway through his second spin, Thompson careened out of control. Fearing he'd lose his grip, gasping onlookers scattered in all directions. The heavy mallet swung upward, although Thompson never let go of the handle—until it landed with a heavy thud on his foot. We all watched in horror when he fell backward; his head slammed against the ground. Dad surged forward to kneel beside him.

"Sasha, call Amy Evans! He's out cold."

"Yep, and I'm calling 9-1-1 too." With my phone glued to one ear, I blocked several people from pushing past me. "Please, stay back."

Jay, Nathan, and Charlie rushed over to prevent curious bystanders from pressing around Dad. He'd pushed the hammer aside but didn't touch Gil's foot or ankle. Gil Thompson groaned aloud, his eyelids fluttering, and let out a deep breath.

"Wha—wha' happened?"

Dad prevented him from raising his head or shifting his shoulders. "Whoa, Gil. Don't try to get up, because you might have a concussion."

"Pulled a muscle, more likely. Damn, my foot hurts."

"Looks like Hunter's questions threw you off your game."

"You can say that again." Gil waved at me, and his deep voice sounded weak. "Sasha, tell Garrett what happened. He'd better find someone else to help at the booth."

"Sure, no problem—"

I fought my way through the mass of people on the field. By the time I finally reached the crowd's fringe, red flashing lights signaled an EMT's arrival. The team rolled a stretcher over the field from the parking lot. I lingered to watch them assess Gil's vitals, then fasten a soft brace around his neck. Once they lifted him onto the flat surface, they raised it and wheeled the upright stretcher over the rough field to the ambulance.

At the Fresh Grounds booth, Garrett listened to my story while he tore off his apron. "Hope he didn't crack his skull."

"It all happened so fast," I said, "but he must have broken his foot."

He stuffed the apron into my hands. "Help Mary Kate until I get back, okay?"

Once he raced off, Mary Kate shook her head. "I'm so glad Mom's with the kids at home today. You don't have to stay, Sasha. I can handle things."

I glanced at the long line waiting for food and drinks, at how exhausted my friend looked, and how her barista looked ready to drop. Then I texted Elle and called Maddie. She rushed over in record time; Mary Kate trained us both on working the coffee machine and cleaning the steam wand in between filling, pressing, and dumping the used beans. Her barista took a much-needed break. I insisted that Mary Kate rest for five minutes, too.

"You can't be Superwoman forever, you know."

"I could say the same thing about you," she retorted, but she sank onto a chair.

Elle arrived with a stack of boxes. "I figured you might be running out of baked goods, so I told the staff to close for the day and pack up whatever was left."

"Good. I'm not sure Garrett would approve, but I'm sure he'll go see Uncle Gil at the hospital." Mary Kate wearily rose to her feet. "I'll handle the cash register. Maddie can fill the orders, and you help Sasha with the drinks."

While we worked as a team, the patient line of customers dwindled at last. We fully caught up when the barista returned from break. Relieved, I turned over the coffee and latte orders into far more experienced hands. Elle soon left for her bookstore, but Maddie stayed on with me to continue helping until Garrett's return.

"Scones to go," I said, filling a bag for a customer. "Enjoy."

"Plus a crème brûlée latte," Mary Kate sang out. "Thank you!"

"It never ends, does it?" Maddie eyed several people heading over to order. "I'm glad we don't sell food. Hey, Sasha, seal up the garbage and take it behind the restrooms."

I didn't mind, until the revolting smell sent me into a dizzy spin. Mary Kate pushed me into the chair, grabbed the trash bag away, and flung it between the trees behind the booth. She shoved my head down to my knees.

"Breathe deep. Deeper, in and out."

I wiped my damp forehead, still shaky. "Yeah, okay. Thanks."

"Something you want to tell me?" Mary Kate whispered, leaning over.

Puzzled, I stared at her. "Huh?"

She winked. "Never mind."

I leaned back against the metal folding chair while Mary Kate returned to fulfill an order. Maddie glanced at me a few times, puzzled, while I checked my cell phone—four o'clock.

I had plenty of time before Jay competed in his events. Despite all the noise surrounding me, I fought a wave of weariness. I could use a nap. But my mind wouldn't stop churning over the recent developments this afternoon.

Poor Gil Thompson. I also couldn't help wondering why Detective Hunter would waste time tracking down the driver of that black Cadillac. What kind of new evidence did he have? If Dad was right, and he was chasing a dead end, he couldn't be close to solving the case.

Unless he was only bluffing.

Chapter 23

Garrett finally returned. "I talked to Uncle Gil on the phone before they drove him to the hospital for X-rays," he said. "Mild concussion, for sure. One of the paramedics said his foot has multiple broken bones. He may end up in a cast up to his knee."

"Or one of those clunky boots with all the straps," Mary Kate said. "He ought to stay off his foot until it's fully healed, instead of waddling around."

"You mean he'd be so unbalanced, he'll fall and break an arm," I said lightly.

"You got that right."

"He'll be a bear, whatever they do." Garrett swiped scone crumbs from the table. "Who can we get to help out tomorrow, Mary Kate? Your mom can't handle two days in a row with the kids, so you better stay home. You can't bring them here."

"Mark can work the booth with you," she said. "Remember he's helped out at fast food places for community fundraisers. Sasha, it's almost five. You don't want to miss seeing Jay in the caber toss."

Maddie shooed me away. "I'll stay and help—you go."

Tearing off my apron, I scurried around clusters of people who meandered around the vendor booths. My feet ached from standing so long behind the table. My stomach grumbled, but the scent of frying grease didn't appeal to me. I hadn't even snitched one of Mary Kate's darling unicorn cupcakes. While I didn't feel sick anymore, something had to be wrong. I never passed up the chance for a cookie.

Dad met me at the edge of the baseball fields. "Where's the fire?"

"I want to see Jay in the caber toss. Do you know why Detective Hunter is so interested in the driver of that black Cadillac?" I asked. "And he mentioned having new evidence in the investigation, too. What do you think?"

"He's grasping at straws," Dad said. "I know Chief Russell put pressure on him to find the killer. I bet Hunter's steamed he can't pin me down. I do feel bad for Mrs. Hartman. She deserves closure."

"Or justice, if she's guilty of murder," I muttered under my breath.

Dad had already walked past me toward the pavilion, however. Halfway to the games, Andrew Kane waved me over to meet him. Wearing casual jeans and button-down shirt, his dark hair mussed, he flashed an easy smile.

"I heard Gil Thompson was taken to the hospital. Is that true?"

"Mild concussion and a broken foot."

"How did that happen?"

I explained the hammer throw accident. "Detective Hunter showed up to question him, and that must have shaken Mr. Thompson's concentration."

Kane nodded sagely. "Oh yeah. Hunter grilled me yesterday. I don't know how many times I've told him that I was
driving to Ann Arbor when Teddy was killed. He must have
checked my phone records."

"Dunno," I said with a shrug.

"I talked to your dad last night, and heard how you solved
other murders around here. Including the previous mayor's
last Christmas. You're a little Nancy Drew, huh?"

I bristled at his mocking tone. "Your client happens to be
an expert at axe throwing, since Lucy won so many trophies.
Why did she pretend otherwise?"

"Teddy wanted her to throw the competition off guard, I
guess. Lucy hated how he kept so many secrets, though.
About his business dealings, bank accounts, failure to get a
loan. And how he cashed out his life insurance to finance the
pet store."

"Lucy must have been angry about that."

"Furious."

"Sounds like the perfect motive for murder," I pointed out.

Kane snorted in derision. "I doubt that. Lucy was always
too scared to do much without Teddy. She relied on him for
everything. Look how her brother's still here, helping her
with the pet shop! She's one of those women who can't func-
tion without a man."

I resented his inference of "those women" even though
his opinion about Lucy might be accurate. "I thought she
asked Whittaker for help before Teddy's death."

"Yeah, because she didn't trust her husband." Kane dodged
a group of teens who rushed past us, shoving each other and
laughing. "All I know is that someone with a big grudge took
Teddy Hartman out."

The lawyer stalked over to greet Lucas Vanderbeek at his
ice cream truck. They seemed on more than familiar terms,
and Kane joined Lucas to help him with customers. I also no-

ticed Isabel French in the distance, staring in dismay, especially when the two men exchanged smiles and deft touches on a hand or shoulder. Uh-oh. Isabel had hoped for more than a friendly chat with the ice cream vendor, but failed to garner any interest.

Andrew Kane had denied any personal involvement with Lucy Hartman. Perhaps he'd told the truth, given his attentiveness to Vanderbeek. But it wasn't any business of mine to pry, or anyone else's for that matter.

Deon Walsh and Chevonne Lang suddenly appeared and dragged Isabel away from the ice cream truck's vicinity. That warmed my heart. Our staff was like family, and the two may have witnessed Isabel's need for emotional support. Figuring they'd take care of the awkward situation, I skirted the soccer ground. A line of women waited to compete in their hammer throw event. Given the large crowd watching, I didn't regret passing up the chance.

The men's hammer throw took place in the first baseball field, and the caber toss in the second one. Jay stood on the sidelines with his brother Nathan. Charlie Volker waited for his turn at hefting the heavy logs. A mass of bystanders blocked my way to their vantage point. I stood on the field's opposite side and mused over Andrew Kane's information about Lucy. I hadn't crossed her off my suspect list, or forgotten about Detective Hunter's new evidence.

So Lucy might have asked for help to murder her husband. Kane had distracted me out front of Vintage Nouveau, after all, while my car had been vandalized. Had Lucy done that? She may have trashed our booth and her own here at the park.

"She fooled Flora Zimmerman, but not me," I said aloud. "What an actress, crying over her trampled banners and ribbons. Big deal."

At the loud shouts and thunderous applause, I returned my attention to the caber toss. Markings littered the field. I crossed the grass to join Jay and his brother. Nathan nodded and then yelled encouragement at the next competitor.

"Come on, Jim, you can do it!"

"Nathan went to high school with that guy," Jay said and squeezed my hand. "No one's beaten Charlie yet. My turn's coming soon. This spot isn't that safe. Better watch from that end, out of range. Over there, by your cousin."

I kissed him for luck and hurried over to join Matt and Elle Cooper. "I didn't know you signed up for this," I said. Matt grinned.

"Yeah, figured I'd give it a shot."

"My husband is a goofball," Elle said cheerfully. "He's been practicing in the backyard for weeks. The kids couldn't play outside, and they're mad at Daddy. He should work for a telephone company and get paid for tossing a pole around."

"I feel like a goofball in this getup," Matt said. "Here goes."

He stepped forward, definitely unique in plaid flannel pajama pants instead of a kilt, a white sleeveless tank, leather gloves, and spiked shoes, with a tasseled tartan cap on his head. Two men in kilts carried the heavy log his way and settled one end at Matt's feet. Once they tilted it against his shoulder, he crouched, gloved hands locked at the pole's base, as if gathering energy from deep inside his gut.

"Heave ho, Cooper," Elle shouted. "Get this over with, bucko."

With a loud grunt, his arm and chest muscles bulging, Matt lifted the heavy log. He took several steps, then increased his speed before he hefted the caber upward. It flipped and then fell forward, inches short of Charlie's marker.

"That's his best throw yet," Jay said. "Too bad he couldn't beat Charlie, though."

Eric Dyer joined our group along with my sister. His pale

blond head glinted in the late afternoon sun, and he watched the competitors with interest.

"I should've entered, the way I lug around those heavy growlers."

Maddie squeezed his bicep. "Yeah, too bad you didn't."

Nathan looked uneasy when he stepped to the line. At a sudden breeze, his Gordon kilt flipped up in back. He flushed beet red at appreciative whistles from some of the women in the crowd. That affected his concentration. Soon after Nathan hefted the caber from the ground, the heavy pole tipped at an angle and fell sideways. Luckily away from any observers.

"Foul," an assistant called out. "Over the boundary on one side."

He walked over in disappointment. "Jay was right. He told me to stick to football."

Elle grabbed my arm in excitement. "Matt's still in second place, and there's only two more guys after Jay. They're awarding gift cards to the top three."

"Hey! I didn't know Dad was competing," Maddie said. "I hope he doesn't hurt himself like Mr. Thompson."

Worried, I watched my father wait for the two kilted men who carried a caber toward him. His old-fashioned knickers, knee-high socks, and plaid vest lent him a jaunty air. Dad swept off his tweed cap with a bow, then allowed the men to place the heavy log against his shoulder. Once they stepped away, Dad took a deep breath and then dodged to one side. The log fell backward, in the wrong direction, with a dull thud.

Everyone in the crowd burst out laughing. "Hold your applause," Dad called out, arms raised, and beckoned to the measuring crew. "Minus twelve feet—a new record!"

"You're in last place, Mr. Silverman," one called out.

"Thank you, thank you! That's great."

Jay bent over, laughing so hard he held his stomach with both hands. Once he finally regained his composure, he rejoined the line. I cheered wildly when his turn came, but fell silent when he prepared himself to toss the caber. Jay had the same trouble as his brother, however. The caber fell toward the side boundary and over by two inches, which disqualified him. He didn't look that disappointed, though.

"Maybe next year." I gave him a consolation hug.

"Charlie will beat us in the hammer toss, too," Jay said.

"Nah. You'll have as good a chance as anyone." His friend held up one hand. "Bent my thumb back so hard, it's killing me. I'm taking myself out of that event."

"Sorry, dude, but not sorry," Nathan said with a wide grin.

I followed the others, with Jay's arm around my waist, to the next baseball field. "I'd like to check on Mom at our booth. She hasn't answered my texts so far. I can't get a good signal to call her, either."

"Plenty of time, so go ahead."

I cut through the back parking lot to avoid the crush of people surrounding the hammer throw. Emily Abbott perched on a stump in a copse of trees with a group of friends, all in their early twenties. They no doubt chatted about the latest bands and online gaming. In my costume and Mom's old loafers, I felt ancient. A few wary glances from the guys confirmed my feelings, but Emily waved me over with a friendly smile.

"Hi, Sasha! The MacRaes hired me on the spot."

"So I heard," I said, and returned her smile. "That's a great schedule, working for the MacRaes and then playing gigs at the pub. The best of both worlds."

Emily jumped to her feet and walked away from the

group, who'd already resumed their conversation. "Gavin and Bonnie think my tats are cool, and I don't have to remove my piercings before my shifts. I always did at the pub. Brian Quinn said they freak out his older customers. Except the guy you asked me about, the tall dude with white hair."

"You mean Kevin Whittaker, Lucy Hartman's brother. What time did he show up that Sunday night, or don't you remember?"

She wrinkled her nose, eyes focused on the sky, before she answered. "After I finished eating a burger. I have to eat before we start playing or I get all shaky. I heard the clock outside while I ate. Pretty sure it struck six times. He walked in half an hour later or so."

"But he said—" I thought back, trying to recall what time Whittaker was supposed to meet his brother-in-law. Was it five or six o'clock? "Did Teddy Hartman ever show up?"

"Nope." Emily headed back to her friends. "See you later, okay?"

"Sure, no problem."

I walked off in a daze, replaying what she'd told me before in my head, and soon found myself on a path between the vendor booths. More people strolled along the blacktop walkway, but their voices and laughter faded. Where had I been when Kevin Whittaker talked about meeting Teddy at Quinn's Pub? I leaned against a huge oak, the rough bark digging into my back, and wracked my memory. Was he talking to Andrew Kane, or my father?

Maybe Dad would remember. I couldn't rely on Lucy's lawyer for a reliable answer, even if he wasn't involved with her on a personal level. She was still a client. Then again, Dad might not believe that Lucy's brother would have helped shield his sister, much less have a motive for murder. Kevin

Whittaker bought Bears of the Heart, after all, and saved it from going out of business. He'd also dropped everything back east to come to Silver Hollow.

Why would Whittaker risk his reputation and community standing? If Lucy was desperate, he might help her divorce Teddy. Dad trusted the businessman, and thought highly of him. I shook myself. Most people would never risk murder as a solution.

Maybe my suspicions were crazy, after all.

Chapter 24

Once I reached the pavilion, I watched a group of young dancers on stage. Eight boys and girls performed in kilts, plaids, and soft shoes, taking careful steps to the lively music from the band behind them. Two dancers came up front and began a complicated routine. The boy and girl focused more on the audience than each other but didn't miss a step. The dance academy they belonged to had set up a sign on an easel as well, advertising lessons.

After they finished, an older teen placed a pair of swords crosswise on the stage. At her signal, a bagpiper started playing while the girl bowed. She began her high steps, leaps, and toe touches in each quadrant of the crossed weapons. That was fascinating.

I noticed that Dad hadn't returned to our booth. Mom bagged a tartan bear for a little girl, while Aunt Eve chatted with her Red Hat Society friends on the blacktop. Vera Adams stepped aside when a couple of rude teens pushed through them to address my mother.

"When is that Hurl the Haggis contest?"

"Later tonight. The schedule is posted at the information booth."

Vera glared at the teen. "As I was saying, Eve, how did you find that pattern?"

My aunt smoothed her full-skirted dress. "I created it myself. We had a few yards of this fabric left over after we made all our tartan bears. I finished sewing last night."

"You're so talented," Shea Miller said. "You should teach pattern-making and sewing in an adult education class, you know. Or sell hand-sewn vintage clothing on eBay or Etsy."

"It wouldn't be as fun. Besides, I have a job already." She sounded modest, her cheeks pink. "I did help Alex sew his first teddy bears to use as prototypes. Not long before he opened the Silver Bear Shop and Factory, because he needed to get investor funding."

"Didn't your niece promise to bring mead?" Vera demanded. "There she is!"

The Red Hat ladies looked my way, clearly enthusiastic. "Who, me?"

"Not you, Sasha," Aunt Eve said with a laugh. "Behind you."

I twisted to see Maddie walking toward us with several dark bottles. Relieved, I caught one bottle before it slipped from her elbow and set it on the table. My sister uncapped one and set out several paper cups. The older women crowded around us.

"Eric wants to know if this mead needs improvement," Maddie said, "so be honest. It's a quick formula, only about six percent alcohol. The fermented honey didn't come from Debbie Davison's bees, though. He had to use a source east of Kalamazoo."

"I hope it has a kick." Shea giggled while Maddie poured the amber-colored liquid into several paper cups. "Mmm. It smells wonderful."

"How can you smell anything with that stuffed-up nose?" Vera teased her.

"Okay, I can't smell it. But why isn't he selling it here this weekend?"

"Amy Evans didn't apply for a liquor license in time."

"The MacRaes are selling malt whiskey—"

"But not for consumption on premise." Maddie passed the cups around. "Eric was so disappointed. He wants to produce enough for this year's Oktobear Fest, so we'll see. This mead should be sweet with a distinct flavor. Let me know if you can tell what he added."

I sipped once, then again. "Apple, for sure, maybe cinnamon. Plus a hint of something else, but I can't put my finger on what it is."

"You mean your tongue?" Aunt Eve teased me. "I agree with Sasha. Definitely apple and cinnamon. Mm, a little nuttiness. Is it almond?"

"You're right! Isn't it good?" Maddie added, beaming. "He's going to try adding pumpkin and cinnamon to his next batch."

"I can't wait," Vera said happily. "I wouldn't mind buying some now if he's gonna sell it at the Silver Claw. I'll stop by on my way home."

"Tell him I sent you, and he'll give you a discount."

I tossed my paper cup in the small trash can under the table. No customers headed to the booth for teddy bears or other merchandise, so I then dragged Maddie away from Aunt Eve's Red Hat friends. They loved to gossip. I wanted to avoid any eavesdroppers.

"Do you remember me telling you about Kevin Whittaker?"

"Huh? What about him?"

Unfortunately, I'd walked in the wrong direction toward the K-9 and Kitty Korner booth. Treat jars lined the table along with piles of colorful print collars. Leashes, thick lead ropes, and retractable nylon ones dangled from the overhead tent poles. Pet toys of all kinds filled rattan baskets. Lucy Hartman glared at the people standing near Wags and Whiskers, her arms folded over her chest. Phil and Jodie Richardson ignored her.

I pushed Maddie past the rescue group until we couldn't see Lucy Hartman. "I know that Kevin Whittaker was supposed to meet Teddy at Quinn's Pub, but I can't remember when he said it, or where I was. It's driving me crazy. Did I tell you about that?"

She shrugged. "I'd have remembered that if you did."

"Mom said that Mark told her the coroner's report established Hartman's time of death between four and six o'clock." I retied my cardigan around my waist, thinking fast, and related what Emily Abbott had seen that Sunday evening. "If she saw Whittaker coming into the pub after six, then maybe he doesn't have an alibi."

Maddie gazed at the clouds overhead when they blocked the sun. "I only saw Whittaker at the Teddy Bear Trot, when he talked to Dad. The day before Hartman's murder. Did you talk to him at the gallery show?"

"No. I saw him there, but only talked to Andrew Kane that night."

"Maybe you overheard Whittaker talking to Dad. Hey, I better tell Eric what the ladies think of his mead. He's dying to hear what they think."

I kicked at a stone on the ground when Maddie hurried away. A staccato beating pierced the air from the pavilion, so I strolled back to watch. Young men with drums strapped to their chests performed onstage, kilts swaying with their frantic movements. The mesmerized crowd applauded when they finished, and yelled for an encore. Emily Abbott's band played next, with a fiddle and tin whistle adding to their electric guitars.

Dave Fox stood talking with my father on the other side of the pavilion. The *Silver Hollow Herald*'s owner and editor wore his usual denim shirt, chinos, and tattered sneakers with duct tape covering a few of the rips and holes.

"That's it!"

The day I'd delivered the press release—both Lucy Hartman and her brother had been at the newspaper office to arrange for Teddy's obituary. Lucy also told me she didn't believe Dad killed Teddy, although that turned out to be a lie. And Kevin Whittaker talked about meeting Teddy Hartman, except he never showed. Did it matter what he said, either five or six o'clock? I'd love to know why Whittaker hadn't arrived at the pub until almost six thirty.

I walked over to Dad, who shifted aside while Dave Fox continued talking. "—can't be everywhere. I don't have much of a budget nowadays." Dave pushed up his dark-framed glasses. "I'll credit any photos I do get, if their shots are clear enough to print."

"Good luck." Dad held up his flip phone. "I'm still in the dark ages, according to my daughters, so I can't help you."

"I took a lot of photographs this weekend." I clicked on my phone's photo gallery app. "The opening ceremony, the bagpipers, fencers, falconer, a weaver—"

"Great! You took a lot that I missed. How about when Gil Thompson got hurt?" Dave frowned when I shook my head. "Too bad. People want to know how he broke his foot."

"I wouldn't report much about his injury. Gil might be embarrassed by any publicity," Dad said. "Even if it is news, Dave."

"Amy Evans might not want a negative spin on the Fling, either, since it might hurt next year's attendance," I said. "I wanted to ask if you remember when Lucy Hartman brought in the obituary for her husband, along with her brother."

Dave shrugged. "Yeah. What about it?"

"That day, Kevin Whittaker said he was supposed to meet Teddy Hartman at Quinn's Pub. What time did he mention?"

"No clue." He waved his camera. "Send me your photos by email, or in a text message. I'll see what I can use for next week's special edition."

"And credit me, if you do."

"Sure, sure."

Dave Fox ambled off toward the pony ride to take photos of teens boosting children into saddles and walking beside them around the ring. Last year Dave used one of Maddie's photos in the *Herald* without crediting her and had to publish a correction.

"I'm sure he'll just happen to forget." I took Dad's elbow. "Oh well."

"Dave's notoriously cheap. He should have enough to pay ten bucks, given all the many advertisements that fill the pages."

"I don't mind, really. Oh, look! How cute is that."

One cluster of three- and four-year-olds holding adorable Highland "coos" stood on the pavilion's stage and managed a few simple tap-dance steps. One sweet kid seemed determined to outshine the others. The audience ate it up, laughing and clapping at her wild antics. They looked so happy, their laughter infectious. A deep yearning for a child of my own welled in my heart. How wonderful to share special moments like this, or an ordinary day-to-day routine.

"I'm curious, honey, about your interest in Kevin Whittaker," Dad said. "What does it matter about his meeting with Teddy Hartman at the pub?"

I tore my gaze away from those sweet toddlers. "Emily Abbott told me that Whittaker showed up around six thirty."

"And this is significant because?"

"Because where was he between four and six, the time of death?"

"Whoa, Sasha. That's a serious allegation—"

Dad suddenly steered me around a clump of rowdy young teens taking swigs from bottles inside brown paper bags. Amy Evans and the security guard hurried to intercept them. I hoped the Red Hat ladies hadn't spread the word about Eric's mead. Dad and I ended up in the crowd watching the hammer throw. Nathan Kirby rolled back and forth on the ground, hands over his face, and moaning in pain. Or was it laughter?

"I hope it's not another accident," I said under my breath.

Jay reached down and pulled his brother to his feet. "Dude, you should've changed to baseball spikes like I did."

Nathan looked sheepish. "I forgot. Not that it matters."

"Are you okay?" I called out.

Jay and his brother both gave a thumbs-up before the next athlete walked forward. The measuring team hadn't bothered with Nathan's attempt, a few feet away from the line. Dad turned back to me, arms crossed over his chest.

"Now what's this theory about Kevin Whittaker? His reputation is flawless. He's won business awards and saved Bears of the Heart from going under."

"Okay, but Teddy Hartman abused his wife," I argued. He looked skeptical, his eyes narrowed, while I explained everything I'd learned so far about the Hartmans. Including their financial problems, the loan failure, and arguments over the pet store. "Vivian Grant said Lucy threatened her with an axe if she ever told anyone what she overheard."

"But she was alone, and didn't report it to the police."

Dad shrugged. "That falls into the territory of hearsay, I'm afraid."

"Oh, come on. There must be something fishy about it," I said. "Jay saw the trophies Lucy won at axe-throwing competitions, only she pretended to be an amateur when we saw her practicing. Who else would frame you and Gil Thompson?"

Dad deliberated in silence, arms crossed over his chest, like he usually did on weighty issues. I gave him time to think. Even if evidence blended with gossip, hearsay, and facts, clear and concise, or a jumbled mess, he loved sorting things into order.

I turned to watch Jay step forward, the wooden hammer in hand. He flexed his shoulders and arms, took several deep breaths, then whirled and let go. The hammer arched high in the air, then down to thud close to the parking lot. One car alarm beeped. He was lucky it hadn't hit the windshield or the pedestrians walking to their cars. Jay shook a hand, his shock clear. Everyone else breathed a sigh of relief.

The final competitor failed to beat the longest measurement. I ran over to hug Jay, aware of his heady scent of aftershave and good clean sweat. Reuben Johnson accepted his trophy, humble and red-faced, then shook hands with the other men. While Jay and Nathan ribbed each other about their poor showings, I walked back over to face Dad.

"So, what do you think?"

"Sorry, but you'll need solid proof for a serious charge like that to stick. I'd also like to see what Detective Hunter's new evidence involves."

"I bet he'll find out it was some innocent guy driving down the road."

"True enough," Dad said with a grin. "Even if Hunter's chasing down crazy leads, at least he's doing his job."

"Yeah, but what if he never solves the case?"

"That happens more often than you'd think." He checked

his watch. "Your mother expects to meet me for dinner. Want to join us, Sasha?"

"No, you go on. Thanks."

"You're supposed to be enjoying the Fling, remember."

"I am—"

"Then forget about the murder and be patient," Dad said.

Discouraged, I headed over to join Jay and Nathan who consoled Charlie Volker. He'd lost the caber toss trophy by mere centimeters to a college athlete from UM, who performed at Greenmead in Livonia for their annual Highland Games.

"And how did Reuben Johnson win the hammer throw?" Nathan kicked a stone with his boot. "He faked us all out, pretending he didn't know what he was doing—"

"What's wrong, Sasha?" Jay asked, and slid his arms around me.

"Not here." I pulled away and ignored Nathan's and Charlie's subtle hints about a lovers' spat. Jay and I walked toward the parking lot. "Dad doesn't think either Andrew Kane or Kevin Whittaker would help Lucy. Hmm. But he never denied that Lucy killed Teddy. Maybe I ought to flat-out confront her over it. What do you think?"

Jay rubbed his jaw. "Remember how she threatened Vivian Grant with an axe? You can bet she's not gonna appreciate you accusing her of murdering her abusive husband."

"Dude, unless it's true!" Nathan had followed us. "Safety in numbers, Sasha. Charlie and me are gonna tag along, because you need witnesses."

"Especially if the chick confesses," Charlie said.

While I appreciated their support, I knew Jay was right. Lucy would fall back on her threat of a slander lawsuit, at least. Without proof, like Dad warned me, I couldn't accuse her of anything. Jay sensed my hesitation, although Nathan paced the ground with restless energy.

"Come on, let's go talk to her —"

"Calm down, bro," Jay interrupted. "She'll deny it anyway."

Charlie held up his bandaged hand. "Well, keep me posted on what happens. I'm off. Catch you later."

Jay turned to me. "Why don't we go over everything from the beginning, Sasha. Maybe we missed something important."

We walked around the field to the riverbank, and found an unoccupied picnic table under a tall elm. The recent rains had washed big branches into the river, along with other flotsam, but a duck and her babies swam by without any trouble. I wasn't in the mood, nor did I have a trash bag handy, to retrieve the litter of renegade napkins, plates, and cups that attendees had tossed around the park.

Since Nathan hadn't heard the details about the Teddy Bear Trot or dog bite, I explained that before we discussed the following day's practice. Jay's brother still resented how Hartman had overreacted to his caber falling the wrong way, and Jay's hammer landing too close.

"Both simple accidents." Nathan laughed. "Bro, maybe you should have beaned the guy after all. Think of all the trouble you could have saved."

"Ha," Jay retorted. "Not funny."

"Let me continue, okay?" I slipped into my cardigan sweater, since the sun had vanished behind a cloud bank. "Right after Teddy and Lucy left with that lawyer, Dad and Gil Thompson arrived to practice axe throwing. While my dad went to the restroom, someone saw Gil standing by the road where the body was dumped. And guess who he saw driving by—Teddy Hartman, who had to be with his wife. That can't be coincidence."

"So let's get the alibis straight. Andrew Kane claims he was talking to clients while he drove back to Ann Arbor," Jay said. "Right?"

I nodded. "Remember we'd gone to get sandwiches at Ham Heaven. Oh! I hope I gave Gil back his change. What's so funny?"

"You, being so honest."

"Someone has to be. Then we hiked around the park until Dad called."

"What time was that, six o'clock? Or seven?"

"Um, I don't know." I dug my cell from my new sporran pouch and then stopped. "This is a new phone, so it won't show the recent call history."

Nathan held up a hand. "Wait a minute. You say Gil Thompson saw Hartman drive past when he stood on the road, but how do you know Lucy was with him?"

"You mean she might not have been?" Jay flexed his fingers, staring at the ground for a minute, and rubbed his bristly jaw. "Where else would she be, back at the pet store?"

"Wait a minute." I thought hard. "Gil Thompson said he saw the dog hanging out the back window. That means Lucy *had* to be in the car with Teddy. No way would Sparky be in there without her. Doesn't that make sense?"

They both nodded. "Yeah, it does," Nathan said.

"Lucy also said that Sparky chewed up the back seat when they left him alone in the car. Without his wife there, Teddy would have abandoned the dog in the park that Sunday."

"No joke," Jay said. "Sparky bit Hartman more than once, after all."

I sighed. "I feel sorry for that poor little dog. I found out Lucy surrendered him to Wags and Whiskers, so maybe Sparky will do better in a new home."

Nathan jumped to his feet and paced back and forth. "So Lucy was in Hartman's car, saw Gil Thompson, and knew where to dump the body. Let's confront her."

"Dude, give us a minute," Jay said. "I still don't get where they were after they left the park. So they dropped Andrew Kane off, but then what?"

"Who cares? There's only one way to find out." He faced us, teetering on the riverbank's edge. "We've got to take the plunge. Let's go."

Jay turned to me. "Did I ever tell you how much of a pain younger brothers are?"

"Younger sisters can be, too," I said.

"Come on! Quit sitting around, take action," Nathan said.

"But three people might spook Lucy and backfire," I said.

"I'm keeping an eye on you," Jay reminded me, "especially after the last few times you messed with murderers—"

At a loud splash, we looked over to see Nathan sitting in the chest-deep water and cursing his bad luck. He rose to his feet, bemoaning his wet boots, and splashed toward the crumbled bank. More dirt slid into the water. He grabbed at solid turf and finally managed to reach more solid ground. Nathan rolled onto his back in disgust.

"Oh, man."

"You wanted action, right?" Jay pulled me up from the picnic table's bench. "Come on, let's see if Lucy Hartman will talk. Better get changed, bro."

"Quit laughing."

Nathan scrambled to his feet, his soaked kilt dripping into his boots, and walked gingerly with squelching footsteps toward the parking lot. I wasn't so sure his plan to confront Lucy was sound, but we had to do something.

How else would we find out the truth about Teddy Hartman's murder?

Chapter 25

Jay and I passed groups of people eating from picnic baskets, weary athletes who rested on the grass or chatted with friends, and children running around. Bonnie MacRae's fragrant shortbread and baking mingled with the scents from pungent herbal wreaths sold by a local farmer, and an essential oils dealer selling lavender diffuser sticks. More shrill music of bagpipes wafted from the pavilion, accompanying a group of cloggers in kilts.

Everyone seemed to enjoy the lingering sunshine and festive atmosphere. Except Lucy Hartman, who stood beside Kevin Whittaker at her booth, hands on her hips, teeth pulling at her lower lip. Her brother looked annoyed. He suddenly stalked off toward the parking lot, where a shuttle bus from the Silver Birches Retirement Home waited. A long line of seniors slowly climbed the short steps into the conveyance.

"Oh, no. Be right back," Jay added, "because Nathan has my keys. Don't do anything without me, okay?"

"Uh, sure. Do you really think—"

He'd already jogged toward the parking lot after his

brother. Sighing, I walked toward the pavilion but stopped. Lucy had started packing up the K-9 and Kitty Korner booth. She filled one large cardboard carton with treat jars, folded the top flaps, and taped them shut. I watched as she fetched another empty box. I couldn't wait for Jay. Lucy might be long gone before his return. It wouldn't hurt to delay her a little.

Lucy glanced up in surprise at my approach. "Did you know it's against the vendor rules to leave early?" I asked. "We have to stay until tomorrow at noon, minimum."

"Who's gonna stop me?" Her vicious tone sent me back a few paces. "Amy Evans can stick those rules where the sun don't shine."

"No, she can't force you to stay—"

"She hasn't done me any favors, either. Wags and Whiskers cut into my business, big time," Lucy said, "so there's no point sticking around until tomorrow. I got the message, loud and clear. I'm not wanted. People are avoiding me on purpose."

I didn't believe Silver Hollow residents knew her well enough to avoid her, but one thing was clear. Her negative attitude turned customers away. I couldn't point that out without her biting my head off once more.

"Let me help, then."

Grandpa T.R. Silverman's old adage of using honey instead of vinegar to catch flies came in handy in this tense situation. Lucy didn't look happy, but waved me around the table to join her. I ducked under the tent flap and sorted a jumble of pet toys and collars.

"Just toss all that junk into a box. I'll organize it later."

"Uh—okay."

We worked in silence until everything but a few items remained. Lucy sank onto the nearest folding chair. She rubbed her face and yawned wide. Lucy's sleek dark hair had been braided once more into short pigtails, and her flannel shirt topped a T-shirt and faded, patched jeans. Her left boot, caked with mud, had one worn-down heel. I'd seen that print before, in the alley behind Mom's gallery.

Now I had solid proof that Lucy vandalized my car. I smiled as a thrill of satisfaction coursed through me. Although Officer Hillerman hadn't considered the print relevant, I hoped he'd noted it on the police report. He had yet to send a copy for my insurance company.

An easy task, once the Highland Fling ended.

"Sasha, didn't you divorce your husband?" Lucy asked. "Flynn Hanson, right?"

"Yes. I filed a few months before our first anniversary after he cheated on me." I leaned against the table's edge. "Flynn often came home late. He'd call me about working long hours or meeting clients, but met his lovers at restaurants or hotels. We lived in the Detroit suburbs back then, not around here."

"So how did you find out?"

Lucy's curiosity sounded genuine, but I wondered what prompted her questions. I had no reason to hide the truth, though. "I was supposed to spend New Year's Eve in Chicago with friends, but bailed at the last minute with a migraine. I drove home and caught him in our bed with one of our bridesmaids. He'd been seeing her all that year."

Her eyes widened. "No kidding?"

That bitter memory rose up in my throat and nearly choked me. Guess I hadn't released my anger after all. I twisted my engagement ring on my finger, wishing I could leave all those bad memories behind me for good, and heard her gasp of surprise.

"Not too shabby—this is new, right? You're engaged."

Lucy had grabbed my hand to eye the diamonds, but I pulled away. Her touch made me uneasy. Along with her rudeness. I'd accepted my ex's bad behavior for too long. After being with Jay, who supported my independence and self-reliance, I was confident to defend my need for personal space. I didn't care if she'd been an abuse victim, either. Lucy had a long way to go when it came to recovering from a bad marriage.

"My sister designed this ring," I said. "We haven't set a wedding d—*ouch!*"

"Wait, your ponytail's caught." Lucy reached behind me and tugged hard, which hurt worse. It felt like she'd ripped my hair from my scalp. She held out a retractable leash with a few blond strands tangled in the metal swivel hook. "Got it free."

Rubbing my head, I forced a smile. "Thanks."

Seeing the thin cord in her hand stirred a memory. Vivian Grant had been nervous while speaking to Detective Mason at her bakery. She'd seen Lucy whip him with a leash in front of the K-9 and Kitty Korner. It had to be the same type in her hand now.

"My marriage was a bust. I wish I hadn't met Teddy," Lucy said mournfully. "He'd just gotten divorced, same as me. We met in a support group. Maybe I shouldn't have started dating someone on the rebound like that."

"Maybe so." I took the leash from her and added it to the box on the table. I reached up to unhook others from the tent pole and packed them. "Did you date long?"

"No. Kevin said that wasn't healthy, and told me to wait before marrying again, but I ignored him. I thought I'd found someone who had it all. A successful business, nice and normal. Boy, was I wrong. Again."

I nodded in sympathy. "People are vulnerable after a traumatic time in their lives. It's why I came back to Silver Hollow after my divorce. I needed my family and friends."

"Smart. Maybe Teddy didn't cheat on me like my first husband, but the last five years haven't been easy."

"You said Teddy didn't trust you." I hoped that sounded

innocent, since she'd started this pity party. "With the bank accounts, right?"

Lucy pushed a few strands of her dark hair away from her eyes. "That got old, fast. He wouldn't let me spend a cent without his approval, too."

"Wow, that's harsh."

"Yep. Clothes, groceries, even the apartment rent. Ridiculous," she said bitterly. "He never told me why he wanted to move here, or about not getting the loan approval for the bed-and-breakfast. I found out when Andrew handed him that big check from cashing out his life insurance. Teddy lost his chance to buy the Richardsons' house by that time."

"So he used the money to open the K-9 and Kitty Corner?"

"He wasn't happy about it, either. I'm not sorry his stupid idea for a B-and-B went down in flames. Imagine me, welcoming guests with muffins, coffee, and a casserole. Gawd, I can barely drag myself out of bed."

Surprised that Lucy shared so much about her personal life, I remained silent. Letting her ramble seemed easier than Nathan's plan of confronting her. She groused about her troubles running the pet store, the vendor booth fee, slow sales— a total waste of time, in her opinion.

"No one wants my homemade dog treats! I spent hours mixing and shaping them. Now I'm stuck with leftovers, and they don't have preservatives."

"They smell good," I said, opening a jar. "What's in them, peanut butter?"

"Natural, of course, without any xylitol. That's toxic for dogs. They have pumpkin puree, whole wheat flour, eggs, too," Lucy said. "Poor Sparky got sick from eating processed treats, so I've been making his from scratch."

"My little poodle has a sensitive stomach, so I'll buy a few jars." I bagged up three along with two plaid collars, then retrieved cash from my sporran pouch. "Rosie and Sugar Bear love peanut butter, so I'm sure they'll enjoy these."

"Thanks, Sasha." Lucy stuffed the money in her jeans pocket. "My brother said he'd find someone to take over the pet store, because I want to go back to New Hampshire for good. That cop better not keep me here—"

"Detective Hunter?" I interrupted. "I saw him earlier near the games."

"He's been bugging me to no end. He wanted to know where me and Teddy were, every minute, after we left the park that Sunday."

"That is his job, after all, to ask questions."

"I told him, fifty times! We dropped Andrew off at the village coffee shop. He should have driven his own car to the park." Lucy ripped several strips of tape and sealed a box of fluffy pet beds. "I was mad at Teddy for staying so long to practice. He didn't care about poor Sparky, and wasn't happy when I wanted to stop at the pet shop, too."

I wondered why Jay hadn't returned by now. Had Nathan lost the truck's keys in the river when he fell in earlier? My thoughts bounced between that and how to ask where else she and Teddy had gone after leaving the park. A third thing also popped in my head. Lucy's voice, to be exact, asking her brother a question at the *Silver Hollow Herald* office.

Wasn't Teddy supposed to meet you at five o'clock, over at Quinn's Pub?

So where was Kevin Whittaker, between four and six? According to Emily Abbott, he didn't arrive at the pub until almost six thirty. Maybe Lucy's brother resented the fact that Teddy failed to tell him that the pedophile case might affect Bears of the Heart's future sales. I had no idea if Detective Hunter bothered to establish Whittaker's alibi for the day of the murder. Maybe Lucy knew what he'd been doing that day.

I listened while she complained about Sparky howling in the car, Teddy's stubborn refusal to leave the park, and then discovering the chewed-up back seat.

"My poor baby! It wasn't his fault he piddled, either," Lucy moaned. "I needed to give him a bath, too, but didn't have any shampoo at home. That's why we had to go to the store. Sparky needed a bath and a good brushing."

"Where was your brother that Sunday afternoon?" I asked.

Lucy stared at me with a deer-in-the-headlights expression. "I don't know. He had a few errands to run, I think. He wasn't interested in watching us practice."

"So he wasn't at the store when you went there with Teddy."

She shifted her gaze to the box, her hands smoothing down the tape. "No, why would Kevin be there? Good thing, because Teddy dragged Sparky out of the back seat, by the scruff of his neck," she said, sounding flustered. "That's why my baby bit him again."

"No dog likes that," I agreed.

"Sparky gets anxious around aggressive men. He went crazy when Teddy argued with the apartment manager. He told me I'd better get rid of the dog, or he'd evict me." Tears trickled down Lucy's cheeks. "I didn't have a choice after that."

"I'm sorry to hear that."

Somehow I had to find out whether Kevin Whittaker had reason to kill Teddy Hartman. How far could I push Lucy, though? Dad always said patience would get a better result. This was turning into my own long, slow death march to the truth.

"Thanks," Lucy said, wiping her face with her flannel shirt. "Kevin's been such a big help. Not like Andrew Kane.

That jerk is representing those creeps who are on trial over using the Benny Bears to target kids."

"But what happened at the pet store?" I asked, since she'd gone off on another tangent. "You wanted dog shampoo. Did you give him a bath in the back room, maybe?"

"Not until I got back to the apartment."

"Your husband went with you, or did he stay behind at the shop?"

I noted Lucy's cheeks flushing crimson, she dodged my question. "I only cared about getting Sparky home, and getting him cleaned up."

Her hands shook, and she wouldn't meet my eyes. Dad taught me that telltale physical signals were often used by liars, along with vague answers and shifting the blame. Her story failed to satisfy me. So she left Teddy at the pet store—alive, or dead? How odd that I didn't get any dangerous vibes from her. Then again, I'd felt safe before Christmas and ended up barely escaping death. Was Lucy fooling me now, like she had Flora Zimmerman?

I understood Lucy better now after this exchange. She'd admitted to Teddy's abuse. Now I'd have to call her out on her own. Especially her threat to axe her husband. Someone had left that hatchet in his back, after all.

At the Silver Bear booth, Karen Anderson chatted with a customer. Maddie wasn't in sight, or Eric, my parents, or Jay. Despite his warning not to do anything without him, I was on my own. Since the caber toss and hammer throw events had ended, the Hurl the Haggis contest should be starting soon. A long row of bagpipers, kilts swaying, shrill music blaring, marched from the closest baseball field. A mass of people followed.

"Can I ask you a question?" I eyed Lucy, my patience gone.

"I heard a rumor that you and Teddy had a huge fight, in front of your store—"

"Listen, I've got to get all this stuff home."

I slapped a hand on the box before she could lift it. "You threatened Teddy, didn't you? Because he hit you that day, and gave you a big bruise. Why didn't you report him, or file for a personal protection order?"

"Like I could really do that." Lucy panted for breath, clearly anxious, as if she'd run in the Kilted 5K. "Don't sound so high and mighty, Sasha. You don't know what it's like living with someone so cruel like Teddy."

"I do know. He hit me at that trade show when I was a kid," I said, watching Lucy as she closed her eyes and turned away. "He was a bully, but you fought back."

"Okay, so I did. What of it?" She lowered her voice further. "You have people who care, who back you up. Some women don't have that option. They can't get out."

"They can by going to a women's shelter, and getting counseling."

"Yeah, yeah. I did that with my first marriage, but it sucked." Lucy shook her head in dejection. "I left, and had nothing—only the clothes on my back. I had to start over. I never thought Teddy would be the same way. So he smacked me a few times—I deserved it. But I let him know whenever he went too far."

"Why didn't you tell your brother? Don't you think he would have helped you?"

"I couldn't tell Kevin."

When Lucy kept shaking her head, I placed a hand over hers. "Abuse is a rotten cycle, but change never happens unless women face it. And end it."

"Whatever." Lucy snatched her hand away. "That's the

kind of crap that people spout all the time to make themselves feel better. It doesn't work for everyone."

"Why didn't you tell your brother about Teddy's abuse?" I asked, refusing to back down.

"You're just like that detective. If Kevin knew the truth, he'd have given Teddy what he deserved. More than a punch in the nose."

With that, Lucy stalked off.

Chapter 26

Now I was getting somewhere. Lucy had almost admitted her brother could have killed her husband—if he'd known the truth. I suspected Kevin Whittaker had found out, and taken matters into his own hands.

"Lucy, wait." I grabbed the box of leashes and raced after her. "How do you know that Kevin wasn't aware of Teddy's abuse?"

She slowly turned around. Eyes huge, her tears spilling over, Lucy gulped hard. "Teddy's dead. I'm free now, so it doesn't matter."

"But it does. You won't be free if you don't face the truth."

Lucy looked confused. "What do you mean?"

"You left Teddy at the pet store, right?" I asked. "You drove home with Sparky to give him a bath. Something happened, because he ended up dead later that afternoon. And you didn't know until the cops came to tell you, right? That Teddy's body had been found."

"With a hatchet in his back." She shook from head to toe, reeling from her emotions, and took a deep breath. "I don't know how he ended up near the park. I don't care what that stupid detective said, either! I didn't kill him."

"But you know who murdered him."

I waited for a denial, but it didn't come. My guess was right—Lucy knew exactly who was responsible. Watching her, I wasn't disappointed when she ignored my last remark and continued walking past the pavilion.

"Things are hard enough right now, Sasha," she called back to me. "I thought you wanted to help, not make all this worse."

I'd followed her to the graveled parking lot. Cars inched past, searching for an open spot. Given the crowds in the park, few people would leave until closing. Packing up this early was a mistake on Lucy's part. The evening schedule was full, with more dancing and music. Due to all the promotion, the Hurl the Haggis contest was a huge draw. I saw teens lugging plastic bags and laughing when they walked toward the park.

Saturday night's attendance was bound to be bigger than any other day of the Highland Fling. Lucy didn't seem to care, however. She'd stopped and looked around, as if searching for her car. The shuttle bus's engine roared past. Its vile smell of exhaust choked me.

"Did Kevin kill Teddy?" I asked bluntly, falling back on Nathan's plan.

"Get out of my way," Lucy said, impatient, and walked down a long row of parked cars. "Just leave that box on the ground."

"You must want closure." I followed her with the box, wincing whenever I stepped on a larger pebble in the gravel lot. Mom's loafers had worn-down soles. "You left Teddy at the pet store, and took Sparky home for a bath—"

"Stop hounding me! That's what Teddy always did. I hated him for it."

I hesitated at her admission. "Did he hound you that Sunday afternoon? Maybe he was mad about the mess in the car."

"Yeah, so?"

"So you fought back. Then what happened?"

She wouldn't meet my eyes. "He fell. Backward on the floor, so I left."

I waited, but Lucy refused to continue. "Was Teddy hurt?"

"He was breathing! I swear to God." Her words tumbled out. "I made sure, and I figured when he woke up again, he'd make me pay. Like he always did. Teddy never let a chance for revenge get away."

Her bitterness was heartbreaking. "You must have locked up before you left for home with Sparky. But it's a keyless entry," I said slowly. "Andrew Kane knew the code, but so did your brother. Kevin closed the shop for you one night."

"Brilliant deduction, Sherlock."

Her sarcasm surprised me. So did the SUV Lucy stood beside—a shiny black Cadillac Escalade. I turned around to see Kevin Whittaker step into view, white hair combed back from his high forehead, his square jaw set. I noticed a sharp, suspicious gaze behind those sturdy black eyeglass frames. He wore another red tie, plain, never striped or patterned, with his tailored suit and polished leather shoes. Power red.

Her brother blocked me. "What's going on, Lucy?"

His low voice sent a shiver through me. I was trapped in the narrow path between the Cadillac and a large van. I'd never be able to flee without one of them cutting off any chance of escape. Lucy's answer chilled me worse.

"Minor problem. We'll just get rid of her before she can tell the cops."

Whittaker was tall and slim but muscular, so I figured I'd better evade him. I turned to face Lucy. My heart hammered in my chest, but I kept my tone calm.

"Why didn't you tell Detective Hunter the truth?"

"Why should I? He's such a jerk."

"So you pretended to be shocked when the police arrived." I shook my head in disgust. "Your brother killed Teddy long before he was supposed to meet him at the pub."

"Hey, wait a minute," Whittaker said behind me, but Lucy waved a hand.

"Shut up, Kevin. It doesn't matter what she thinks—"

"You both vandalized my car, right?" I demanded, my back flat against the van, and hoping someone would come by so I could scream for help. "You did that, Lucy, because you left a boot print. While Andrew Kane talked to me in front of Vintage Nouveau."

"That was my idea," Lucy said, her eyes gleaming. "Fun, too. I put the red slime on the table at your booth, the perfect touch. But I didn't know what Kevin was gonna do. He's the one who left the axe in that piece of firewood. That sure scared me when I saw it."

"You said to make it look realistic," Whittaker said.

"You probably thought killing Teddy was long past due," I said.

"I told you I didn't kill Teddy," she snapped. "Kevin got rid of him for me."

"I didn't kill him!" Whittaker sounded desperate. "I went over to the shop like you said, after you called me. I found him on the floor, but Teddy was already dead."

Lucy shook her head. "He was alive, Kevin, when I left."

"You choked him with that dog leash," he spat back. "I saw the mark on his neck."

"Only until he passed out! You hit him, too." Her tone

had a cunning edge. "You left that dented trophy right beside him. I had to throw it in the trash."

Whittaker didn't answer back at first, his gaze darting around, until he focused on me. "Listen, Sasha. I didn't murder Teddy, you gotta believe me. He was breathing."

"Did you check for a pulse?" I hated how my voice squeaked, but he ignored that.

"I couldn't let my sister go to jail, not after how she suffered. Teddy was horrible to her. He bragged about smacking her around all the time."

"So one of you murdered him."

"You don't know that for sure," Lucy said. "He had to be alive when Kevin left him by the roadside. Teddy must have died afterward."

"The cause of death was either a brain bleed or asphyxiation." At that news, I noticed they exchanged guilty looks but plunged on. "Neither of you called 9-1-1 for help, either at the store or when you left him to die by that road. Half-hidden under the shrubbery, too, so no one driving past would see him."

Lucy looked triumphant. "You think you know so much! Andrew told me once that under Michigan law, people can't be charged for not helping an accident victim. So there."

"That doesn't apply this time." I pulled out a thin cord from the half-open box. "Teddy wasn't a car accident, not if you choked him with this kind of dog leash. And then your brother hit him with a trophy? That's intent to do bodily harm. Manslaughter, at the very least. But I'm sure any lawyer would go for felony murder."

"Shut up! It wasn't like that at all. I looked up murder on the internet—"

"You researched that, Lucy?" Whittaker smacked his Cadillac's hood in disbelief. "The cops will check your search history, you know. Damn."

"I lost Teddy and gave up my dog," she said, eyes narrowed in anger. "I'm not about to lose my brother, too! I don't have anyone else in the world. Teddy deserved what he got, Sasha. Nobody's gonna tell the cops, not you or anyone else."

Whittaker's anger receded. "But what can we do with her?"

"Put her in the trunk, Kevin. Just do it." Lucy's voice turned brittle. "I'm not going to jail, and neither are you. You said last night we had to figure out a way to get out of this mess. So that's what we're gonna do."

"Oh, for God's sake," he said. "How the hell do you think we're gonna get away with this? She's Alex Silverman's daughter."

"I don't care—"

I snapped the dog leash at Lucy's face, hoping she'd recoil. Lucy stumbled backward and fell, screaming profanities. The box in her hand flew into the air, but I dodged it. Treat jars spilled out from the loosened tape and smashed around her on the gravel. Maybe that would keep Whittaker from following me, given all the shattered glass. No such luck, since he grabbed my sweater while I sprinted between the next two cars.

Twisting, my sleeves slipped from my arms. I raced to the left, but halted when Lucy emerged a few cars away. Somehow she'd recovered fast, although blood trickled from one hand. Whittaker panted behind me and grabbed for my ponytail. I lunged over a small car's trunk and slid down, running back the way I'd come.

"Help! Help me!"

I didn't see anyone around, however. This time Whittaker succeeded, yanking my hair and swiveling me around to face him. Pain seared my scalp. He grabbed my throat.

"I can't let this get out about Teddy—"

Another loud yell, from a distance, rang out. Out of pure

instinct, I obeyed the command to duck. A plastic-wrapped bomb smacked Whittaker's forehead. Dazed, he dropped to the ground without another word.

The haggis had burst open on impact, too. Its contents coated his face and hair, puddling around his head. Amazed, I rose to my feet when a kilted figure raced past, barreling in fury toward Lucy Hartman. Screaming, she turned to flee.

Nathan half-tackled her with one arm, snagging Lucy by the waist, and rolled onto the ground. He jumped to his feet, however—a classic football move. Jay suddenly pulled me away from Kevin Whittaker's spread-eagled form. He let out a few low moans amidst the splattered mess of oats, sausage, and spices. I didn't feel sorry for him or Lucy, who spewed curses and threats. Nathan stood guard over her, however, fists ready.

"You broke my arm—"

"Cops should be here any minute." Jay hugged me tight. "Are you okay?"

I gulped, unable to speak, as the last bit of adrenaline faded. My knees wobbled, too. But I felt better when I freed my hair from the elastic ponytail holder and shook out the tangles.

"That was one well-timed fastball, Kirby."

"I almost missed," he murmured against my ear. "Tell me how this all happened. I was going crazy. When I got back, you'd disappeared."

"I'd been talking to Lucy, like forever," I said with a laugh. "Nathan's plan to confront her didn't exactly work out the way we hoped. Although once we got here to the parking lot, things got way out of hand."

"Good thing I guessed right. This park is long and skinny. If we'd gone the opposite direction, you'd be toast."

At the sound of police sirens, relief surged through me. Two cruisers, blue and red lights flashing, stopped in a swirl of gravel. All I wanted was to sit down. Anywhere, far away from Whittaker and his murderous sister. Thank goodness for Jay's skill as a pitcher, and haggis. Now I'd have to give in and taste the Scottish delicacy at the Kilted Scot's booth.

It had saved my life.

Digger Sykes emerged from the first patrol car. He quickly ran over to Lucy, who'd been struggling to get up while cradling one arm. "What happened?" Digger asked.

"Get away from me, you big lug," she said, glaring at Nathan. "I want to press charges of assault and battery, officer. He broke my arm!"

Officer Hillerman walked over from the second car. "Police—show your hands."

Nathan raised his in the air. "I don't have a weapon. That guy over there, flat on the ground, and his sister, Lucy, killed her husband, Teddy Hartman. Ask Sasha. She knows the whole story. They were gonna kill her—"

"First they tried to kidnap me," I said, clutching Jay, "and then kill me."

"That's a lie," Lucy yelled. "She can't prove anything."

A group of people streamed over to check out the commotion. Where were they when I'd needed help? I was glad when Hillerman intercepted with a warning to keep their distance. He soon returned to assist Digger, who'd been struggling to subdue Lucy; she batted the handcuffs away and managed to kick Nathan in a tender spot. When she continued to resist, Hillerman used his Taser. That finally worked.

The EMT crew arrived and rushed over to Kevin Whittaker, who remained prone. Digger and Hillerman dragged Lucy to her feet. Her flannel shirttails flapped around her; bits of glass sparkled on her jeans, and dirt smeared one side of her face.

"We're placing you under arrest, ma'am, on suspicion of kidnapping and murder," Hillerman said, and helped Digger lead her toward a patrol car. "You can contact your lawyer when you get to the station."

"Some people," Nathan said, shaking his head. "How did you like that tackle?"

Jay grinned. "I bet that football coach might still take you on, even if it's been over a year since he offered. So it's one of the Big Ten colleges—"

"—didn't kill my husband, I swear it!" Lucy's howls escalated. "Look what that jerk did to my brother, that's assault! Is he dead? Kevin, can you hear me?"

"He's awake and responsive, ma'am," Hillerman said. "Watch your head." He pushed her into the cruiser's back seat and shut the door, although that didn't drown out her protests.

"Oh, man," Whittaker said, his voice weak. "What's all this gunk in my hair?"

He pushed the female EMT away, but she ignored him and checked his pupils and pulse. Her partner swiped at the worst haggis bits. Disheveled, his suit stained, his white hair stringy with brown goop and flecks of oatmeal, Whittaker insisted on standing. Together the technicians helped him to his feet and walked him to the police cruiser.

"I-I'm all right." He brushed off his tie and slacks. "I'll go peacefully, officers. I know it's all over."

"So you admit to killing Teddy Hartman?" I asked.

Whittaker fixed his gaze on me, bleary-eyed. "I never said that."

Jay squeezed my waist. "He must be all right, if he's smart enough to deny it."

"Is he good to go?" Digger asked the EMT crew. They nodded and headed back to their truck. "I'm placing you under arrest, sir, on possible charges of kidnapping and murder—"

The two policemen supported Kevin Whittaker when he swayed, still groggy, and then guided him to the second cruiser.

I leaned against a nearby car, wondering what Phil Hunter would think when he heard the news.

"So much for his new evidence," I said under my breath. "Imagine how much fun they'll have questioning those two. It may come down to the exact time of death, in terms of which one is guilty of murder. I don't much care, though."

"They'll blame each other, no matter what the truth is," Jay said. "Maybe that plan to confront Lucy wasn't so smart. Remind me to never listen to my brother again."

"Okay, it was a stupid idea." Nathan sidled over. "I got a kick in the nuts for my trouble. Lucy Hartman spit on me, too!"

"Digger can add assault to murder and attempted kidnapping charges."

"So will you go to college?" I asked Nathan. "Jay told me you aren't happy working at the Quick Mix factory."

"Dude." He glared at his brother. "I just don't like the supervisor."

"You're only there for the free doughnuts," Jay shot back.

"Stop bickering," I said with a smile, "but it's worth exploring a new career."

We watched both policemen take photos of the scene and collect evidence—the broken glass from the jars, dog treats trampled over the lot, the spatters of haggis. I had to answer plenty of questions about my chat with Lucy, how things escalated when Whittaker appeared, all while Officer Hillerman took notes. Digger snapped photos of the black Cadillac SUV and then took Lucy to the station, his police cruiser lights flashing.

Hillerman turned to me. "You're sure you're okay, Sasha?"

I drew a shaky breath. "Yes, and thanks for everything."

"I'll contact the county sheriff." He pocketed his notebook. "I can't wait to hear what Chief Russell will say about this."

Nathan snickered. "That smart-mouthed detective won't be happy."

"I hope this is the last case you solve, Sasha," Jay said. "At least for a while."

Silently, I seconded that hope. Nathan followed us while we slowly walked to join the crowd watching the Hurl the Haggis contest. I'd avoided another close call, all due to a bad case of rabid curiosity.

I had to break that habit, and soon, before my luck ran out.

Chapter 27

"Hey, guys!" Jay's brother Nathan waved in our direction. "Over here, come on, quick. Before he starts playing."

"Before who starts playing?" I asked, hurrying to follow Jay.

"No idea what he's talking about—"

Up ahead, Maddie squealed and clapped her hands. "The Unipiper! He's actually here," my sister crowed. "That is so cool! I don't know how he can keep balanced on that thing while he's playing, though."

We watched a kilted musician on a unicycle ride along the blacktop oval. He adjusted the bag under his arm and pumped until a low hum rose into shrill music. A crowd gathered on either side of the walkway, applauding whenever the pipes against his shoulder—drones as my sister identified them—spouted flames. He performed excerpts from popular music, including "The Imperial March" from *Star Wars* and the ending of Tchaikovsky's *1812 Overture*.

"Totally cool," Eric said. "I could learn how to ride a unicycle."

"Good luck with the bagpipes," Maddie teased him.

"How about a kazoo?"

She flashed him a sour look, but I laughed. "Sounds like great entertainment for the next charity event we put on. Kazoos and Fourth of July teddy bears."

Jay and I soon slipped away and headed back home. Exhausted, elated that I'd arranged for others to staff the booth tomorrow, I brushed my teeth and crawled into bed. Jay snuggled close. He murmured something, but his voice quickly faded. Bright sunshine woke me. Groggy, half-remembering yesterday's crazy confrontation with Lucy Hartman and her brother, I rolled over to stretch. Then bolted upright. Oh, no. Not again.

A few minutes later, Jay knocked at the bathroom door. I couldn't answer, however, until I'd rinsed my mouth and scrabbled in a drawer for a sealed package. I couldn't ignore obvious signs. I needed an answer. It took less than ten minutes to get one.

I opened the door to see Jay, who rubbed his stubbly jaw and blinked, still sleepy. "Um, happy early Father's Day." I handed him a plastic stick.

"Huh?"

Hand over my mouth, I raced back into the bathroom. By the time I'd finished, Jay had a mug of hot tea and crackers ready. "Thanks."

"Stale, though. Sorry about that." He blinked. "So, that thing means—"

"I'm pregnant, yes. I'm sorry," I said, biting my lip, "because I've been so busy, and forgot to refill my prescription, and now what are we gonna do?"

Jay had looked "gobsmacked" as Bonnie MacRae would

say, but he puffed out his chest with a huge grin. "Are you kidding me? That's amazing! We're gonna have a baby."

"Are you sure you're okay with that?"

"Hell yes." He hugged me tight while I sipped tea and chowed down more crackers. "Too bad the dogs aren't here to clean up the crumbs."

"They'll be waiting under the high chair for anything that drops."

"Your mom's gonna be over the moon, Sasha. She seemed disappointed about us not wanting a big wedding."

"Trust me, this news will erase all that." I leaned against the sink, exhausted once more. "Mom's bugged me about grandkids for years."

Maddie tiptoed into the bedroom. "What's going on—hey!"

I'd slammed the door shut, fighting another bout of nausea. At last I emerged to find Maddie jumping around and waving the pregnancy stick with its positive stripes. She rushed over and hugged me so tight, I felt dizzy.

"Oh my God, Sash, how wonderful! I knew something was up when you didn't drink any wine at the Guilty Pleasures Gossip Club."

"Yeah," I said, sitting down on the bed's edge. "When I'm not sick in the morning, I'm craving ChocoLair's truffles."

"I'll get you a big box. And I'm throwing a baby shower with a teddy bear theme." My sister danced out of the bedroom. "I'm calling Mary Kate and Elle, right now."

Jay sat and drew me close into his arms, his chin resting on top of my head. "This is fantastic timing, Sasha," he said. "I wanted to surprise you later with my news, but I guess I'd better tell you now."

"What news?" I shifted to meet his eyes, my heart beating

faster. Jay never showed much excitement, but for some reason I dreaded the mix of emotions that showed in his eyes. Not only excitement but satisfaction. "You're going up north to teach again?"

"Nope."

"Don't tell me you're getting a new job, Jay Kirby. Not after you've worked so hard to establish your studio—"

"I bought a house." He laughed at my open-mouthed shock. "You didn't want to keep living here at the Silver Bear Shop, right? With people tramping through the backyard to the factory for tours, and we'd only have the back half of this house to ourselves. It's nice, but not that much room, right? So I put in an offer and just heard from the realtor this morning, while you were busy. The owner accepted."

"Why didn't you tell me?" I demanded, "and where is this house?"

"Right over there," Jay said and pointed out the window. "I found out Mary and Tyler Walsh bought a condo. Your mom talked Barbara Davison into selling me that Cape Cod. I know how much you loved it, along with the picket fence and yard."

I threw my arms around him, but then had to duck back into the bathroom. Weak, my stomach hurting, I slipped back into bed. Jay squeezed my hand and smoothed strands of blond hair out of my eyes, his hazel ones full of joy and love.

"Are you sure you want to live in that house?"

"I love it, Jay," I said, squeezing his hands with so much happiness. "It's perfect, and so close to your studio. Will you carve our baby's cradle, with teddy bear cutouts on each end? But no claws or teeth marks, please."

We both laughed at that. Maddie burst into the room again, carrying a bag in one hand. "Like I said, I had a suspicion about you skipping breakfast a lot lately. You always look

tired, Sash. Totally wiped out. Last weekend I bought a few
things at the Kilted Scot."

"You're already giving us presents for the baby?"

"Aunt Maddie's gonna spoil your kid, to the max, so get
used to it."

I glanced at Jay. "We're in big trouble."

Maddie didn't give me a chance to open the bag, drawing
out a handful of baby onesies, rompers, and sleepers in plaid
and tartan patterns. One had a fuzzy brown teddy bear, another had a black Scottie, and the footed sleeper proclaimed
"Baby Bear" in white letters. She also brought forth a hand-
sewn teddy with corduroy fabric, a worn-out nose, and dull
eyes, and placed it on the dresser. Next to the Highland
"coos" and Jay's kilted bear.

"Grandpa T.R.'s old bear for the wee new bairn."

"Thanks, Mads," I said, wiping my tears. "There's nothing better than a teddy."

AUTHOR'S NOTE

The character "Jim Perry" is based on a brilliant artist and friend, Jim Pallas, whose artwork is shown in detail at http://www.jpallas.com.

My husband once worked with Jim, writing the computer program for the Century of Light, the "world's first large public permanent electronic interactive sculpture" that was originally located on Washington Boulevard in Detroit. Unfortunately, the artwork fell into disrepair and was dismantled. Jim donated the Century of Light to Ann Arbor's Hands-On Museum, which includes the cabinet of electronics and the Progmod. They will have to reconstruct the mandala of 144 lights to revive the complete sculpture. We hope that happens one day.

Thanks for the inspiration, Jim.

Readers and fans of teddy bears—check out the history of how they first were produced, some adorable crochet patterns to make, and my personal collection of bears on my website: megmacy.com.

Connect with Us

Visit us online at
KensingtonBooks.com
to read more from your favorite authors, see books
by series, view reading group guides, and more.

 Join us on social media
for sneak peeks, chances to win books and prize packs,
and to share your thoughts with other readers.

**facebook.com/kensingtonpublishing
twitter.com/kensingtonbooks**

Tell us what you think!

To share your thoughts, submit a review,
or sign up for our eNewsletters, please visit:
KensingtonBooks.com/TellUs.